KATHY LOVE

BRAVA

KENSINGTON PUBLISHING CORP.
www.kensingtonbooks.com

Thank you to Erin McCarthy for the chat that led to the creation of Finola White.

A very special thanks to my editor, Alicia Condon for her input, patience and support.

Thanks to the Tarts, for the shared plotting, laughter, desserts and wine.

And finally, thank you to all my friends and family who deal with me dropping off the radar before every deadline.

Devilishly Hot

Prologue

Winter, 2008

"Couldn't you just have fired her?" Tristan looked down at the motionless body of yet another of Finola's personal assistants.

Finola lifted her herbal relaxation mask from her eyes and made a rueful face. "I suppose. But if you had seen what she'd done," she sighed deeply, "Well, you'd have had a hard time thinking rationally too."

Tristan, still contemplating the body, raised a dubious eyebrow. "I highly doubt it."

Finola sighed again. "That's true. You are so much more judicial than I am."

Was that what she was going to call it? Tristan would have gone with *sane*, but tomato/tomahto.

Finola retrieved her crystal champagne flute from the glass end table beside her massage chair. She sipped her Dom Perignon White Gold Jeroboam. A sure sign Finola wasn't pleased. The champagne always came out when she was feeling stressed. He'd call it petulant, but there was no point in mentioning that to Finola. Best to just let her soothe herself with her $40,000 bottle of bubbly.

"Honestly though, Tristan," she said once she'd drained her glass and poured herself another, "she was utterly incompetent. I mean, she couldn't do a single thing right.

And it wasn't like I was asking for the moon. I just expect that when I ask for something to be done, it be done on time."

Tristan, only half listening, made a sympathetic noise. What the hell was he going to do with *this* one? Getting a grown woman down from the fifteenth floor of a busy building out to the even busier streets of Manhattan wasn't easy, even for a demon. Add to it that this one didn't appear capable of moving on her own two feet—and it was a real pain.

Really, he was the one who deserved the damned champagne.

"I simply asked her to get me the fabrics that an artist in Milan was creating specifically for the Alber Elbaz photoshoot. This was not an unreasonable request."

"When is the photoshoot?" Tristan asked, considering the white handwoven Persian carpet in Finola's office. It was big enough to wrap the body in, but Finola would have a conniption that he was using her handmade original flown in directly from Nain, Iran. But then again, this was her doing. He couldn't help it if her damned rug was another casualty of her temper.

"It's tomorrow," Finola said, a hint of peevishness making her tone a little defensive. "I didn't say it would be easy. But it was absolutely doable."

Tristan looked from the carpet to the body, then back to the carpet. "What time did you tell her about this absolutely doable feat?"

Out of the corner of his eye, he saw her wave her hand, "Oh, I don't know. Probably one-ish."

His gaze shifted from the rug to the cabinet behind Finola's desk. That would be heavy all on its own, and with a body in it . . . he returned his attention to the carpet—also heavy, but the best bet.

"When is the photoshoot?"

"Eleven," she answered, topping off her glass again, the golden liquid sparkling, bubbles dancing.

Tristan didn't feel like dancing. He was furious, but he pushed it aside, remaining cool. Giving in to his own emotions wouldn't help the situation.

He returned to the body, crouching down to slide his arms under its neck and knees. With only a slight grunt, he hefted it up. Thank Lucifer and his many minions, this one was thin. The last one had been a good twenty-five pounds overweight, which hadn't helped her with Finola's wrath and ultimately was a large part (no pun intended) of her . . . early retirement.

"You do realize that gave her less than twenty-four hours to get the material for you, don't you?" he said, his tone breathy as he struggled to carry the body over to the rug.

"Well it can't be impossible. It could have been flown on the Concorde or something."

Tristan dropped the body rather unceremoniously onto one side of the carpet. "The Concorde stopped flying about five years ago."

"Oh," Finola sighed, clearly weary of their conversation, "well, whatever, she was a terrible assistant."

She settled back in her lounger, replacing her mask over her eyes. Tristan arranged the body so the limbs were straight, then he lifted the edge of the carpet and started to ease the carpet and body over, rolling the body up like the filling of a jelly roll. A very complicated, costly jelly roll.

Finola lifted the edge of her mask and peered at him. "What are you doing?"

Saving your ass.

"Playing it safe," he said, with a grunt, shoving with both arms to finish rolling the carpet. "You should really require height and weight to be included on all your employee résumés."

"You are so right," she agreed, but not for the reason he wanted the measurements there.

He rose, running his hands down the front of his Armani trousers, smoothing any wrinkles. Ah, there was a metaphor there.

"I quite like that carpet, you know," Finola said, but then released her mask back over her eyes.

Well, at least she'd accepted that better than he'd expected.

"I'm going to have to go get one of the moving vans to dispose of this," he told her.

She made a noise of acknowledgment, uninterested acknowledgment. But why would she care? Finola just made the messes; he cleaned them up.

He strode across her office, heading out to get the van and get this done.

"Wait," Finola said, sitting up, her voice suddenly panicked, "I don't have a personal assistant."

"No," Tristan agreed, his voice wry, "this is true."

"I need an assistant. I mean, look." She took off her eye mask and waved it in his direction. "My mask is absolutely cool now. A cool mask is not going to help this wretched headache behind my eyes. I need someone to warm my mask."

Tristan fought back the urge to roll his eyes. Instead he walked over to the cabinet he had considered using for the body disposal. He opened the bottom drawer and pulled out a thick manila folder. Then he went to Finola and placed it on her lap.

"Pick one."

She considered the file for a moment, then opened it. She flipped through several of the résumés, scanning them very briefly.

Finally she sighed, and randomly tugged one out of the dozens. "Hire this one."

She held the page out to him without even glancing at the person's education, abilities or experience.

"This could be why your assistants never work out," he said dryly, but accepted the resume.

He raised an eyebrow as he perused the information there, but he walked over to Finola's desk and picked up her phone. After punching in the numbers, he waited as the phone rang.

Finally, just when he would have hung up, a woman answered, her voice breathless, and heavily laced with a Southern drawl.

Tristan cringed. Not a good start. Finola wasn't fond of the South. Too hot—ironic, he supposed.

"Hello," he glanced back to the page in front of him, "I'm trying to reach Annie—Lou," *Lou?* Really? "Riddle."

Oh yeah, this was *not* going to go well.

The woman on the other end told him that was she.

"My name is Tristan McIntyre and I'm calling from *HOT!* magazine. I'm pleased to tell you that Ms. Finola White has decided to hire you as her personal assistant."

Tristan nodded impatiently as Annie Lou thanked him profusely—and lengthily.

"Great," he said, finally cutting off her sweet, golly-gee gratitude. "We'll see you tomorrow morning. Eight o'clock sharp."

Annie Lou Riddle was still drawling away as he hung up the phone.

"Done," he said.

"You are the best, Tristan."

Yes, he was. But he didn't say anything, he just left the office. As he strolled past the large, ultramodern assistant's desk, he made a note to himself that he had to get rid of all of the last assistant's personal items that were still there.

Annie Lou Riddle. She had no idea that by accepting this job, she'd just sold her soul to the devil. Literally.

* * *

Annie stared at the receiver still clutched in her hand. The faint dial tone hummed, signifying no one was on the other end of the line, but she still didn't hang up.

Finola White's assistant. *HOT!* magazine. *HOT!* magazine!

She managed to pull herself together enough to press the OFF button on the cordless phone and drop it back into the receiver. Then with total abandon, she started to hop and dance around the tiny living room, laughing like a madwoman.

HOT! magazine! Finola White!

"Oh my God . . . oh my God," she repeated over and over, still dancing.

Only the pounding from the downstairs neighbor on his ceiling, her floor, made her stop her happy dance. She collapsed onto her worn, circa 1970s tweed couch, still grinning.

This was amazing. Just amazing.

She let her head fall back against her sofa, closing her eyes and still smiling. This couldn't come at a better time.

When her phone had rung, she'd been in the middle of packing her suitcases to head back to Magnolia, Mississippi, her small hometown where there were no prospects for a woman with degrees in fashion design and journalism. Oh sure, there was a local small-town paper she might work for, if she wanted to write articles on exciting things like the pros and cons of adding a stoplight on Main Street or who got into a fight at Sonny's Bar and Grill this week.

But she didn't have to worry about that now. She was officially an employee of *HOT!* magazine, the number one fashion magazine in the U.S. And not only that, she was going to be personal assistant to Finola White, magazine owner, entrepreneur, fashion icon herself, and one of the most powerful women in the fashion industry.

"Maybe the world," she said aloud to herself, then giggled.

Amazing.

She opened her eyes and sat up as she heard a key in the door lock. Her smile growing even wider, she jumped up and raced to the door.

"Hey, there," Annie's boyfriend, Bobby, said, his blue eyes wide with surprise and confusion to find her waiting for him on the other side of the door. Or maybe it was because she was grinning like a fool. Heaven knew, it had been a long time since either of them had been light-hearted.

She flung herself into his arms, laughing.

"What's going on?" he asked, once he'd recovered from his astonishment.

"I got a job!" She released him, hopping up and down in her excitement. The downstairs neighbor immediately thumped as if waiting with a broomstick or whatever was handily poised at the hint of the first noise.

Annie didn't care today; nothing could ruin her joy.

"Really?" Bobby said, a wide smile of his own revealing his gleaming white teeth and the boyish dimples on either side of his perfect lips.

Annie told him how she'd been packing when she'd received that call.

"It was like providence," she ended with a happy sigh.

Bobby frowned. "Is that a TV show or something?"

Annie laughed. Bobby was beautiful with his thick tawny hair and blue eyes. The all-American boy. And that would take him places, even if he was a little confused at times.

"This could be good for you too," she said, "You never know, maybe you could get some modeling jobs through the magazine."

Bobby raised an eyebrow. "I'm an actor."

"I know," Annie said automatically, although she suspected he'd do a lot better as a model. His acting was . . . painful, at best. But she knew it was his dream and she would certainly support him.

"When do you start?" he asked.

"Tomorrow."

"Awesome." He headed to their "kitchen," a corner of the one room where they had a mini fridge, a hot plate and a microwave. He pulled a package of bologna out of the fridge, curling up a slice and taking a bite.

"We should celebrate," he said, then popped the rest of the luncheon meat in his mouth.

She laughed and joined him to steal one of the slices. "I think this is going to be the extent of our celebration tonight."

She raised her bologna in a toast. He smiled and joined her.

"But things are about to change," she said with excited conviction. "Soon we'll be able to afford a real celebration."

This was it. She knew it. Their lives would never be the same.

Chapter One

Three years later . . .

"Anna!"

Annie started at Finola's voice bellowing over the intercom on her desk phone. How it still managed to startle her after all these years was a mystery. Maybe it was more of a Pavlov's dog thing. Whenever Annie heard that demanding voice disguised in a lilting, melodious tone, she knew she was in trouble.

But just like the obedient dog she'd become, Annie jumped up from her huge desk in the reception area outside Finola's office and hurried through a glass maze to her boss's office.

She stepped into the office, greeted by Finola's fluffy white maltipoo, Dippy, who was considerably less obedient than Annie. The dog jumped up and down, and the beast's surprisingly sharp nails threatened to snag the material of her skirt and make runs in her stockings, but Annie tried not to react. Finola didn't like anyone to reprimand her pet.

Finola stood in the center of her office, debating between two items in her assistant editor Tristan's hands. As Annie got closer, she saw her boss was trying to choose between two diamond-encrusted necklaces.

"This one," she said, pointing to the one that dripped

with dozens of perfect, glittering diamonds. Tristan nodded, then turned to return both of the pieces to their blue velvet boxes.

Finola still didn't acknowledge Annie as she walked behind her ultramodern white desk. Actually, everything in Finola's office was white, including the woman herself with her alabaster skin and pale, pale blond hair.

And Annie, with her mousy brown hair, simple brown cashmere sweater and tweed pencil skirt, was fully aware that she was like a glaring mole on the façade of Finola's perfection.

Finola leaned forward to scoop up Dippy, setting the little creature on her lap before she finally looked up at Annie. Immediately a grimace pulled at her ruby-red lips, the only vivid color on her face. Her gray eyes, as light as bleached marble, narrowed as she inspected Annie's clothes.

"How many times do I have to tell you I do not like brown?"

Annie smoothed her hands down her skirt, not because the expensive garment had any wrinkles but because her palms were sweaty. After three years, this woman still had that effect on her.

"It's part of the newest Chloé collection," Annie said softly, even though she knew Finola wouldn't be impressed. She was rarely impressed with anyone but herself.

"I don't want to see brown again," Finola repeated and Annie nodded. You did not cross Finola White. Annie knew that very well.

"I need you to go to the design house and pick up the new spring pieces that will be highlighted in the April issue of the magazine. And as you will see, there is no brown in the collection."

Annie nodded, not inclined to point out that it was a

spring collection, which would be unlikely to feature brown anyway.

"I need those items delivered to the photoshoot on Staten Island. By one."

Annie glanced at her watch. It was already 11:30. By the time Annie made it to the design warehouse, got the clothing loaded into a cab, then drove to the ferry and made it to Staten Island, even with taxis and traffic on her side and a prompt ferryman, she'd be pushing it. But she didn't even bother to be amazed. Finola always made impossible demands. Annie suspected the woman sat up at night thinking of tasks that Annie couldn't help but fail— or at the very least, would send Annie's blood pressure and stress to dangerously high levels.

Annie didn't bother to point out the logistics, either. She didn't have the time. She simply nodded and rushed for the door. Dippy leapt down from Finola's lap, bouncing and yipping like Satan's very own purse dog.

Finola's cultured, beautifully accented and utterly irritating voice called after her. "And bring us back lunch from Raimondi's."

Because you don't have enough stress, Annie muttered silently to herself, not slowing her frantic pace. Fortunately, she didn't need to waste precious time asking Finola what they wanted from the restaurant or who "us" was. It certainly wasn't Annie, that was for sure. Finola referred to herself, Tristan . . . and Dippy. Finola and Tristan always got the ahi tuna tartare with the Asian salad . . . and Dippy liked the goose paté.

But now Annie also knew, even if she got the clothes to the photoshoot on time, the lunch would definitely be late.

There was no pleasing Finola. Annie lived for the woman, and the woman was never happy. At least not with her.

But Annie didn't let that slow her down. She would do her best, just as she did every day. She stopped at her desk to grab her purse and coat, tugging it on as she zigzagged her way through the busy hallways like a Navy SEAL racing through an obstacle course.

She was relieved to see that the elevator doors were open as she approached, her only thought to make it inside before they slid shut, forcing her to wait, shaving off precious minutes from her nearly impossible time limit.

So she wasn't even aware of the man still on the elevator, just stepping out as she was rushing in, until she plowed into him, both of them nearly toppling over upon her impact.

Miraculously, the man not only managed to keep his own balance but maintained hers, too. Strong hands curled around her upper arms, steadying her. She got the impression of a broad, hard chest and the scent of something manly. Leather? A rich woodsy scent? Something more subtle underneath that? A distinct, wonderful scent, but one Annie couldn't put her finger on.

"Whoa there, are you okay?"

Annie's body further jumped to awareness at the husky, rough tone of the man's voice. She looked up at him.

Good Lord, this man was beautiful. Not the model type of beautiful Annie had grown oblivious to over the past couple of years. This man's beauty was tough, masculine, a little gritty. This guy got his hands dirty for a living; he wouldn't pose pretty in front of a camera.

Not that she was jaded or anything.

The corner of his mouth lifted in mild amusement, and Annie realized she was staring.

"Um, yeah. Yeah, I'm fine. Just not paying attention to what I'm doing. Sorry."

"Well, you are clearly in a hurry."

"I am."

"Then I will let you get to it." But his hands lingered on her upper arms, and she could feel his heat all the way through her layers of clothes. Then the elevator bell dinged, snapping them both out of the moment. He bowed his head by way of good-bye and stepped out of the elevator. The door closed, blocking him from her sight.

Annie sagged against the elevator wall, breathing in deeply. For the first time in a long time, her body felt heavy with something aside from stress or exhaustion or worry. She actually felt . . .

She frowned, disconcerted. She felt attraction. Maybe even lust.

"Who knew?" she mumbled to herself, then chuckled. She certainly didn't know she still had the interest for that kind of emotion, much less the energy.

The elevator bobbled to a halt and the doors slid open. Annie forced the rather nice sensation aside. She didn't have time for arousal. Not unless it was written into her schedule or Finola gave her the okay. And Finola would never concern herself with someone else's enjoyment.

At the thought of Finola, she got back to her plan of attack for today's impossible task. First, flagging down a taxi.

She hurried out to the street, praying the taxi gods would be on her side. She stepped off the curb and waved at the first one heading in her direction. It slowed and pulled up beside her.

"Good start," she mumbled to herself. "*Good* start."

She scrambled into the back as quickly as her pencil skirt would allow, giving the driver the address of the design house.

She fell back against the vinyl seat, the scent of stale smoke wafting around her from the tatty material. Sighing, she ignored the unpleasant smell and tried to formulate the best strategy for getting the clothes loaded into the taxi, then the best route to take back through the city. But untypically, her mind wouldn't stay on task.

Instead, visions of the man from the elevator kept creeping in to distract her. Even the memory of his scent somehow blocked out the smell of the stinky cab. Who was he? Working so closely with Finola and Tristan, Annie met—or at least saw—just about everyone affiliated with the magazine. But she supposed he could be someone new.

God knows, if she had met him, she would remember. Even now, her skin tingled in the places where his hands had grabbed her arms to catch her. And she was in a wool coat and it was January.

He'd definitely made an impression.

But there's not one single point to thinking about him. Even if you did find him again and he was interested in you, you don't have a life. Finola White owns you.

And there was still the little matter of Bobby. Their relationship wasn't exactly a dream, but he was still her boyfriend.

So, stop fantasizing about the rugged, very, very attractive man from the elevator and start concentrating on how you are not going to incur Finola's wrath.

Like the good little servant she'd become, she pulled out her smartphone and checked the time. No messages. That was a relief, but she could see time was ticking by. Quickly.

Focus. Focus.

She leaned forward. "Could you drive a little faster, please?"

"Ms. White will be right with you, if you'd like to have a seat."

Nick Rossi stopped surveying the lobby to look at the blond receptionist. Her smile widened invitingly, and though she gestured toward the sitting area, he didn't think a seat was all her smile was offering.

But he only accepted that, wandering over to the waiting area, taking a seat in one of the red velvet chairs that looked like something straight off the set of a Tim Burton movie. He sank into the overstuffed cushion, feeling a bit childish, like he was at a mad hatter's tea party or something.

He glanced back over at the receptionist. She smiled again, and apparently she didn't think he looked quite so ridiculous. He smiled back, but reached for one of the magazines on the glass table in front of him.

HOT! magazine, of course.

He only glanced at the pages as he surreptitiously watched and listened to the receptionist. She answered several calls, directing them to the appropriate people. Several other *HOT!* employees came and went through the large double doors at the end of the lobby. All of it seemed like the typical comings and goings of any business.

Not that he expected anything different. It was hardly as if anyone would be doing something illicit right out in the open in the middle of the workday. But Nick felt very certain nefarious things were happening at *HOT!* magazine.

The elevator chimed, and Nick straightened in his huge chair, the magazine forgotten completely.

An elderly man pushing a mail cart ambled out. Nick frowned as a feeling akin to disappointment caused a slight drop in his stomach.

Who was he expecting? Of course he knew he wasn't expecting anyone. He was hoping. He was hoping it would be the woman with big, stormy gray eyes and brown hair pulled back into a tight little bun.

He frowned, letting his attention drift away from his surroundings and back to her. What had it been about that woman? She'd been pretty enough, but really there hadn't been anything particularly unusual about her. Of course, his dick had had a totally different opinion about that. As soon as he'd touched her, his body had reacted. He couldn't recall that happening in years. That kind of instant attraction.

It's because you never get laid, dumb ass.

He worked most of the time. Maybe his libido was finally realizing the lack of attention.

Hardly rocket science, Rossi.

He glanced back to the receptionist, who still wasn't attempting to hide the fact she was watching him. She smiled, definitely giving him another silent invitation.

Maybe he should take the offer that was clear in her gray-blue eyes. She was beautiful, in that tanned, manicured, my-boobs-are-so-damned-perky-they-could-stand-up-and-do-a-cheer sort of way.

She could be amusing. But something about her caused a prickle across the back of his neck. And not a good prickle. It was a sensation he'd come to think of as his "cop sense." And this woman tripped it. He couldn't imagine why. She hardly seemed like the type who could be the mastermind behind what seemed to be going on here. But still, he got the feeling something wasn't quite right about her.

He shifted, the prickling sensation actually making him uncomfortable, and just when he would have stood up to shake off the strange feeling, a movement beyond the blonde pulled his attention away from her. Nick realized that the older mailroom clerk was staring at him. But when the man saw that Nick had noticed, he immediately turned his attention toward organizing his mail cart.

Nick narrowed his eyes, considering the man. Something

was odd about him too, although he didn't get that same strange vibe from the man as he had from the receptionist. In fact, that prickly feeling abated as soon as Nick turned his attention to the mail clerk.

Then after a few seconds, Nick recognized what he found out of place about the man. He was old.

So far Nick hadn't seen anyone in the office who was older than their early thirties. This man was much older, stooped a little, his face weathered, his hands slightly gnarled.

Nick certainly hadn't seen all the employees of the magazine, but he got the distinct feeling this guy was an anomaly. Finola White was a woman who venerated youth and beauty. The older man didn't exactly fit that image, but then again he was just a lowly mailroom clerk.

The old man's gaze met his again, just for a second, but though his eyes were hazed with old age, Nick got the feeling the old guy didn't miss much.

The old man intrigued him, even though Nick wasn't exactly sure why.

Nick watched him until he finished messing with his cart and disappeared through the double doors into the magazine's main offices.

Nick rose, deciding to ask the receptionist a few questions about the old guy, when the double door opened again. A tall man dressed in an expensive black suit with a bright bluish-green shirt underneath. What was the color called? Teal maybe.

Nick supposed if he was going to describe a man as elegant, it would be this guy. As he walked toward Nick, the red recessed lighting that highlighted the walls glinted off his polished, alligator-skin oxfords.

Nick glanced down at his scuffed leather boots. Yeah, this was a different world.

The man stopped in front of him. And the first word

that came to Nick's mind was vampire. He was reminded of Dracula from the old movies—of course, this guy was an updated version, with a trendy haircut and designer clothing—but the pale skin and eerie, unreadable eyes were just the same as the classic movie monster's.

His neck prickled, and Nick disliked the other man instantly.

But when the man offered his pale, long-fingered hand to him, Nick didn't hesitate to accept it. His palm was cool and his grip surprisingly strong. Again the thought of vampires popped into Nick's mind. Nick scoffed silently at himself. He never liked those silly monster movies. He saw plenty of real-life horror, inflicted by real people, so he didn't find much appeal in imaginary monsters.

But for just a moment, a memory flashed in his mind. A snippet of memory he'd told himself couldn't be real and one that he'd forcibly learned to repress.

Because it's not real, Rossi. It's just some figment of your imagination.

"My name is Tristan McIntyre," the man said, his deep, cultured voice driving out the rest of the memory. "I'll bring you back to speak to Ms. White."

Nick nodded. "Nick Rossi, nice to meet you."

"Likewise." Tristan looked composedly affable, but Nick was certain neither actually meant what they said. Nick followed the man as he pushed open one of the huge doors that led into the inner sanctum of the *HOT!* offices.

Stepping through that door was like falling down the rabbit hole, at least for a guy like Nick. The whole place was abuzz with eclectic people in equally eclectic attire. It was surreal even to someone who had seen plenty.

The red lighting and strange, oversized yet modern furniture followed from the lobby into the offices and it was actually hard to decide where to look first.

"So you are a detective?" Tristan asked over his shoulder as he led Nick down a cavernous, glowing red hallway. "What brings you here today? Nothing unpleasant, I hope."

Nick stopped peering around him.

"Um—" he inwardly cringed at his confused reaction, but it took him a moment to rally his overwhelmed senses. "There's no need to go into it twice. I'll explain once we reach Ms. White."

Tristan smiled back at Nick, revealing white, surprisingly even teeth. No fangs like Nick had suspected. "Well, how very succinct of you."

They reached a different section of the offices. A group of rooms sectioned off by glass walls. The effect was even more disorienting than the outer offices. Nick felt as if they were now entering a carnival funhouse.

The red lighting was now gone and the whiteness of their surroundings was almost blinding. Nick followed Tristan, looking through the glass at what was obviously a boardroom with a long glass table. Past that, more offices. And farther beyond that, a huge office that seemed to glow in its whiteness.

He realized that was where they were going and as he looked more carefully, he realized he could finally see a woman who was obviously Finola White seated at a glossy white desk. Even with the glass walls, the maze design somehow kept her office private until you were very close to it, like some odd chrysalis keeping her hidden in its translucent shell.

But now that he could finally see her, she was every bit as striking as her photos in the newspapers and magazines. Her skin and hair were so pale, she almost disappeared amid all the white of her office.

They continued down another hallway, and again Nick had that funhouse feeling. He could see where he wanted to go, but couldn't quite seem to get there.

"Ms. White is waiting to see you."

Nick didn't respond. After all, he could see her through the crazy glass walls.

Finally they navigated the maze, and Tristan rapped on the glass door. Finola White straightened as if she hadn't noticed them at all.

She smiled and waved for them to enter.

Tristan held open the door for him to enter first. Nick stepped into the room and approached the desk, again struck by how fair she was, as if dressed up in a costume.

Surely she must be albino, except Nick suspected albinos had more color than this woman. Even the irises of her eyes were a pale, pale gray, just a shade or two lighter than the whites of her eyes. Only her lips held any color and they were red. Bloodred.

Yet, despite her odd coloring, she was truly beautiful, like a classical artist's sculpture come to life.

To Nick's astonishment, a growl came from her, low and menacing.

"Oh, you silly baby," she then crooned and Nick realized that the rumble didn't come from the fashion icon, but the small fuzzy dog on her lap. The small beast's white fur blended almost completely with Finola's white skin and suit.

"Ignore him," she said, baring teeth as white as the rest of her. The wide smile looked far more predatory than her lapdog's snarl. "Dippy is my delicious new pet, and he's still getting settled in."

She didn't break eye contact with Nick, nor did that hungry smile slip, as she lifted the puppy up to nuzzle its fur against her cheek.

Nick found the action oddly unsettling. Even the dog looked a little uncomfortable.

But finally she lowered the animal back to her lap and said, "I'm sorry, I didn't even introduce myself. I'm Finola White."

Nick stepped forward to accept her extended hand, her fingers long and delicate against his—and as icy as her coloring.

"I'm Detective Nick Rossi."

"A detective?" She tilted her head, clearly intrigued, as her pale, pale gray eyes roamed over him. "Please have a seat and share with me why you are with us today. I'm very curious."

Chapter Two

Her gaze continued to move over him, intense and aware, as he took a seat in a white velvet chair. He was relieved that piece of furniture had more normal dimensions than the ones out in the lobby and his feet didn't threaten to swing off the ground when he sat. He already felt at a disadvantage in this world without the furniture being as unusual as the people themselves.

"So Detective, please tell me what brings you here. I cannot even begin to imagine why." Finola smiled that predatory smile again, and before he could answer, she added, "Of course, if Tristan hadn't told me you were a detective, I would have thought you were one of the male models here for the new Zeke Hoffstead photo layout for the May edition of *HOT!* You know his clothes, they are so rugged and masculine. Perfect for a man like you."

Nick didn't know. He'd never heard of Zeke Hoffstead. But he did know when a woman was flirting with him. And Finola wasn't being remotely subtle.

He glanced at her assistant editor, who stood beside her desk like some sort of sentry. While his expression was stoic, totally unreadable, Nick got the impression he didn't quite agree with Ms. White's opinion of him.

Nick pretended to be oblivious to her overture, and pulled out his badge. It was always best to keep things on a professional level. At least at first. He wasn't such a prude that he wouldn't use attraction to get the answers he needed. Especially if he knew it would help the greater good.

But for now, he kept his tone serious. "I'm here from NYPD to talk to you about several of your past employees."

Finola's barely glanced at the silver badge as she met his gaze, her finely arched brows drawing together. "My past employees?"

"Yes, it seems that Finola White Enterprises and specifically *HOT!* magazine has quite a track record of strange occurrences."

Finola looked totally unsurprised by that. "Well, I'm sure that is true. Fashion is a strange industry. Why, remember just a few editions ago—" she glanced over to Tristan as if he would verify the story she was about to share—"when culottes made a resurgence. We actually did a four-page spread on them. That was a very strange occurrence, indeed. Culottes."

She shook her head, looking truly baffled and dismayed. "So yes, I readily agree odd things do happen here. But not the type of things that would require the attention of the police—well, aside from the fashion police maybe."

She smiled widely at her own joke.

Nick stared at her, trying to decide if her silly storytelling was genuine or an attempt to distract him. He honestly wasn't sure.

Nick glanced at Tristan to read his reaction, but the man's expression remained deadpan. Nick got the feeling Tristan wasn't as indifferent as he appeared. Something about his stance, though it looked relaxed enough, hinted at the fact he wasn't as calm as he appeared.

Nick's neck prickled.

Nick returned his gaze to Finola.

"Well, I won't presume to say I know anything about the fashion industry, but—"

"You are doing just fine."

Nick frowned. "Excuse me?"

"Your understanding of fashion. You are doing fine," Her gaze roamed over him, and there was definitely no mistaking the interest in her pale eyes now.

"Thanks," he said, again feeling that he should keep things on a professional level. Her interest made him uncomfortable. More prickles needled his neck and this time even down between his shoulder blades. He held still, determined not to try to shake off the sensation.

Instead he refocused on the task at hand.

"So am I to believe you are not aware of the disappearances of several of your past employees? Twenty-one of them to be exact."

Finola's eyes widened. "Twenty-one. Really?"

Nick nodded, trying to read her reaction. Her wide-eyed expression looked sincere, but something about it seemed not quite right.

Then she glanced toward her assistant, who still remained expressionless, but Nick got the impression that something had passed between them.

"That does seem like a lot." She returned to Nick. "What happened to them?"

"Well, that's it. No one knows. They simply disappeared."

Finola made a face then, one of dismay.

"Disappeared," she whispered. "That's awful."

"Yes," Nick agreed. "All of them gone with the exception of one."

The dismay disappeared from her face as she shot a glance back to Tristan. This time an actual frown marred the polished man's perfectly serene expression.

Interesting.

"One?"

"Yes," Nick said, feeling as if he was getting somewhere. Both Finola and her assistant editor seemed—surprised by this news. Not the disappearances, but that one had resurfaced. These two definitely knew something.

Nick pulled a small notebook out of the pocket of his leather jacket, flipping it open to the names of all twenty-one past employees. He leaned forward to slide it across Finola's glossy white desk. He tapped the last name on the list.

"Jessica Moran. She was discovered wandering the streets after being reported missing almost a week before."

Finola stared at the list, but he got the feeling she wasn't really seeing it. The white dog on her lap growled.

"Jessica Moran," she finally repeated, her tone vague as if she was trying to recall who that might be.

"She was your personal assistant."

Finola's eyes widened again. "Oh, of course. Although as I recall she only worked for me very briefly."

"It appears most of these people only worked for you very briefly. And some of them were reported missing shortly after leaving the magazine. Sometimes within a day." Nick told her.

Finola slid the notebook back toward him. "The magazine industry can have a very high rate of turnover. It's a stressful job. Very competitive."

"I'm sure it is," Nick said. "And I suppose twenty-one people quitting their jobs, or even being fired, wouldn't be so strange in a five-year period. But twenty-one disappearances—now, that does seem strange, doesn't it?"

Finola met his gaze, her gray eyes unflinching. "Yes, that does seem strange. But technically it would be twenty disappearances, wouldn't it? The one was found, right?"

Nick nodded. "Yes, she was, but I've met with the woman and you can't really say that she's 'back.' Not truly."

Finola frowned, just a brief creasing of her brow, over

almost before it began. "What do you mean she's not truly back?"

Nick shifted in his chair, uncomfortable with what he was about to say. After meeting Jessica Moran, he'd had prickly feelings in droves, and he hadn't liked it one bit. But he knew there had to be a reasonable explanation for the behavior he'd witnessed in the young woman.

"She seems to be suffering from some kind of post-traumatic stress or something."

Finola frowned again, another brief crease. Then her pale face returned to its lovely flawlessness. She waited for him to continue his explanation.

"She reacts to demands. She will do whatever you tell her, but when you look in her eyes, it's like no one is in there. And when she isn't following instructions, she simply sits as if she can't think on her own. It's . . ." he hesitated to use this description, but it was the only way to really describe what he'd seen, "it's like she's a zombie."

For a moment, Finola didn't react, then she straightened in her chair, her expression incredulous. "A zombie?"

She glanced toward Tristan, whose lips twitched slightly. Of course the vampire would react to that. When Finola's eyes returned to Nick, they twinkled with amusement.

"I'm sorry, Detective," she said, attempting to smother back her amusement with her fingers to her lips. "I don't mean to make light of the situation, but you have to admit this all sounds pretty far-fetched."

Nick gritted his teeth, but nodded. A familiar feeling—one from long ago—tightened his chest. He didn't like the description either. He knew it was far-fetched. But he also knew what he'd seen.

Just like you know what you saw all those years ago.

No. He wouldn't go there. He had imagined what he'd seen years ago. And this time, well, there had to be a medical explanation for the young woman's condition.

And while Jessica's case was weird, Nick was really here to focus on the missing people. Something was going on at this magazine. And the only common denominator among all these people was *HOT!* magazine and Finola White.

Finally Finola realized that Nick wasn't sharing any of her amusement and she immediately sobered.

"Nick—it is Nick, right? I realize what you are telling me is serious. Certainly I'm sympathetic and highly concerned. My employees are like family."

Nick remained silent. He didn't know Finola White, but he knew enough of her reputation to know that this woman would hardly consider her employees, her underlings, family.

He glanced at the vampire. Okay, she might consider that one family. And Nick didn't believe for a moment Finola didn't know about these disappearances and that she wasn't somehow involved.

"So how can we help you?" Finola asked, those pale eyes eating him up, almost as if she was reading his mind. She pushed the notebook across the desk again.

Nick pushed it back.

"Look at those names again, and tell me anything you can about them. What departments they worked in. Anything you can recall about their work, interactions with other employees. With you. Anything." He pushed the notebook back.

Finola reached forward to take it again, her French-manicured fingertips grazing his. He felt nothing but the coolness of her skin.

He instantly thought of the woman in the elevator. How even touching her arms through layers of clothing brought his body to sudden awareness.

He was here to work, to figure out what the hell had happened to all these people. And that was the only thing he needed to be focused on.

Finola read the list again, then finally shook her head, giving him an almost woeful sigh. "Again, many of these people must not have worked here very long, because most of the names don't even ring a bell with me."

So much for the "family" comment.

"Do you do the hiring?" Nick asked.

"I make the final decision, but often Tristan does much of my hiring, and of course certain departments such as the art department do their own interviewing, again just running the final decisions past me."

Nick nodded. That made sense.

Finola handed the notebook back to Nick, and again her fingers brushed his. This time, they lingered even after he accepted the book. He immediately rose and walked over to Tristan, holding the pad out to him.

Tristan raised an eyebrow, seeming reluctant to accept the notepad. Then he uncrossed his arms and took it, his eyes scanning the row of names.

"Yes, I recall several of these people," he said, meeting Nick's gaze, his eyes cool. "Finola was correct, many of them actually did not work here very long."

"Many people think the fashion business is going to be all glamour and fun with fabulous perks," Finola explained. "But running a highly successful business is hard work with long hours. Many people just don't work out, or simply quit."

Nick nodded, then turned back to Tristan. "I'm assuming you can give me a list of who you hired and whether they were indeed in *HOT!*'s employment on the dates they were reported missing or . . ."

"Turned zombie?" Tristan suggested, another smile tugging at his lips, but he again managed to repress it.

Nick stared at the man for a moment, silently warning him that he didn't see the humor in this at all.

"I'd also like lists of who hired these people and who they would have worked with closely."

Finola made a small noise of displeasure. "This will be a bit time-consuming, won't it?" She made a slight face, one that looked remarkably like annoyance, but it was quickly masked behind a sigh of sorrow. "But it must be done. We have to find out what is happening here."

Nick nodded, wishing he believed she really felt that way.

"I appreciate that," he finally said. "Is there any chance I could speak to other employees now?"

"Of course," Finola said without hesitation, then she grimaced. "Actually, I forgot, today isn't the best time. I have a large staff meeting taking place in—" she looked down at the thin silver watch on her left wrist—"my goodness, in about twenty minutes. And unfortunately this one is going to include most of the people you'd want to talk with. All the heads of the different departments."

Nick nodded, undeterred. "That's fine. I wouldn't have had much time myself. But if it's okay with you, I will be back, hopefully tomorrow."

Finola smiled, the gesture almost—sweet, if that was possible for a woman who was notorious for being de-manding and a diva. "That's fine. I should warn you, it will be chaos here. It is our busiest time of the year."

She seemed to be waiting for him to react, but he didn't recognize what was of such importance.

"It's New York Fashion Week," she said as if he was a total dolt.

"Oh, right." He had heard of the event, although he didn't know much about it. But he supposed for a fashion magazine that would be a huge and important occasion. It also meant the *HOT!* staff would be very busy.

Oh well. His investigation was important too.

"I appreciate your meeting with me," he said, offering her his hand. Instead of accepting it from where she sat, she stood and came around the desk, and now Nick got the true impact of Finola White. She was tall, only a few inches shorter than his 6'2". And she had a killer body, there was no denying that. Every lithe curve was perfectly displayed in a simple snow-white sheath that somehow managed to accent her pale skin rather than blend with it. She was so unusual-looking that she was totally stunning. He might not feel any reaction as he looked at her, but he also couldn't deny she was beautiful.

And Nick didn't trust her any more than he did her sidekick, who continued to watch them with his usual deadpan expression. How could they not realize what had happened to her employees?

Oh, she did. She might be self-absorbed, but even she couldn't ignore twenty, twenty-one missing employees.

"I look forward to seeing you tomorrow," she said, smiling wide, her ruby-red lips parting to reveal teeth that perfectly matched her hair, skin and dress. She shook his hand. He repressed a shiver that wasn't totally due to her cool skin. Her dog rumbled grumpily from its place tucked under her arm.

"Great," he said, ignoring the grouchy little mutt. "I will be in touch."

She smiled widely. "I'm counting on it."

Yeah, there were no double entendres in that exchange.

Nick extricated his hand from hers, nodded toward the vampire, then left, weaving his way slowly through the disorienting glass hallways.

Well, he'd learned only one thing from his meeting with Finola White. Dealing with her was going to be interesting, very interesting.

★ ★ ★

As soon as the detective disappeared, Finola spun on Tristan. "How did you let one of them get away?"

Tristan wanted to point out that cleaning up after Finola's impulsive behavior wasn't the easiest thing. Not to mention, the soulless did have a tendency to wander. It was a wonder that more of them hadn't resurfaced.

"This makes me very unhappy," she said, walking over to her wet bar in the far corner. She set down her dog, which immediately shook itself as if to cast off Finola's touch. Then the animal scooted to its white velvet and Swarovski crystal–encrusted bed, settling in with an annoyed huff, its dark eyes moving back and forth between them like it was actually following the conversation.

After a moment, Finola returned with a bottle of champagne, handing it to Tristan to uncork. He noted it was only the Bollinger, which meant she wasn't that mad. Tristan had long since learned to gauge Finola's ire by the expense of the champagne she drank while distressed.

This one meant she was barely irritated. Interesting, since he'd have expected her to be royally pissed. A rogue soulless body was a huge deal.

He popped the cork from the bottle, then crossed over to the bar himself to pour the golden liquid into one of her crystal champagne flutes.

"I'm sorry, my dearest," he purred as he handed her the glass, betting that a little groveling would calm her. "I'm sure this will blow over. There are no clues to be found. And certainly none of your employees would dare speak. No one will ever figure out what's wrong with the mortal. At best, their medical science will pronounce her catatonic or demented or something. But still, I will make sure the others are where I placed them."

Finola took a long sip of her bubbly, then nodded. "Of course it will be fine." She wandered over to the necklaces she'd been admiring earlier that morning. The two exquisite pieces were each worth over a million. The perfect diamonds shimmered and shone as she took a leisurely sip of her champagne and ran her long, white fingers over them.

Again, Tristan was surprised she was taking this so well. Too well, really.

"I want him," she said suddenly.

Tristan frowned, sure he'd misheard. "You want the Dior parure? I like it the best too."

She took another sip, then shook her head, her gaze still focused on the spill of precious stones in front of her. But now, Tristan realized she wasn't really looking at the necklace. The wheels were turning in her head.

A tightness filled his chest.

Damn it. It was never good when she got that look.

Then her icy gaze met his, and she smiled sweetly.

Damn. Another bad sign.

"I do want this one," she said, tilting her head to study the necklace she still stroked. "But I also want Detective Rossi, and I will have him."

Chapter Three

"I don't think that's a wise idea," Tristan said before he thought better of it. Then he remained absolutely still like a person who'd accidentally provoked a wild animal. One that could strike if he wasn't careful.

"I don't recall asking for your opinion," Finola said, her smile withering to a look of irritated arrogance. "As you just said, there isn't anything for him to discover. Now is there?"

Tristan lowered his gaze, then shook his head. The submissive act required every bit of his control. He was finding it harder and harder to submit to her, even though she was his superior.

But superior or not, she was an impulsive, careless and arrogant demon. And all those traits made her dangerous. More specifically, a danger to their mission.

"I'm sorry, Mistress." His voice caught on the title of submission and respect. "I'm just afraid he will somehow use your attraction to him to garner information."

Tristan instantly realized he wasn't making any reparations by continuing to question her.

But this attraction was very dangerous. Even in the short time he'd seen Detective Nick Rossi, Tristan could tell he was a smart, perceptive guy. The detective's career revolved around getting a person to talk and using whatever means necessary to do that.

And whether Finola wanted to admit it, which of course she didn't and wouldn't, she did have her weak spots. Her ego being one. And her certainty that she was superior to everyone else.

Still he couldn't stop himself from saying, "He's here to investigate you and the magazine. Letting him too close is like playing Russian roulette. What if you slip and reveal something?"

She made a disparaging noise, then waved one of her elegant hands in the air, a huge, multi-carat ruby ring flashing on her middle finger. "I haven't done anything wrong. So what is there to let slip?"

Tristan regarded her, glimpsing what had gotten her to the powerful position she held in Hell. No remorse, no sympathy, no sense of right or wrong. Evil in the truest sense. He admired that.

"Plus he'll soon be so smitten with me, he won't even consider that I could be involved. What is that adage? Keep your enemies close? Very close."

Not exactly, but Tristan didn't bother to correct her. He could see from the glitter in her pale eyes, as hard and uncompromising as the diamonds beside her, that her mind was made up.

Which meant his only way of survival, and keeping their assignment on track, was to simply run interference. Just like he always did. They were headed into Fashion Week, critical to their plans for a demon takeover. He couldn't let Finola's capricious desires ruin their scheme.

Tristan simply nodded then, again dropping his gaze.

But as usual, Finola's arrogance knew no bounds, and she came over to him, pressing a cool palm to his cheek.

"Wait, my beautiful Tristan, are you jealous?"

His gaze shot up, denial nearly spilling from his lips, but

instead he looked away. He knew it was a long shot, but maybe if she thought the idea of a tryst with the detective hurt him, she would reconsider.

He feigned his best pained look.

"Oh my poor baby," she cooed, "are you afraid I will lose interest in you?"

The hand caressing his jaw forcibly lifted his face to meet hers. "You know I treasure you above all else."

Tristan's gaze roamed her face, flashing emotions in his eyes. Need, hunger, even the desire to please. To please his ultimate master, Satan. Even if it meant groveling to Finola to keep them on task.

She smiled, clearly liking his display of vulnerability. As she always did.

"I keep you here with me because I can't exist without you."

That was true. She couldn't exist without him, but he simply nodded, not saying a word, although his eyes shone with humility and gratitude.

His submission aroused her and she kissed him then, her lips moving over his possessively, her teeth tugging roughly at his bottom lip. She bit until he moaned with a mixture of pleasure and pain.

For a moment, he thought maybe, just maybe, his game had worked, but as soon as they parted and he still saw the hardness in her eyes, his hopes vanished.

"But you know I like my diversions," she said, gently caressing his cheek again.

"Yes," he said, his voice low, passive.

"After all, he was quite delicious. In an unpolished, very manly way."

Now, that Tristan wouldn't deny. There was no question that Detective Nick Rossi was a very attractive specimen of human male. And very dangerous. Tristan had recognized that as soon as he'd seen him in the lobby.

"Perhaps I will share him with you," she said with a sweet smile as she crossed back to her desk and reached for her cell phone. "You'd like that, wouldn't you, dearest?"

He nodded. As a demon of lust, he would. That he couldn't deny. But his thoughts weren't on his carnal needs, not at the moment. They were on making sure Finola's lust didn't out them all.

She smiled, pleased by his compliance. She walked to her desk and picked up the phone. She pressed in a number, then waited. Her smile faded and the softness left her voice as she spoke to the person who answered, "Anna, where are you? Are you nearly done?" She made an impatient face, cutting off her assistant's response. "Fine, fine. But get back to the office. ASAP. I have a job for you."

Annie pressed the END button on her phone and didn't bother to contain her frustrated growl.

The taxi driver glanced at her in the rearview mirror. "Bad news?" he asked in a heavy accent.

"Always," she muttered, glaring down at her phone, her electronic shackle to Finola. God, it was such a temptation to just open the window and pitch the damned thing out. But that wouldn't free her from her bonds. She was owned—completely. And the worst part was that Annie had done it to herself, willingly, gladly.

If only she'd truly understood what she'd gotten herself into when she'd signed on the dotted line and agreed to become Finola White's personal assistant.

She dropped her phone back into her purse and sighed. What did Finola want now?

She leaned her head against the cold glass of the window, staring blankly at the world passing her by. Hopelessness drained away all her energy and she could only think one thing over and over.

I can't do this anymore.

★ ★ ★

By the time the taxi pulled up to the large warehouse, Annie had rallied herself yet again, telling herself she could survive whatever Finola threw her way. Annie was tough, determined, and frankly, she wasn't going to let evil win.

She rushed toward the warehouse where the photoshoot was being held, arms overflowing with designer clothes. Probably only three or four of them would be used for the photo spread in the June issue of *HOT!*, but all designs had to be available. As she fought to open the heavy metal door, she wrestled with the slippery, plastic-protected garments, hoisting them up to keep them from dragging on the ground. But her attention was quickly diverted from her struggle as she entered the building.

Greenery hid the industrial metal beams and ductwork. Real palm trees swayed in a warm tropical breeze created by portable heaters and fans. Annie could hear the rush of a waterfall, glimpsing blue water through the jungle of verdant leaves and undergrowth. A brightly colored parrot cawed, only to be answered by another one.

"Amazing," she murmured to herself, recalling why she'd wanted to work for *HOT!* in the first place. For these moments of magic.

She wandered farther onto the set, taking in every detail. That was until she squealed and stumbled backward, realizing the "hanging vine" near her left shoulder was actually a snake. A real, live, tongue-flicking, ginormous snake.

"Don't worry. I've been assured they are all friendly and nonpoisonous."

Annie turned to find Charlie Bowen, *HOT!*'s up-and-coming new photographer, headed in her direction.

"They?" Annie peered around her nervously. "Well nonpoisonous is definitely good. But I'm not convinced that anyone can know for sure if they are friendly."

Charlie chuckled as he took the majority of the garments from her arms.

"Right this way." He jerked his head toward the other side of the warehouse, where a makeshift wardrobe and makeup area had been made.

"Thanks for getting these here," he said, giving her a friendly smile over his shoulder while managing to negotiate electrical wires and other builders' disarray without effort. Annie picked her way behind him, more aware of needing to watch her footing. Never mind that the snakes could have slithered anywhere.

"I'm sure Finola was fit to be tied when she realized they weren't here already," he said.

Annie glanced up, just for a moment, then shrugged, her attention back on her footing. "She's always fit to be tied about something." Then she shot a look at Charlie, afraid she might have said too much. Much like the snakes, she wasn't sure who at *HOT!* magazine was friendly. If anyone at all.

Charlie shot her a sympathetic smile, which again looked sincere, but Annie decided the best bet was to keep her mouth shut. Always the safest strategy at *HOT!*

"Just one minute," Charlie said as he strode to where about a half dozen models were seated, getting their hair and makeup done. Charlie spoke with each of the makeup artists, gesturing with his one free hand, clearly telling them what he liked and didn't like. Then he stopped beside one particular model. Ava Wells. His girlfriend.

Ava and Charlie were *HOT!*'s "it" couple, their romantic tale sort of a Cinderella story in reverse. The mailroom clerk discovered to be an amazingly talented photographer who gets the dream career and the girl. And the girl's a supermodel to boot.

Annie watched, the sight bittersweet. Annie had given

up everything for the same dream. To have an exciting, successful career. To have true love. To be happy. And here she stood, overworked, with nothing to show for her suffering and hard work but long hours, stress, exhaustion and headaches. There was no glamour, no respect. There was no true love. And what rewards she had gotten came at a very steep price.

No, Finola White wouldn't break her. Yet deep inside her, in a darker, more cynical place, Annie wondered what the "It Couple" had sacrificed to obtain their dreams. And would the cost really be worth it in the end?

She watched them a moment longer, finding herself hoping it was worth it. She needed to believe life could work out and be better. She needed to believe happy endings did exist, even after bad choices.

Annie shifted the remaining clothes from one arm to the other, telling herself for the umpteenth time that things would work out. She had to believe that.

Charlie returned to her, directing her toward the dressing rooms. Outside was an improvised clothing rack, which was nothing more than the rods and framework from the tropical rainforest set.

"Roget would have a stroke if he saw his pieces hanging on old theater scaffolding," Charlie grinned.

"But he'll be thrilled with your work when you are done." Annie put the last of the garments on the bar. She brushed down the bags to keep the clothes as wrinkle-free as possible, then turned to Charlie. "Okay, I've got to go."

Charlie stopped inspecting the different pieces and frowned at her. "Aren't you going to stay a bit and see how these look?"

Annie laughed humorlessly. "Yeah, right. Finola has another task awaiting me, pronto. See you later. Good luck with the shoot."

"Annie," Charlie called as she began to pick her way back through the cords and wires. She turned to look at him. He walked across the several feet, his usually amused hazel eyes serious.

"You will be free of her one day soon."

"Of course," she said readily, although she wasn't sure what he meant.

He nodded at her as if they'd just shared a private promise of some sort. One that she didn't understand. But she forced another smile, then hurried back to the waiting cab.

Once she had settled in the seat and given the office's address to the driver, she leaned back, contemplating Charlie's words.

You'll be free of her one day soon.

Did he know what Annie had done to get her job at *HOT!*? Probably. People just didn't go from the mailroom to successful photographer overnight. He must have made a deal of some sort himself. The deal no one ever discussed. That was part of the pact too.

Which made Charlie's comment all the more disconcerting. He had to know he could be risking all the happiness he'd acquired with comments like that. And happiness was surprisingly elusive when you made a deal with a devil.

Suddenly a chill crept over her like the devil was standing right beside her. What if Charlie was one of *them*? What if he was a demon, trying to trick her into breaking her pact? Wasn't that the game? Make her trip up so she would break contract, and they would get her soul?

She'd learned pretty quickly to trust no one within Finola's company. Yet she had stupidly begun to trust both Charlie and Ava, because they'd been so warm to her. Maybe that was just some sort of setup. A way to see if she was really loyal to Finola. For all she knew, Charlie could report everything she said back to Finola.

None of the *HOT!* staff were her real friends. Hadn't

she learned anything over her years of working for Finola?
She had to keep all her cards close to her chest. Be careful
who you trust. Be careful what you say. Do your work.
And try to avoid Finola's wrath as much as possible.

That was how she planned to survive. She only had
seven more years until her contract was paid in full.

She groaned. "Seven years."

Chapter Four

"I need you to find out everything you can about a Detective Nick Rossi."

Annie stared at her boss, not sure why the request surprised her. Finola had asked her to do many strange things over the past three years, not the least of which was locating hundreds of lovebirds in the greater borough of New York for a photoshoot. Tracking down a specific silk weaver who raised a particular, preferable type of silkworm and lived in a remote part of China. And the worst being when she insisted that Annie purchase the original celluloid reels of *Casablanca* so Finola could have a designer make them into a dress that she would then wear on the red carpet for the Oscars.

Needless to say, Annie hadn't managed the last one, but she did manage to save her immortal soul by getting the original reels from *Night of the Demons*, which, not surprisingly, was also one of Finola's favorite movies, so her demanding boss was appeased. And actually did look quite stunning on the red carpet.

So strange requests Annie had handled. But Finola's requests had always centered around the world of fashion and her place in it. Annie didn't know what to make of investigating an investigator. Why would Finola want her to do that? Was she in trouble? Could a detective even be a threat to a—creature like Finola?

But she knew better than to ask questions like that. Instead she asked, "What do you want to know?"

Finola didn't answer her right away. Instead she wandered over to her desk, not taking a seat, but absently running her fingertips along the edge of her desk, then over the back of her leather desk chair. Her movements had an almost daydreaming, sensual quality.

Annie found her motions almost entrancing, even as she found them odd. She'd never seen Finola act this way.

Through the glass walls, Annie could see Tristan in his own office, seated at his desk. He spoke on the phone, but his attention appeared more focused on their boss than his conversation. His unusually beautiful face was marred by a frown and his own expression looked as vexed as Annie felt. Clearly he was aware of Finola's strange behavior too.

What was wrong with her?

Finally she turned back to Annie as if she'd just realized her assistant had asked a question.

"I want you to find out everything," she said as if that were the most obvious thing in the world. "Where he lives. Where his office is. What he does in his spare time. About his family."

Annie couldn't suppress her frown. Family? She didn't think she'd ever heard Finola say that word before. It sounded almost like a foreign term when passing over Finola's bloodred lips.

Then as if the word disturbed her too, Finola's wistful expression hardened and she clearly considered something she hadn't thought of until that moment.

"I want to know whether he's married. Or if he has a girlfriend."

Ah, realization hit Annie. Her boss was romantically interested in this man. Annie had never seen Finola act this way over a man before. She seemed outright—smitten.

Finola always had men. They flocked to her. And usually she just treated them like entertainment and accessories. This was definitely different.

Finola might be evil, but she was beautiful. And she could be charming. And seductive. Men came as soon as Finola crooked her finger. Surely this man would too.

So why the research? Was it because Finola was truly interested in this man? Could a demon feel genuine love and affection?

"I want the information on my desk first thing tomorrow morning," Finola said, the dreamy quality gone, replaced by the demanding diva Annie knew so well.

Annie nodded, all thoughts about what a demon could or couldn't feel gone. She had another task, and all her concentration had to be focused on that. This was just another job to be done and done well to keep herself safe.

"I'll get right on it," Annie assured her boss, turning to leave Finola's office.

"Where is lunch?" Finola asked, halting Annie's retreat instantly. "I did tell you to get takeout at Raimondi's, did I not?"

Annie gritted her teeth, wanting desperately to remind Finola that she'd also demanded that Annie return directly from the photoshoot. But Annie was damned if not getting lunch was going to be the thing that got her soul damned for all time.

She turned back to her boss, keeping her expression carefully contrite. "I'm sorry. I will go there right now."

She hurried from the room before Finola could react more.

But of course, Finola had to have the last word.

"Be quick about it, Anna," Finola called after her. "We

have enormous amounts of Fashion Week details to go over. Pick up some lattes too. It's going to be a long afternoon."

Annie raised a hand to acknowledge she'd heard, then dropped it back to her side, fisted, her nails digging into her palm.

Seven years. Just seven years.

"What do you mean she isn't staying on task?"

"She's wasting her time on frivolous things. Clothes, jewelry, all manner of human indulgences."

Satan looked up from adjusting his ski boots. He raised one of his distinctively arched brows in that condescending way only he could.

"And what's wrong with that?" he asked, his voice rumbling through his cavern like thunder. Then he glanced pointedly at his own attire. Human skiwear.

"Nothing, Master. Nothing. But she gets distracted by them. And she loses her focus."

Satan rose from his throne, walking over to a large oval mirror that two small goblin-like demons struggled to hold upright for him. He turned from side to side, admiring his new ski apparel. The human clothing looked odd against his red skin, and the knit cap didn't fit quite right over his horns. But overall, the look wasn't too bad.

"Do hold the mirror still," he growled at the goblins. The goblins instantly braced their tiny bodies, levering the mirror straighter. Their lean, reptilian muscles quivered under the strain of obeying his command, but they did manage to keep the large glass oval motionless.

After a moment, and apparently satisfied, he turned his attention back to the topic at hand. As soon as Satan looked away, the goblins nearly dropped the mirror in their relief. But they didn't. Luckily. A broken mirror would not please Satan. Even he was superstitious.

"Tell me more," he demanded, his voice echoing around them again, startling.

"She also seems to be attracted to a human. A detective who is asking questions about the missing employees."

Satan frowned, then stroked his pointy goatee.

"How attracted?"

"Very."

Satan considered this, then nodded. "Thank you for letting me know. You will come right back to me if she does anything too reckless. We're coming up to the most important event of our takeover. Her actions had better not interfere with that."

"Yes, Master. Of course, Master."

Annie stepped into her apartment, not containing her groan of relief at being home. Finally. She dropped her briefcase in the small coat closet by the door. Automatically her high heels followed. She moaned again with relief, flexing her sore feet against the cool wood floors.

"Annie, is that you?"

Annie closed her eyes at the sound of Bobby's voice and silly question. Who else would it be? But she shoved the snippy comment away. After all, Bobby wasn't to blame for her exhaustion.

She pulled in a calming breath and managed to answer, her tone not precisely happy, but at least pleasant. "Yeah, Bobby, it's me."

"Wow, you're home early."

Annie raised an eyebrow at that as she hung up her coat, but she supposed he was right. It was a little after nine, which was actually an early day for her. But it had been a high-stress day. And she was beat.

"Did you bring home dinner?" he called. "I'm starving."

Annie walked down the small hallway that opened up

into a large living room. Large even by Manhattan stand-
ards. Bobby lounged on the sofa, his feet on the coffee
table, and his attention on the large-screen television
mounted on the wall. A video game controller was clutched
in his hand.

Annie dropped down onto the oversized chair that
matched the rich, warm brown material of the sofa.

"No, I didn't stop to get anything. But I could order
pizza or Chinese, if you want."

He didn't look away from his game, making faces and
jerking the remote as his computer self sped wildly
through the city streets on a motorcycle. Wreaking havoc
as he went.

Absently she watched the game, too tired to do anything else.

Finally, he won—or lost, Annie wasn't exactly sure—
and he tossed the remote onto the coffee table, a cool
piece Annie had found at a flea market and refinished herself back when she'd first started at *HOT!* and had been
excited about this nice apartment and decorating it.

She still liked her place, with its eclectic décor and rich,
warm colors. Browns, rusts and warm beiges, accented
with cool pillows and artwork and lighting. A sort of
bohemian feel, comfortable, but stylish. Fun but calming.
A haven from the outside world. But it wasn't a haven she
got much time to enjoy these days.

"I guess Chinese would be okay," Bobby said with a
sigh, stretching his arms over his head as if he'd been hard
at work himself. The muscles in his broad shoulders
flexed. His T-shirt strained against his sculpted torso. He
yawned, running a hand through his naturally tousled
blonde hair.

He was so good looking—a perfect combination of California surfer and boy-next-door. He would be just about

any red-blooded woman's fantasy, and Annie wondered why, as she watched him, she felt nothing. Her pulse didn't even jump, much less speed up.

Exhaustion, she told herself, just like she did every time she didn't react to him.

Bobby finished his long stretch, then looked at Annie. "You look wiped out."

She nodded, surprised he even noticed. "Yeah, I am. It was a rough day." Another rough day.

"Then you'd better order the food before you totally crash."

She stared at him for a moment, the irritation she'd first felt when she'd entered the apartment returning. But again, she tamped it down.

Bobby didn't mean to be thoughtless. Sure, he'd been home all evening and he could have picked up something for dinner. But she knew he simply didn't think of things like that.

Annie was the organized one; he was the creative one. His struggle to get acting roles took up most of his attention and his time. He'd made the decision not to get a job for that very reason. He needed to be available to make auditions. And he did take a lot of acting classes. His quest for success made him a little absentminded; she understood that.

Annie forced herself up from the soft comfort of her chair to go back to the front closet to retrieve her phone from her bag.

She scrolled through her list of contacts to find the number of the Chinese restaurant that was Bobby's favorite. She placed the order, knowing what he liked. Once that was done, she headed toward the bedroom to change out of her work clothes, imagining the comfy warmth of her fleece pajama bottoms and a nice thick hoodie.

"You didn't even ask me about my rehearsal today," Bobby said before she could make it to the door.

She stopped in the doorway to turn back, giving him a pained look. Bobby had just gotten a part in an Off-Off Broadway play. It was not a huge role but he was still excited about it, and Annie couldn't blame him.

"I'm sorry," she said, trying not to show any of her exhaustion. "I forgot. How did it go?"

"Rehearsal was great," he said, smiling. A million-dollar smile, as they say. "I really think all my acting classes are paying off. I'm totally getting into this character's head."

It couldn't be that difficult, Annie thought. He played a deliveryman with only four lines.

Not kind, she instantly admonished herself. She knew Bobby was working hard, taking his work seriously, and she should be happy for him.

"Listen to how I've changed this one line to put my own spin on it. This is the original. 'Hey, mister, where do you want me to put this?'" He cleared his throat and shook out his long limbs, more like he was heading into an intense Shakespearean soliloquy than a single line.

Then in an awful Brooklyn accent that couldn't even begin to mask his Southern drawl, he said, "Hey, buddy, where do you want me to put this?"

Annie waited, not sure what to say. Then Bobby grinned, clearly pleased with his performance.

"See what I did there? I changed 'mister' to 'buddy.' I think it makes it more current. The director was pleased with my interpretation—and my initiative."

She forced a smile. "Nice."

He nodded. "This is really a great opportunity. A good solid piece for me."

"That's good." She offered him another smile, then headed into their bedroom.

She looked longingly at her bed, imagining how good the thick comforter and soft pillows would feel. But she bypassed it to go to her dresser to find her pajamas.

As she searched, her weary mind wandered. Thinking about the fact that she still needed to "research" Detective Nick Rossi, and how she was going to do that. Then her thoughts moved to what Charlie had said about being free of Finola. What had he meant? And why had he said it to her?

Finally, completely unbidden, her thoughts came around to the man from the elevator. His handsome face. His dark eyes. The naughty tilt of his lips as he'd talked to her. The slightly raspy quality to his deep voice.

Even now, the memory of him was enough to make her skin prickle with awareness and certain parts of her body tingle in a way they hadn't in a long time. After a moment, she realized she was just standing there like a silly school-girl, her pajamas clutched to her chest.

Guiltily, she glanced toward the doorway. She couldn't manage to muster attraction to her handsome boyfriend, the man who'd been her first love, and her boyfriend since her junior year in high school. Yet she could fantasize about a total stranger. Surely that didn't say very good things about her.

She quickly changed into her favorite fleece sleep pants and a comfy sweatshirt, then padded back to the living room.

She was about to curl up on the sofa next to Bobby, determined to have a nice night with him. To actually take the time to enjoy his company and not let her stresses and worries distract her, even if just for a couple of hours, when the apartment phone rang.

"You going to get that?" Bobby asked, even as she'd already started in the direction of the cordless handset, his attention back on his video game.

She didn't bother to respond, answering the phone instead.

"Hello?"

"Hello," answered a female voice on the other end, and for a second, Annie feared it was Finola. "Is Bobby there?"

"Umm, yes. Just a moment." She frowned at the receiver, wondering to whom the silky Southern-accented voice belonged.

"Bobby, it's for you."

He didn't respond for a moment, finishing up his game, then he accepted the phone.

"Hello?" Annie watched as Bobby instantly recognized who the woman was. "No, no. You aren't interrupting anything. Just hanging out."

Annie frowned, feeling a little hurt that he didn't say more. That he didn't tell the woman he was getting ready to spend a night in with his girlfriend, eating Chinese and cuddling.

Not really fair, her conscience said. Most nights, she and Bobby didn't spend the evening together. Usually he was out doing things related to his acting or hanging out here and she was working late. So he probably didn't even think before he answered.

Annie wandered into the kitchen and poured herself a glass of wine. Then she waited in the kitchen, not wanting to be hovering around like some nosy girlfriend, even though she could still hear his whole conversation.

"Thanks. I thought rehearsal went well today too," Bobby said, and Annie realized that this woman must be involved with the play as well. Annie took a sip of her wine, then got down plates for the Chinese food.

"I know," she heard Bobby agree to whatever the other woman said. He laughed. "It will be something if that happens."

Annie grabbed some silverware from the dishwasher.

She'd run out of time this morning and the clean dishes still needed to be put away.

She did the chore now, absently listening to Bobby chat.

"Really? Yeah, I'd love to do that. Sure. Yeah, that won't be a problem. Great. Okay, great. See you there."

Annie returned to the living room, setting the dishes on the coffee table.

"Who was that?"

"Ally," he said, placing the phone on the coffee table. "She's in the play with me."

Annie nodded. "It sounds like she is just as excited about the production as you are."

"Definitely. She's the lead. Remember her? She's a pretty amazing actress."

He reached for the television remote. He turned it off.

She nodded, although she couldn't really picture the woman.

Annie sighed, appreciating the silence. She was glad to have a quiet night with just Bobby. They really needed this, she realized.

But as she settled down among the pillows of the sofa, he stood. He crossed the room to grab his leather jacket, which hung on the back of the computer chair at her desk in the corner.

"Where are you going?" she said, frowning, confused.

Bobby slid one arm and broad shoulder into his coat, then the other. "Ally was calling to tell me there's this improv group meeting tonight at the Bleecker Street Playhouse. So I'm going to go check it out."

Annie looked down at the dishes she'd placed on the coffee table. "But I just ordered Chinese food."

"I know," Bobby said, "but I can just grab something on the way there. A sub or something. And the Chinese food will keep."

She nodded, her eyes suddenly misting over, surprising her as much as it surprised Bobby.

He frowned, looking around for an exit like a man trapped with a crazy person. Of course, the sudden display of emotion made her feel a little crazy. Irritated with her lack of control, she swiped at her eyes, determined to stem their flow.

"Annie," he said slowly as if he had no idea what to say.

She spared him from struggling for words. Raising a hand to cut him off, she sniffed slightly, then managed a tremulous smile.

"Of course you should go. I'm just overtired from work. That's all."

Bobby stared at her, then glanced toward the door, then back to her. "It really is a good opportunity for me. You know, both to improve my acting skills, and also to meet other actors. Networking does pay off in this industry."

"Absolutely. I'm fine. I'll just go to bed early." She laughed, albeit weakly, "Obviously I need a good night's rest."

Bobby studied her for a moment, then nodded. He came over and leaned down to give her a kiss. Their lips met, the touch so familiar to Annie it was like second nature. Yet even as she thought that, an image of the man from the elevator popped into her head.

She instantly pulled away, and Bobby frowned down at her. Shame burned her cheeks. But she fought to give him a normal smile.

"You should get some rest," he told her and she could see the concern in his eyes. "You look a little flushed."

"I will," she assured him. Her voice sounded strained, but Bobby didn't seem to notice. He grabbed his cell phone and waved good-bye.

As soon as he was gone, Annie made a noise low in her throat.

"Forget him," she muttered to herself. After all, who fixated on a man she'd met for less than five minutes in an elevator?

A sharp rap on the door snapped her out of her guilty reverie. She jumped up and retrieved her wallet from her purse, then answered the door, her assumption right. The Chinese food was here. Food for two, now for one.

Annie tried not to allow the hopelessness she'd been struggling with all day to creep back in. She focused on preparing a plate of Kung Po Chicken and spring rolls. Then she switched on the radio, changing the station when she realized Eric Carmen's "All By Myself" was playing.

"That's a bit too Bridget Jones for tonight," she muttered, switching to a station that played a still bitter, but at least not maudlin, song by Pink.

She poured herself a bit more wine, grabbed her laptop and curled up on the couch, food, wine and Internet within reach.

"Well, Detective Nick Rossi," she said to her computer screen, "let's see what we can find out about you."

Chapter Five

"Nick, what are you still doing here?"

Nick's head snapped in the direction of the gravelly voice behind him. Captain Joseph Brooks leaned against the doorway to Nick's office. He frowned, his gaze moving to what Nick had been studying so intently that he hadn't even been aware of his boss's appearance. Nick wondered how long his boss had been there watching him. He wondered how long he, himself, had been studying the computer printout photos that lined his office wall. Twenty of them. With one, number twenty-one, set slightly to the side of the others.

"Just getting caught up on some work," he said, turning his back to the photos as if that would somehow prove he hadn't been standing there obsessing over them.

Nick wasn't sure how long he'd been staring at these people, but he was sure it was a long time. But this case astounded him. So many people, working in one place, yet no one from *HOT!* magazine had ever reported their disappearance. Family and friends had reported them missing. It was almost as if no one at the magazine even knew or noticed. That couldn't be.

Something was very amiss at *HOT!* magazine.

But what?

Captain Brooks wandered over to the pinned-up photos, his gaze moving slowly over each face.

"Any leads?" he asked.

"No, but I only got to talk to Finola White and her assistant editor. They claim to have no knowledge of the disappearances."

Brooks glanced over his shoulder and snorted. "Likely story."

"Exactly."

Brooks returned his attention to the pictures. "With this many people in one company missing, someone has to know something."

"Definitely. I'm heading back over tomorrow to talk with some of the employees. Here's hoping someone talks," Nick said, his tone already dubious.

Brooks turned back to Nick, crossing his arms over his barrel chest. "That's always the trick, isn't it?"

Nick nodded.

"You finished up now?" Brooks asked, although Nick got the impression it was more an order than a question.

Nick glanced to the folder on his desk; inside were the notes he'd made thus far about the *HOT!* case. He wanted to look over the profiles of the missing people again, but instead he nodded at his boss.

"Yeah, I was headed out." How long would it be before Brooks and his follow coworkers no longer thought Nick needed to be handled with kid gloves? He'd been back almost four months. He was fine.

"Good, I'll walk out with you," Brooks said, waiting. Again, Nick felt his boss was only leaving with him to make sure he actually left. Next thing he knew. Brooks would be coming over to his apartment to make sure Nick was eating balanced meals and going to bed on time.

But Nick kept his disgruntled thoughts to himself and reached for his coat.

"Have you found any connection between the missing people aside from the magazine?" Brooks asked as they wove through the cubicles where many detectives and officers continued to work. One officer led a ranting detainee toward the interrogation rooms. Several distraught victims talked to officers. The place was abuzz, but then it was never quiet in the 18th Precinct.

Nick glanced over to see a woman who'd been here many times before for domestic violence. Maybe this time she'd actually press charges. Maybe.

Nick turned his attention back to his boss. "Not really. The only thing they all have in common is *HOT!* magazine."

Brooks nodded, then fell silent.

They stepped out of the precinct and the winter night enveloped them, frigid enough to take their breath away. But the busy street still felt more peaceful than headquarters.

He breathed in deep.

They started down 54th Street, still not talking.

After nearly a block, Brooks asked, "How are you feeling, Nick?"

Nick should have guessed this was coming. Maybe checking on his diet and sleep patterns wasn't so farfetched.

"I'm fine," he said, keeping the frustration out of his voice. After all, he couldn't exactly blame his boss. The man did need to know that one of his detectives wouldn't suddenly go crazy on him.

"This is a big case. Are you sure you're up to it?"

More irritation roiled in the pit of Nick's stomach. He was annoyed that his captain, who'd known him for nearly fifteen years, would doubt his ability. But he was even more annoyed with himself, that he'd given his boss cause to doubt his abilities. His sanity.

"I'm fine. I want this case."

Brooks shot him a glance, but then nodded. "Good."

They fell silent again, but after a few moments, Brooks asked, "So did you meet *the* Finola White?"

Nick smiled, glad to be off the topic of his sanity.

"Yes, I did."

"And?"

"She's as—unusual—as you would imagine."

Brooks chuckled, but then after a minute added, "Her photos make her look pretty attractive, though."

Nick nodded. "She is." But even as he agreed, his thoughts didn't actually go to the tall, striking blonde, but to the harried woman with the brown hair in a bun and big gray eyes. The small woman had managed to invade his thoughts many times since he'd left the magazine's offices. Charging right into his memory as she'd done to him physically on the elevator.

"Well, this is my station," Brooks said, startling him out of his thoughts about the petite brunette. Brooks paused at the top of the stairs that led down to the subway stop. "Let me know what you find out tomorrow. Twenty people, that's a damned lot."

Nick opened his mouth to say "twenty-one," but stopped himself. Captain Brooks didn't consider the last woman to be a missing person. But if he'd seen her, he'd realize she was as missing as the others. Oh, she was there physically, but that was it. As soon as Nick had looked in her eyes, he'd seen she was gone. Vanished.

But there was no way in hell Nick was going to tell his captain that. And he especially wasn't going to use the description he'd used with Finola and her assistant editor. Referring to that woman as a zombie was exactly the kind of comment that would have his boss very, very worried about his mental state.

"Well, I'll see what I can find out tomorrow."

"Keep me posted," Brooks said as he started down the stairs. "And go home and get some rest. Forget about all this for the night."

More worry. Damn, he hoped his fellow officers would realize he was perfectly fine, and soon. "Will do."

Brooks nodded and disappeared underground.

Nick turned down 46th Street, heading toward his small apartment on 10th Ave. The *HOT!* offices were in the opposite direction on 46th. He considered turning, just to wander by the building, but stopped himself.

See, that was the kind of behavior Captain Brooks would worry about. And maybe his boss was right. Maybe he did have to pace himself. Something had made him crack—even he couldn't deny that. Maybe he did need to let his cases go when he was off the clock.

He'd go home and actually get a decent night's sleep if he could. He already knew who he planned to talk to first tomorrow. Since a couple of the missing persons had been Finola White's personal assistants, it only seemed reasonable to talk to the present assistant.

That would be one Annie Lou Riddle. He felt certain if there was anything odd about *HOT!* or its owner, this woman would know.

"Well, Detective Nick Rossi," Annie said, scanning another interview article, "you are a pretty busy and pretty controversial guy."

She took a sip of her second—maybe third—glass of wine as she read. So far she'd learned that Nick Rossi was a well-respected detective, involved in bringing down some of New York's worst drug dealers, murderers, etc. In fact, in his earlier career he seemed to be a favorite with the police commissioner and the mayor, until around 2009, when the press releases changed. Suddenly most of the articles seemed to imply that the commissioner and the police chief were not supporting Detective Rossi's erratic behavior. And by early 2010, articles appeared saying Detective Rossi had been pulled from cases and had actually taken a leave of absence. It didn't say the leave was forced, but the articles and comments from Captain Brooks of the 18th Precinct certainly implied that was the case.

She went to the drop-down menu on her computer and clicked PRINT. Across the room, her printer clicked and hummed to life.

Why would Finola be interested in this guy? He must be very attractive. That was the only reason Annie could think of. She'd never been interested in blue-collar men before. She then clicked the link to bring up images of the man. But interestingly, she couldn't find any, except a few where he was hardly visible behind the captain or the commissioner.

Annie sipped her wine, studying one picture that showed him in shadowy profile. She held the glass to her lips, considering the straight nose and one brow she could make out. This man did look vaguely familiar. Had she seen him on the news?

She tilted her head, trying to make him out better. Then her thoughts drifted to another man. One who also had a straight nose and dark brows over laughing brown eyes. A man who had a naughty smile that immediately had made her think of equally naughty things.

Lifting the glass to her lips again, she clicked on another picture. As the photo enlarged, taking up most of the computer screen, she nearly choked on her sip of chardonnay.

No. It couldn't be.

There in front of her was the face she'd just been imagining.

Detective Nick Rossi was the man from the elevator.

★ ★ ★

"Do you have it?"

Annie hurried forward to place a folder on Finola's desk. Tristan leaned against the edge of the desk, his long legs crossed at the ankles, a cup of coffee in his hand. When Finola flipped open the file, he leaned in, his expression bored as always, to peruse the contents along with Finola. They both read the typed page of stats.

Annie watched both their expressions, but couldn't tell what either was thinking. She did know what *she* was thinking. She could not believe Finola White was stalking, or rather making Annie stalk, the man she had thought about far too much yesterday. And today.

Finally, after scanning the page, Finola slowly closed the file.

"This doesn't tell me what I want to know."

Annie had expected that response, but she quietly asked, "What did you want me to find out?"

"I told you. Everything. Personal information," she said, her voice losing just a little of its melodious tone.

"I searched, but I couldn't find anything online aside from what I gave you."

Finola stared at her for a moment, then sighed. "Anna, you are a very resourceful woman. By far the best personal assistant I've had."

To some employees a comment like that from a boss might have filled them with pride, but for Annie the compliment only filled her with dread. With each task Annie achieved, the stakes went up. Because Finola ultimately didn't want Annie to succeed. Finola was banking on her failing.

"And I expect you to figure out a way to find out the personal information I want to know. I want to know as much as I can about him, down to the smallest detail."

Annie nodded, but she couldn't help asking, in the most flattering way possible, "But why don't you discover the details about him for yourself? I'm sure if you asked him out, he wouldn't even consider turning you down. Men are crazy about you."

Apparently she'd layered her question with enough compliments, because Finola's expression remained calm, a mask of loveliness.

Annie noticed that Tristan raised an eyebrow, however.

But when Finola answered, Annie realized her compliments might have saved her from Finola's wrath, but they hadn't saved her from the task.

"I've made it very clear what I want, and I'm assuming you can do as I ask. If not, then perhaps you are not the personal assistant for me."

Genuine fear tightened Annie's chest, making it hard to breathe. She glanced at Tristan, even though she already knew there would be no help or sympathy there. In fact, his usually unreadable face looked almost amused.

"Yes, I can get the information."

"Good. Now go away," Finola said with a wave of her hand. "I have work to do, and so do you."

Annie nodded, wasting no time leaving her boss's presence and making her way back to her own desk. She had no idea how she was going to get this information, short of actually stalking the man. Sadly, she knew if that was what she had to do, she would.

Seven years. Just keep ticking off the days, the hours, the minutes.

Chapter Six

"Excuse me, I'm looking for Annie Lou Riddle."

"Just one moment, please," Annie answered without looking up from her computer. She was right in the middle of searching city records to see if Detective Nick Rossi was or ever had been married. She typed in the last word of her search, then hit the ENTER key with a resounding tap.

Ah, cyberstalking at its best.

She spun in her chair, preparing to get rid of this person as quickly as possible, since she knew Finola would expect new information in her usually unrealistic amount of time.

But as it turned out, her search had come to her.

Detective Nick Rossi stood on the other side of her desk, waiting patiently, watching the bustle of the *HOT!* staff.

But as soon as he saw her, recognition dawned in his dark eyes and that naughty smile that she was sure she must have idealized in her memory appeared. Nope, she hadn't improved him with memory; he was every bit as attractive as she remembered.

But he was the focus of Finola's interest. Not hers.

"Hey there," he said, his voice deep and husky, also just as appealing as she remembered. "I know you. We've bumped into each other before."

She blinked, amazed at how even his voice made her body react.

Her bewildered gape didn't deter him. "Are you, by chance, Annie Lou Riddle?"

It took her another moment to gather herself, but then she nodded.

Get focused here. His arrival had just made her life a lot easier. Now Finola could find out *everything* about him herself. Certainly a much better option than Annie having to walk into a police station to interrupt his work and ask him important questions such as what his favorite color was and could she have the names of all his childhood pets.

"You must be here to see Ms. White." She automatically reached for her phone to page Finola, but his rich, throaty voice stopped her.

"Actually, you're the lady I came to see," he said, with another charming smile, his nicely shaped lips framed by a goatee that just made him look more enchantingly rakish. His brown eyes, the color of sweet tea, twinkled. And for just a moment her belly fluttered like a teenage girl, discovering for the first time that the boy she had a crush on liked her back.

Stupid, she told herself. So, so stupid. He wasn't the boy she had a crush on. He didn't like her. She was a grown woman with a boyfriend, an all-consuming career, and a demon boss who *did* have a crush on him.

But he'd said he wanted to talk to her.

"Are you sure you aren't here to see Ms. White?" she asked again, still holding the phone receiver.

A smile tugged at one side of his lip. "I'm definitely sure."

She hesitated a moment longer, then hung up the phone.

"Okay," she said, knowing she didn't sound pleased. "How can I help you?"

His eyes twinkled at her resigned tone. "Why do I get

the feeling you aren't happy to see me? Was our elevator collision that unpleasant for you?"

"No," she said automatically.

His smile widened and he moved a little closer to her desk. "Yeah, it wasn't in the least bit unpleasant for me either."

Annie felt her cheeks grow warm. Was he flirting with her? Again her stomach did little somersaults.

No. No, she warned herself again. He wasn't, and even if he was, she wouldn't react. She couldn't react. And whether this man knew it or not, he belonged to Finola White.

"I never thought I'd see you again, actually," he said, drawing her attention back to him.

"You didn't?" she said, knowing she sounded as bemused as a silly schoolgirl.

Stop it, Annie! Now.

He shook his head, then leaned forward to add, "But I wanted to."

Her whole body tingled at his admission, her heart joining her tumbling stomach. She stared into those golden brown eyes of his, wondering what it would be like to be with a man like him.

"No," she stated, not realizing she'd even said the word aloud, until his smile faded.

"No, what?"

"No—" She struggled to collect herself, to find something to say that would make sense and stop this man from looking at her as if she was the most beautiful woman he'd ever seen. "That is—no, I didn't expect to see you again either."

"But you wanted to, too, didn't you?"

Annie was sure if any other man had said that it would have sounded arrogant and cheesy, but this man made it sound adorable.

Annie, you have got to stay focused.

"No, I'm just surprised. That's all," she said, managing to sound calm and not in the least bit interested.

He feigned a brief look of hurt, but then nodded, accepting her explanation without further comment. Probably sympathy for the poor muddled woman.

They both regarded each other for a few moments, then she again managed to rally her thoughts.

"So what did you want to talk to me about?"

He sobered completely, his expression now all business. "I wanted to talk to you about the disappearance of several employees over the last few years."

He was here doing an investigation. That was why he'd been here yesterday. He must have come to talk to Finola about these missing people. Funny, she hadn't even considered why he'd been in the elevator or how Finola had met him. But suddenly it all made sense.

"Missing employees?"

He nodded, his brown eyes regarding her for a moment, assessing her reaction. But she couldn't tell what he was thinking as he said, "I know you are working, but it would be great if maybe we could go get lunch and talk."

Her first instinct was to say no. Go to lunch? She didn't have time for that. She usually wolfed down a sandwich whenever she could find a minute. Her days were too busy for things like actual lunch breaks.

But then she realized this was the very person Finola wanted to know about, and going to lunch with him would be an easy way to find out all the details of his life.

Of course, she didn't want to answer the questions he'd likely have for her, but maybe she could keep him busy with questions of her own. She told herself she wasn't agreeing because she wanted to know more about him herself. This was work. Work and keeping her soul one more day.

She managed a slight smile. "Sure. Lunch would be great."

"So what's your favorite food?"

Nick looked up from his turkey sub, getting the definite impression he was the one being interviewed here. On the walk to the small diner just a few blocks from both her work and his station, she'd asked him at least a dozen questions. Did he live in Manhattan? Did he have family in New York? Did he have siblings? When was his birthday? Did he like winter? What was his favorite season? What were his hobbies? Did he have pets? What was his favorite color?

"I like just about everything. I'm not a very picky eater," he said, not bothering to hide his wry smile.

She nodded, oblivious to his expression, her own very serious—focused, even. She took a bite of her chef's salad, then reached for her cell phone, acting as if she was simply checking her messages. She typed something on the screen, just as she had after every few questions since they'd left the office. She might think she was being subtle, but he'd long since figured out she was making notes about his responses.

As if reading his mind, she looked up, giving him an apologetic smile. "Sorry, I just need to answer this email."

He nodded, not keeping the amused disbelief from his eyes, but again she didn't seem to notice. Whatever she was doing, it was her total focus.

She looked up from her phone. "Do you drink?"

This time he openly grinned. "Every day."

Annie's gray-blue eyes widened with dismay.

"Oh," he said slowly, pretending to just now understand her question, "you're referring to liquor. Yes, I do, sometimes."

She nodded, again oblivious to the fact that he'd been teasing her. She typed on her phone.

Well, one thing was for sure, Annie Lou was living up to her last name. He definitely didn't understand what she was doing, but he planned to find out. He took a bite of his sandwich, chewing slowly, watching her as she now focused on her lunch again.

The only thing he knew for sure was that she was just as pretty as he remembered. Wide eyes the color of stormy skies, long dark lashes, full lips, her brown hair pulled back from her face to reveal lovely cheekbones and a perfect complexion.

She might possibly be the nosiest woman he'd ever encountered, but her constant, random questions didn't bother him, especially asked in that sweet voice with just a hint of Southern twang softening the words. And her occasional smiles that made her face even more adorable. Although so far, her smiles had been far too infrequent. And laughs, well, he'd definitely like to hear more of those.

"Oh, I forgot," she said suddenly after swallowing a bite of her salad. "Are you married?"

Forgot? He frowned, now truly curious about what was motivating all these questions, but he answered her, because this one he definitely wanted her to know.

"No, I'm not married."

Another nod, and she was back to her phone. She glanced up at him, giving him another pained smile. "I'm sorry. Another email. You know how it is, always something."

"No problem," he said. "Although I didn't notice your phone signaling you received one."

Her finger paused on the touch screen.

"It's, um, on vibrate," she said.

He nodded, and for the first time, she seemed to realize he might not be buying her explanations. Still, it didn't stop her.

"Do you have a girlfriend?" Her fingers paused on the

touch screen as she waited for his answer. Did she really think he couldn't tell she was taking notes?

He stared at her until she realized it had been several seconds, and he still hadn't answered. She met his gaze, her eyebrow cocked as she waited.

"Why are you asking all these questions?"

She hesitated, then offered him a weak smile. "Just curious."

He leaned against the booth seat, resting his arm across the back of it, regarding her for a moment. She regarded him steadily, but he could see their shared look was making her uncomfortable.

"You know," he said, "you'd make a terrible spy."

She looked away, her cheeks tinting to a delicate pink.

"So why are you asking all these things?" he asked again. "I'd love to believe it's because you're wildly attracted to me and want to know every little detail about my life, but I don't think that's the case. Is it?"

Her cheeks grew rosier. She blushed easily, another thing that was very cute about her. One of the many things.

"No, of course I'm not attracted to you," she said glancing at him, but then she quickly looked back to her salad, using her fork to roll a cherry tomato around her plate.

"So you just interrogate everyone?" he asked softly, not wanting to put her on the defensive. He was good at reading people; it was part of his job. And it was easy to see that Annie Lou Riddle had a wall around her. Her guard was always up as if she didn't feel comfortable relaxing or letting anyone see too deep into her. And he was afraid if he pushed her too much, she'd simply shut down and he wouldn't get any information at all. He didn't want that. In fact, he'd like to see her open up to him a lot more.

His gaze dropped to her mouth as she nibbled at her bottom lip, an action Nick found so fascinating that for a moment, he forgot he'd even asked a question.

But then she stopped worrying her lip and straightened in her seat. "I'm just trying to make small talk."

He didn't believe a word she said, and he didn't think she did either, but he'd definitely give her an A for effort.

"Annie, you do realize what I do for a living, right? I'm really pretty good at reading liars."

Instead of blushing, this time her cheeks blanched, her eyes wide with worry and indecision.

"So why all the questions?" he asked, again keeping any confrontation from his voice.

She toyed with her tomato again, then to his surprise, she caved.

"I'm finding out information for Finola."

Finola? He shouldn't be surprised, but he was. "Why?"

"She asked me find out more about you." She hesitated, worrying her lip again briefly. "Because she's interested in you."

He'd been aware of Finola's interest yesterday, but he was shocked that she would go to these lengths to find out more about him.

"Finola White does not strike me as the kind of woman who'd really care about things like my favorite food or what season I like best. Is this really what she wanted you to find out about me?"

"I don't know," Annie admitted, her tone a little desperate. "She just told me to find out everything about you. So I was just asking anything that came to mind."

He couldn't help laughing, both with amusement and amazement. "And I take it you do whatever she asks."

"Yes, that's my job," she said, her tone resigned, bordering on hopeless.

His laughter died instantly. All bosses could be demanding, but Finola's expectations seemed to go beyond just being demanding. And he knew in his gut, past employees had paid a steep price for not doing whatever Finola demanded.

He did not want to see Annie come to the same fate as those others. Suddenly this strange task wasn't so funny, but a sign that others would suffer—or even die—if he didn't figure out what was going on at this company. Possibly Annie herself. That idea was very, very sobering.

Definitely time for him to get back to business himself. He reached for his messenger bag, opened the flap and pulled out his notebook. He pushed the list of victims' names toward her. This page contained only seven names— all past personal assistants of Finola's.

"Was doing whatever Finola asked these people's jobs too?"

She scanned the list briefly, then looked back to him. Her expression was guarded, but she nodded. "If they were Finola White's assistants, then yes, their jobs were to do what she asked."

"And what kind of things do you think she asked?"

She shook her head. "I don't know. I only know what she asks me to do, and while sometimes her requests are outlandish, they haven't been illegal."

He studied her, his gut saying she was telling the truth. But he still believed that if anyone knew private things about Finola White, it had to be Annie. She worked very closely with the woman. In fact, he'd already deduced that the two people most likely to be aware of Finola's nefarious deeds, if there were any, would be Annie and Tristan McIntrye. But even from just the brief meeting yesterday, Nick got the feeling he wouldn't get any straight answers from Finola's right-hand man. That left Annie.

"Did you know any of these people?"

She glanced at the list again, then shook her head. "No." Again, he believed her. Why would she know them?

They had already disappeared before she was hired. But she needed to see the list and realize that this could be her fate too if she didn't help him.

"You were hired to replace this woman," he said, pointing to the last name on the list. Jessica Moran.

"She'd moved here from New Hampshire to start a career in the magazine industry. She majored in journalism with a minor in sociology. She wanted to work for one of the newsmagazines, *Time* or *Newsweek,* but *HOT!* was the magazine that hired her. Fashion wasn't her area of interest, but she thought working for the great Finola White would be a wonderful experience, and in truth, she needed the job."

He paused, watching Annie's face, trying to see if any of this sounded familiar to her, but she just continued to stare at the list.

Only a slight nibbling at her lower lip revealed any sign that the story was affecting her. And he knew for certain she identified with the other girl's story. He'd already done a little background check on Annie Lou Riddle. He knew where she grew up, what college she attended, her major—or rather majors—even her grades.

She, too, was a girl from a small town, looking to make it big in the world of publishing. Her story differed from Jessica's because *HOT!* magazine was totally Annie's dream job. She'd majored in fashion design and journalism. But overall, their backgrounds were very similar.

"Jessica must have seen the position of Finola White's personal assistant as a godsend. But her good luck didn't last. She only worked for *HOT!* magazine for a total of two months. Then she was gone. Her family reported her missing, and just a few weeks ago, she was found."

Annie's head popped up, her gaze meeting his, almost as if she was surprised to hear that news.

"That's good. Isn't it?"

He nodded. "Well, it's good she's alive, but she's not the person who disappeared. She's in this strange almost catatonic state."

Annie grew wan, looking almost as pale as her employer. Her eyes shone with dismay.

But what interested Nick most was that her reaction didn't seem to be one of surprise or shock, but rather dread.

"I'm very sorry to hear that," she finally said, her voice even. She still didn't make eye contact with him. "I would like to be of some help, but I didn't know any of these people."

Nick nodded as if he accepted her response, but then he turned the page. "And what about these people? Anyone you recognize here?"

Annie stared down at the second page of names, nausea gripping her stomach. So many people. So many bargains made and lost. As selfish as it was, she couldn't allow herself to be one of them.

She started to shake her head, when her gaze landed on Sheila Bernard. *Sheila.* All these months, she'd wanted to believe Sheila had decided working in the mailroom at *HOT!* just wasn't her thang, as she would have said.

I tell you, girl, this mailroom gig, it ain't my thang.

Annie shook her head slightly, hearing Sheila's sassy voice as if the feisty, fun and truly nice woman was sitting right beside her. Sheila had been one of the few people at *HOT!* who'd reached out to Annie with any type of friendship.

She'd delivered the mail daily—and every day she'd have some funny story or comments or just a big smile for Annie. That smile had been so welcome, especially in those early days when Annie had first realized what she'd gotten herself into.

Then one day, Sheila was gone. Annie had told herself that she'd had finally made good on her constant threats that she was going to quit. Sheila had wanted to be an artist. Annie had seen some of her paintings and they were amazing. She had a real eye for seeing the small things, the details others might have missed.

Had that been the very thing that had gotten Sheila into trouble? Had she seen too much?

No. Even now, even seeing her name printed on that page, Annie didn't want to believe she wasn't out there somewhere. Of course she probably was out there somewhere. A body without a soul. Just like the personal assistant who'd worked for Finola before Annie.

A cold chill snaked down her spine and she didn't manage to suppress her shiver. Soulless. She wouldn't let that happen to her.

"So do you see someone you know?" Nick said, his voice like her own conscience.

Annie stared at her friend's name a moment longer, then shook her head. "No. I don't know any of these people."

She forced herself to calmly push the notebook back toward him and return her attention to her lunch, but the vegetables might as well have been straw in her mouth.

I'm sorry, Sheila, she said silently. I wish I could help, but I have to look out for myself.

The things going on at *HOT!* were so much bigger than Nick could imagine. Certainly the police weren't going to be able to protect anyone.

She prayed that, wherever Sheila was, she understood that.

Chapter Seven

Snowflakes drifted through the air when Nick and Annie stepped out of the diner.

"Wow, it's beautiful," Nick said, hoping to engage Annie's attention again, but since she'd looked at that list, she'd been quiet. His earlier suspicions about her reactions had been right. When pushed, Annie shut down. All her walls were up, not even allowing small glimpses of the sweet woman he'd seen here and there throughout their lunch.

Hell, he actually found himself missing the random questions she'd been firing at him earlier. In truth, he'd rather enjoyed them, the surprise of what she might ask next. Of course he *had* liked them better when he'd thought they were to satisfy her own curiosity, not for the benefit of Finola White.

He also would be willing to bet Annie had developed these walls to keep herself safe. Seven of Finola's personal assistants had met awful ends; that alone had to be enough to make Annie wary. To make her careful and closed.

He'd also bet money, big money, that she knew a lot more than she was saying about the past employees and about her current employer. But he couldn't fault her for keeping quiet about what she knew. After all, she could be in danger if she talked.

He considered telling her that he understood her hesitation, but he decided now wasn't the time. If he pushed any more right now, he suspected she wouldn't ever talk.

She stood on the sidewalk, waiting for the light to change so they could cross the street. Her arms were crossed over her middle, not from the cold, but because she was subconsciously trying to protect herself. And she still wouldn't look at him.

She was scared.

He wanted to tell her that he could keep her safe, but that was a big promise to make, especially when he didn't even know what he was dealing with yet. Instead he decided it would be better just to get her talking about anything other than the case, what she might or might not know, and especially her boss.

"So what is *your* favorite food?" he asked, hoping to distract her and hoping to hear her pretty voice. It was amazing he could miss it so quickly. Besides, he really did want to know things about her too.

She glanced at him, her cheeks pink from the cold air, snowflakes clinging to her hair.

"Crawfish."

He smiled at that. "A real Southern girl, huh?"

She wavered for a moment, then managed a small smile back, something akin to gratitude in her gray-blue eyes. She seemed to realize that, at least for now, he was going to drop any talk about the disappearances at her workplace.

"And what's your favorite season?" he asked, his voice just a little teasing.

"Well, I have to admit, most of the time, I don't love the cold."

"Southerner," he teased.

"*But*," she continued, giving him a warning look that made him smile even wider, "when it snows like this, it is pretty beautiful."

She lifted her face toward the sky for a moment, then smiled at him. Snowflakes clung to her thick eyelashes, while others melted and glittered on her creamy skin like precious jewels.

Nick felt his body react instantly. Annie Lou Riddle fascinated him. She'd intrigued him from the first time he saw her, in a way he couldn't explain and had never experienced before.

They headed slowly down 8th Avenue, neither of them in a hurry to get back to their lives. It was as if they believed that if they stayed in this snowy world, reality would be held at bay.

"Do you have any pets?" he asked, and she shot him a sidelong glance.

"Do you really care if I have any pets? Or are you just teasing me about all the silly questions I asked you earlier?"

He turned toward her, walking backward, pressing a hand to his chest as if mortally wounded. "How can you ask that? Of course I care."

She laughed then, and two of his organs leapt in response. One in his chest, the other in his jeans.

"No, I don't have any pets. But growing up I had a pet pig named Tootsie."

"After Dustin Hoffman?"

Annie laughed again. "No, after Tootsie Rolls. She loved them."

Nick nodded, looking impressed.

"Why would you want to know anything about me?" she said after a moment, and he could hear suspicion in her voice.

It didn't take a rocket scientist to realize she was still uncomfortable with him and what his motivation might be.

"Maybe I just want to get to know you," he said, his words utterly honest. "Maybe I'm interested in you the way Finola is interested in me."

She came to a stop, her expression one of surprise and concern, but he could swear he saw flickers of longing in her wide gray eyes too.

Before he thought better of it, he walked back to her and caught her hand. Her fingers were freezing against his warm palm and he instinctively took both her hands in his, rubbing them.

She looked down at their joined hands, then up at him. Her eyes darkened to the same color as the sky above them and this time he was certain it was with desire. The same desire that zinged through his body like some crazy electrical current.

"Speaking of your earlier questions, you do realize I never answered the most important one you asked," he said.

She stared at him expectantly, her gaze only leaving his for a moment to again glance at their hands.

"What question is that?" she asked, her Southern accent more pronounced than usual. Her cheeks flushed pink. Pretty, pretty pink.

"No," he said and he leaned in closer to her. "I don't have a girlfriend."

And he kissed her.

Annie froze as Nick's lips brushed against hers. For just the briefest moment, she told herself to pull away. That she couldn't do this. But those thoughts drifted away as easily as snowflakes in the breeze around them. His lips moved over hers, slowly, perfectly. Just like that her mouth softened, molding to his as if she'd been made for him. As if he was made for her. She could feel the coolness of the winter air, the taste of snow on his lips, then his tongue slipped inside her mouth, so sweetly hot, and she melted.

She made a small noise, but her arms came up to circle his neck, trying to find purchase amid the desire that swirled around them, a storm of its own. Only the longing deep inside her wasn't delicate or gentle like the snow around them. It was powerful and pounding, threatening to overcome her.

Suddenly the force of that need frightened her, bringing her to her senses. She pulled away from Nick, stumbling backward, bumping into a man passing by.

"Hey," the man muttered, stopping to glare at her.

"I—I'm sorry," she said, flustered from the kiss and her clumsiness.

"Watch what the hell you're doing," the man said, his eyes flashing with more than irritation.

Nick came forward, tucking Annie against his side, his eyes hard and fierce.

"There's no need to get so worked up. It was an accident."

The man glowered at them for a moment longer, but then he moved on, clearly not willing to tangle with Nick. Although he couldn't resist muttering "damned fools" over his shoulder once there was more distance between him and Nick.

"You okay?" he asked, still holding her, but leaning forward to study her face.

She nodded, far more affected by their kiss than by the belligerent man. And equally affected by Nick's protection. Protection. When was the last time someone stood up for her, defended her, made her feel safe? Safe, what a wonderful feeling, as wonderful as his amazing kiss.

"Not everyone can be as charming as me," Nick said, giving her one of his crooked grins.

A much too tempting grin. Annie moved out of his hold again, not wanting to leave the safe haven of his arms, but also knowing it wasn't really her safe haven.

Nick Rossi couldn't be that to her. Ever.

"Annie," he said, concerned by her withdrawal, but she raised a hand to stop him. She felt too raw, overcome by longing, desire, sorrow, guilt. It was all too much. She couldn't even pull in a full breath. This was too much. Way too much.

"Annie," he said softly, stepping toward her, but he didn't touch her. Fortunately. She couldn't handle his touch. Not with the way she wanted it and feared it. But he did say her name again, making her look at him. All the naughty glint and charm was gone from his golden eyes, replaced by uncertainty, concern.

"Annie, are you okay?"

She shook her head. "You should have asked me that last question, too."

He frowned, clearly not following.

"You don't have a girlfriend, but I do have a boyfriend."

With the disclosure, she fled, dashing away from him as quickly as her high heels and the snow would allow.

She was relieved that Nick didn't follow her.

"Where have you been?"

Annie winced at the deceptively melodious voice behind her as she hurried back to her desk. Annie turned to find Finola—and the ever-present Tristan—standing in the doorway that led to the *HOT!* boardroom.

"I'm sorry," Annie said automatically, shedding her coat and dropping her purse beside her office chair. "I was meeting with Detective Rossi."

Tristan straightened from where he leaned on the door-frame. All signs of world-weary boredom vanished from his eyes.

What caused that reaction? Did Nick have him nervous? But Annie didn't have time to consider that idea or what it might mean, because Finola had also moved to stand directly in front of her.

"What did you find out?"

That he was an amazing kisser. The thought popped unbidden into her head, just as it had many, many times since she'd left him standing on the sidewalk. But she forced the thought aside, praying her embarrassment and guilt didn't show on her face.

"I found out he's single."

Finola smiled, her ruby lips curling into a self-satisfied grin as if he was already as good as hers. "And what else?"

Annie sorted through what she knew. That he had a naughty smile that was so very charming. That his dark eyes twinkled like he knew a joke and he was sharing it no one else but you. That he liked autumn best of all the seasons, because he liked the crunch of fallen leaves under his feet and the smell of them in the crisp air. That he himself seemed to smell like autumn, clean and earthy and so masculine. That he was protective and strong, and he could make a woman feel safe just by putting an arm around her. And she would remember the feeling of his mouth against hers for a long, long time.

"He likes turkey subs with extra lettuce and mustard instead of mayo."

Finola tilted her head, clearly confused. "What?"

"I—I didn't get to ask him too much," Annie finally said, puzzled by her own answer. She had asked the man plenty of questions, but she chose his lunch choice as the fact to share?

Because you don't want him with Finola. It's that simple.

Finola held Annie with her icy gray stare for a few more moments, then sighed. "Well I suppose you did manage to find out the most important thing. Not that I would have cared if he was involved with someone or not. But it does make the situation less complicated."

Annie didn't react to her callous words; they didn't surprise her. Finola would destroy anyone to get what she wanted. Of course she would. She was a demon. It wasn't like her moral compass was set due north. In fact, she didn't even have a compass.

Not that Annie was feeling very good about her own moral compass today. Never in her life had she seen herself as a woman who could kiss one man while involved with another. She'd been faithful to Bobby all the years they'd been together.

Until today.

She looked away from Finola and Tristan, somehow sure they could see her shame.

But right now her shame didn't really matter. Keeping Nick away from Finola was her bigger concern. At the very least, she couldn't willingly hand Nick over to her boss.

Because Finola's a demon, she told herself. Not because the idea of Nick being with another woman made her so jealous she could hardly breathe. Definitely not that.

"What else did you learn? Surely something more valuable than what condiments he favors," Finola said, her irritation with Annie clear, even though she kept her tone light.

Before Annie could think better of it, she nodded. "I did find out a lot, and the truth is, though he's attractive, I don't think you'd really be all that interested. He's very— blue collar."

"Blue collar?" Finola said, tilting her head as if she'd never heard that term before, and maybe she hadn't.

Still Annie's heart pounded painfully in her chest. Fear that she'd said far more than she should made her remain utterly still, awaiting her boss's potentially lethal reaction.

But instead of getting angry, Finola's expression shifted from confusion to something that looked decidedly like intrigue. "Blue collar? How interesting."

"Interesting maybe," Tristan said from beside her, "but I'm sure he will bore you to tears very quickly. He certainly won't fit into your world."

Annie blinked at Tristan. Was Finola's toady actually agreeing with her?

"Of course he will," Finola said confidently. "But maybe first, I need to learn how to fit into his world."

"What?" both Annie and Tristan said at the same time.

Finola smiled, turning her full attention on Annie.

"Surely a girl like you comes from blue-collar stock. You can show me how to be the kind of woman Nick Rossi would want."

Annie gaped at her employer. Was she joking? Finola wanted to be schooled in how to be blue collar? This was—unbelievable.

Finola giggled then, lifting her little dog from her oversized dog tote and cuddling her little dog against her cheek. "This will be perfect. I will learn how to be what he's comfortable with, and then when he's besotted with me, I can work on making him what I want."

Annie opened her mouth to argue, but Tristan spoke first. "Finola, you will never be comfortable being common. You know that."

Finola frowned at her assistant editor. "I don't believe this is up for debate."

Her little dog growled as if agreeing with its owner.

Tristan glanced at Annie and for the first time ever, Annie almost got the feeling the man—the creature—was sympathetic to her. But he didn't say anything further.

Annie's heart sank.

"I must go to meet with Ralph Lauren now," Finola said, "But when I get back I want you to have contacted Nick and set up a date. You will go out with us."

Annie didn't respond, still trying to find something to say to bring this awful twist to an end. But what? Finola had made up her mind.

"But Nick will think it's odd to be on a date with two women," Tristan pointed out, and again, Annie had the feeling they were on the same side.

Finola was silent for a moment, then shrugged. "Well, we will make it a double date. Nick will think you and Annie are on a date with us."

Annie's heart sank even more, like it was dropping to her toes.

"Finola—" Tristan started, but Finola snapped her fingers and he stopped. Annie watched in horror as Tristan's mouth snapped closed and seemed locked that way.

The demon even touched his lips as if wanting to pry at them.

Finola sighed them. "Now I hate to be this way, but neither of you is listening. I've told you what must be done, and that's that."

"Yes," Annie said automatically. If a fellow demon couldn't fight Finola, then she certainly couldn't.

Finola glanced toward Tristan. He stood in a position of submission, his gaze barely meeting their boss's, but he too nodded his assent.

Finola snapped her fingers again, and Tristan's face noticeably relaxed, his lips parting. He pulled in a deep breath through his mouth.

"Good, I have to leave now. I'm meeting with Ralph Lauren to discuss his Fashion Week show," Finola said with a sweet smile, and no sign that she'd just done something supernatural to Tristan. No sign that she remotely thought her demands were strange at all.

She removed her dog from her oversized purse, and handed it to Tristan. A small grimace tugged at his mouth as he reached out to accept the beast, but Tristan clearly wasn't going to deny Finola anything. Not if he didn't want a worse punishment than his lips being forced shut.

The little white dog growled, which seemed to be about all the creature did, but Finola didn't seem irritated by its complaints.

"I know, sweet baby," she crooned to the dog. "I will be back soon." She wasn't nearly as sweet sounding as she turned back to Annie and said, "So have a date arranged for tonight by the time I return."

Annie nodded again, realizing this would probably be the task where she finally failed. How was she going to convince Nick to go out with Finola, then teach Finola White to act like a normal person, while also making Nick believe she was on a date with Tristan?

She should just hand over her immortal soul now.

Finola started to leave the reception area, then paused. "Oh, I almost forgot. Here is the list of things that need to be arranged for my end of Fashion Week party."

She dug into her non-dog purse and pulled out a piece of paper.

Annie accepted the white sheet, reading down the list written in Finola's loopy, swirly handwriting.

Six dozen white candles.

White linens with silver overlays

China with silver detailing

Four cases of the German wine (the same vintage I had at my Fall Equinox party)

Use the same caterer as well

12 dozen white lilacs

Annie stared at the list. So she was supposed to find lilacs in the dead of winter, and make Nick fall for Finola. Oh sure, this would all be a piece of cake. Man, she was screwed.

Through her swirling, panicked thoughts, Annie vaguely heard Finola talking to Tristan.

"You stay here and work with Carrie on the layout for the 'An Orgasm a Day Keeps the Wrinkles Away' article."

"Yes," Tristan said dutifully.

"Good. Now I must go. Ralphie hates to be kept waiting."

Annie snapped out of her overwhelmed reverie in time to see Finola saunter away, her tall, lithe body in a perfectly fitted, ivory white business suit that would arouse the jealousy of even a supermodel. She seemed completely unconcerned with the fact that she'd just made demands that were impossible.

But Annie was going to have to make them possible somehow. Part of her was desperately afraid for her own soul, but most of her still just didn't want Nick succumbing to Finola and the dark temptations she offered. The idea depressed Annie and triggered another, sharper, more painful feeling that she didn't want to explore.

But as usual, Annie had no choice but to do what she was asked. It wasn't as if she could stop her boss. Nor could she tell Nick the truth. First of all, he'd just think she was crazy.

By the way, Nick, HOT! magazine is run by demons. Flee for your life.

Yeah, that would go over well.

But the truth was, even if he did believe her, what could he do to protect her or himself? Even the NYPD couldn't stop demons. She was pretty sure of that.

So she had to do what Finola asked.

She sighed, staring down at her list of tasks, more guilt choking her. She felt helpless. Selfish.

You are just trying to survive this, she reminded herself. It was all she could do.

She turned to go to her computer, only to start when she realized that Tristan still leaned in the doorway of Finola's office, watching her. The little white dog watched her too with small, black eyes.

"I'm sorry. I didn't mean to startle you," he said although, as usual, Annie could not read any regret on his face. His strange, vividly blue eyes just studied her, unreadable. Almost empty looking.

He pushed away from the doorframe and sauntered over to her desk, his long legs encased in a pair of designer trousers. His broad shoulders and lean torso were displayed impeccably in a vintage-style button-down shirt, untucked and with the sleeves rolled back over his forearms, making him look expensive, hip and casual all at the same time.

Tristan was beautiful. Annie remembered the first time she saw him. She'd been stunned that any man could be so pretty and masculine at the same time. But even then, three years ago, she'd been wary of him. He was hard and cold, and Annie got the feeling he could be just as dangerous as Finola, even though Tristan had never done anything to substantiate that feeling. At least not that Annie had ever witnessed.

Maybe it was because Finola's evil was close to the surface. Even though she was unpleasant, Annie usually knew what to expect. Tristan was like trying to read a faded newspaper in a dark room. Impossible.

Annie forced a smile, trying to hide her wariness. "I just didn't expect you to still be standing there."

He stopped at the edge of her desk, suddenly seeming

to realize he still held the cranky little mutt. He quickly lifted it out of its tote and set it down like something particularly nasty, and it trotted off to sniff around the reception area. When he straightened, he studied her for a moment, his strange sapphire gaze moving over her in the most disconcerting way.

Annie fought the urge to fidget under that intense stare.

"You need to make Finola realize she can't tolerate being an average person."

"Excuse me?" she asked, confused by Tristan's comment. Confused that he was talking to her at all.

He frowned at her, something akin to impatience flashing through his eyes—just a flicker—then emptiness again.

"Finola might lose interest in this detective if she realizes he's too uncouth for her."

"But he isn't uncouth," Annie said, thinking about how funny and charming Nick was. Finola wouldn't miss that. She must have seen it already, or why would she be so determined to have him?

"But we can *make* her think he is. Get in Finola's head and think of the worst place she would want to go on a date. And we do that."

Annie blinked at him. Was Tristan actually trying to help her? But why? And could she really trust him?

As if he read her mind, he said, "Her interest in the detective is a bad idea. I'm sure you'd love to hear I'm working with you to sabotage this because I'm concerned for you, or the detective. But that isn't the case. I'm concerned with what we've worked so hard to set up here. Satan has his plans. I can't let Finola's sex drive throw a monkeywrench into them. But getting rid of the detective will also keep you safe. It's a win/win situation."

Annie stared at him, this beautiful façade before her that hid so much evil. "Well, when you say it like that, how could I not ally myself with you?"

Just for a second, Tristan actually appeared amused.

"Good. I'm glad you realize this is the only way."

Annie nodded. It was the only way, and even that wasn't guaranteed to work, but what other options did she have? None.

She also had no choice but to trust that Tristan was really on her side, sort of, in this plan. Again, what choice did she have?

Chapter Eight

"Good evening, Master."

Satan looked none too pleased at the interruption. Perhaps it wasn't the most opportune time to come to him, while he was in a hot tub with two buxom blondes. But seeing as he was in the tub with them in his natural state, his red skin slick with water, these women, or whatever they were, wouldn't be shocked by his sudden materialization.

In fact, they were too busy draping themselves over Satan's body, their hands stroking over his powerful, muscular chest.

"Why are you here?" Satan demanded, making it evident he wasn't happy with the intrusion.

"I just wanted to let you know that action is being taken to get Finola under control and stop her interest in the human."

Satan nodded, although he still looked uninterested. "Fine." He returned his attention to his women and his own pursuit of carnal pleasure.

Perhaps it hadn't been necessary to report in, but it was his job. And he was very diligent, taking very seriously his mission to keep an eye on things.

Still, he didn't say anything else, leaving Satan to his hot tub fun.

★ ★ ★

The phone on Nick's office desk rang, and he picked it up on the second ring. He'd been waiting for a call from one of the witnesses in a case involving a stabbing in an apartment building.

So he was very surprised when it was Annie's voice that answered his clipped greeting.

"Hi, Nick. This is Annie."

He leaned back in his chair, her lovely voice shooting through the line and directly into his body, warming him.

"Annie. I have to admit, I'm surprised to hear from you."

"I'm surprised to be contacting you."

"So why are you? Is it too much to hope you missed me?"

"Yes," she said and he smiled at her frankness.

"So what's up?"

"I'm actually calling on behalf of Finola. She's hoping you will go out on a date with her."

Nick raised an eyebrow. "First she makes you stalk me, and now she's making you ask me out—for her. You have a pretty odd job, Ms. Riddle."

There was a moment of silence, then Annie said flatly, "You have no idea."

"When does your boss want this date to happen?"

"Tonight?"

"I can't do tonight. I have some casework that I need to get done."

"Tomorrow?" she asked, and he could sense the subtle change in her voice as agitation set in.

Finola definitely scared Annie. That was very clear, and he didn't want to add to her anxiety, or worse, put her at risk in some way, but he didn't know whether seeing Finola on a social basis was a good idea. He didn't want to complicate his investigation of her and *HOT!* Or create any conflicts of interest.

Jokingly he asked, "I don't know, will you be there?"

"Actually, yes."

Nick paused, surprised. Finola didn't seem like the type of woman who would share the limelight with anyone else. Especially on a date.

But the fact he would get to see Annie again definitely made the idea of the date more appealing. He'd done little but think of her since their kiss.

"Will your boyfriend be there?"

"No," she said.

Hmm, now that was interesting.

Without further thought, he said, "Sure, I'll go on a date tomorrow."

Annie gave Nick the details about when and where they would meet him, then quickly ended the call, finding it hard to hear his husky voice without reacting to it. But when she hung up the phone, instead of feeling relief that he'd agreed to go, she felt more dread.

She wanted to believe her plan with Tristan would work, but she wasn't sure. Finola seemed determined, but she supposed Tristan was right. It was worth a try.

But what she feared even more than Finola at this very moment was the idea of seeing Nick again. And not being able to keep her attraction to him hidden.

This was going to be like making her way through a minefield.

But for today, her work was done, and she was going to head home where, maybe for just a moment, she could feel safe and forget this long and dreadful day.

But she found she didn't feel much better as she stepped into her apartment and closed the door tightly against the outside world.

She leaned against the door and for just a moment, she

recalled how she'd felt in Nick's arms, his strong body beside hers, his words and demeanor so protective and comforting. Safe. For a brief moment, Annie had remembered what that felt like. And how much she had missed it. Missed everything she'd felt in his arms. Being safe, happy, aroused, sexy. She'd felt none of those things in so long.

Then a sound invaded her thoughts. Bobby's voice.

Instantly she was ashamed. Ashamed that she was standing here thinking of another man while her boyfriend was in the next room. She sighed, telling herself to get it together. Nick was off limits for so many reasons.

She kicked off her shoes and headed into the living room, only to realize Bobby was in the bedroom. She paused outside the half-closed door, listening.

"Oh yeah? You'd like that, huh?"

Annie frowned, instantly aware of his tone, low, teasing, flirty. She straightened, then leaned a little closer to hear better.

"You want me to come over right now? While no one is home?"

Annie stopped, unable to believe what she was hearing. Who was he talking to?

"If I come over there, you'd better be ready for me. And by ready I mean naked."

Annie gaped at their bedroom door, shocked. But anger quickly replaced shock, and she no longer remained in her hiding place. She shoved open their bedroom door, standing in the doorway, glaring at Bobby where he lounged on their bed, wearing only jeans. The cordless phone was pressed to his ear.

He startled at Annie's sudden appearance, clapping a hand to his bare chest.

"Annie," he said, his voice breathless. "You surprised me."

"I bet." She glared at him.

He pushed himself upright, frowning at her. "What's wrong?"

What's wrong? She widened her eyes. She knew Bobby wasn't always the sharpest tool in the shed, but . . .

"Do you really need to ask?" she said, shaking her head with disgust. "I just heard everything you said."

He still looked confused, then looked at the phone still held loosely in the hand resting on the bed. Then he laughed. Actually laughed.

More anger and hurt filled her.

"Annie, I was rehearsing."

Annie stared at him, sure she couldn't possibly have heard him right. Then when his words finally sank in, she wasn't sure if she could believe him.

She'd heard his lines from the play many times, and what he was saying into that phone wasn't what he'd been practicing for his role as deliveryman.

He saw her disbelief and chuckled again. "Annie, I was practicing lines for a new part I got today. For a horror movie. An actual movie."

He levered himself off the bed, enthusiasm in his every movement. Then he rushed to her, giving her a big hug.

"An actual movie," he repeated, his light blue eyes dancing with excitement.

Annie gaped at him a moment longer and finally the news sank in, and along with it shame. She'd been so easily convinced he was doing something bad and now she felt awful for even thinking such a thing about him. Bobby would never do that to her, but she realized her own guilt must have helped her jump to that conclusion.

Her cheeks burned, shame and regret filling her heart. How could she doubt Bobby? How could she have done what she'd done to him?

She threw her arms around Bobby's neck and hugged him.

"That's so wonderful," she said, squeezing him even tighter. "Really wonderful."

She pulled back from him, happiness and apology in her eyes. "I can't believe I thought . . . that I thought that."

She couldn't even say the words aloud. It was too embarrassing, her lack of faith in him, which made her own weakness glaringly awful.

Bobby grinned, blessedly oblivious to why her cheeks were stained deep red and her eyes were a little too bright.

"I can only imagine how it sounded," he said. "But I bet you could hear it's a great part. I mean, it's a horror flick, but it's a good script, right up there with *Halloween* and the classics. I play the bad girl's boyfriend, so that means I get it in about the middle of the film. Really gory, really scary. It's going to be killer!"

Annie laughed. "Good pun."

Bobby's tawny brows drew together as he regarded her quizzically. "What?"

Nick would have gotten the joke, she thought, then instantly berated herself. How awful to compare the two men. "Nothing. I think it's great you are so excited."

He nodded, his full grin returning. "It's a real break for me."

She smiled, having heard him say that many times before, but this time it really did seem as if his luck was changing. And she planned to support him every step of the way. She did care about Bobby. Maybe they had gotten a little complacent about their relationship because of work and other stresses, but she wasn't going to let that happen any longer.

Would you ever get complacent about Nick? Annie caught herself, sick at her own train of thought. That answer did not matter. She'd made a mistake. She wouldn't do so again.

She smiled at Bobby, focusing all her attention on his handsome face, his golden beauty. He was her first love.

She hugged him again.

"So how did you hear about the role?" she asked, her head resting against his bare chest, hearing his heart beating in a steady rhythm.

"Ally. She's been such an amazing help."

Annie lifted her head, a moment of misgiving seizing her, but she simply smiled. "She has. That's great."

She was being ridiculous—any niggling mistrust she was having was because of her own behavior. She knew that.

"She is great," Bobby agreed, pulling away from Annie to go to his dresser and take out a shirt. He held it loosely in his hand as he turned back to her.

"In fact, she got cast in the movie too."

"Really? That's fabulous for both of you."

He nodded. "She's actually playing my girlfriend. The bad girl."

Annie had another ripple of unease, but again she told herself she was being ridiculous. She walked over to him, filled with the need to be close to him, to feel the way they had when they first fell in love.

She reached for the shirt, tugging it out of his grasp and tossing it on top of the bureau.

"What are you doing?" he said with a small, knowing smile.

"I was thinking we should celebrate," she said, pressing a kiss to his collarbone.

He stood still, his arms loosely around her waist as she continued to kiss his neck, along his collarbone, down his chest.

"Annie?"

"Mmm?" she answered, smiling against his skin.

"I'd love to take you up on this celebration, but—"

Annie lifted her head, frowning up at him.

He smiled, the gesture sweet, apologetic. "But the director of the movie is taking some of the cast out for drinks to celebrate. And I don't want to miss a chance to talk with him and the other actors."

Annie didn't react for a moment, then she nodded. "Sure. You can't miss that."

Bobby grinned again. He released her and grabbed his shirt, tugging it over his head. "You are the best, Annie."

She nodded, feeling so far from the best it was scary. He started for the door, then paused.

"It would probably be okay if you wanted to come along."

Annie could hear the reluctance in his voice. Her heart twisted, but she shook her head.

"Nah, this is for you and the movie cast. And you know me, I'm always glad to get a good night's sleep."

He readily accepted her excuse. "Okay, get some rest."

She nodded, offering him a smile filled with calmness she didn't feel.

He disappeared out of the bedroom and Annie couldn't help noticing he didn't even give her a kiss good-bye. And she thought of another kiss she'd had today. Her toes curled into the carpet at the memory. A memory she had to forget . . . she had to, not only because it was the right thing to do but because it was the only way to keep them safe.

"Hi." As soon as the single word was out of his mouth, Nick wished that he'd come up with something cleverer. But he hadn't expected to see Annie in the front lobby. He'd figured she'd be at her own desk, and he'd simply avoid her as he went to talk to a couple of the other *HOT!* employees. He knew he was going to see her tonight, but he'd thought it best to give her a little space today.

So much for that.

Annie swung around from her conversation with the lobby receptionist to greet him with those wide, stormy gray eyes of hers.

"Hi," was all she managed back, but then maybe because she realized the blond receptionist was watching them, Annie smiled, the gesture a little stiff.

"Are you here to do more questioning?" she asked, her voice polite and distant.

"Yes." He nodded, wishing he could take his eyes off her lips and stop thinking about how wonderful they had tasted. How amazing she'd felt against him.

"Questioning?" the blond receptionist asked, leaning forward on her desk, the pose making her low-cut sweater even more revealing. "What kind of questioning?"

She smiled at him as she waited for him to answer. That same hungry smile from the other day.

"I'm investigating several former employees that have gone missing over the past few years," he explained, keeping his tone professional, disinterested. Which wasn't hard with her, but with Annie . . .

Damn. Here the blonde was throwing her assets out there for the world to see, yet it was Annie in her simple black turtleneck sweater who kept his gaze returning again and again to her.

She was lovely.

But he needed to stop. Last night, awake in his bed, his whole body recalling their kiss, he'd realized he couldn't push himself on Annie. She didn't deserve that.

Yet here in her presence, he only knew one thing. He wanted her. But he had to stay focused on why he was here and on making sure she was fine and knew she could trust him to behave himself.

"Missing people," the blonde said, her blue eyes wide. "That's pretty scary."

Nick forced his attention away from Annie and on to the receptionist. "Yes, it is."

The blonde started to ask something else, but the phone cut her thought short. Nick would have liked to have thanked the caller on the other end personally, and as soon as the other woman was distracted, he turned his attention to Annie.

"How are you?" He needed to know.

"I'm fine." Her voice was cool and clipped, her sweet Southern twang almost gone. "And please don't let me keep you. I know you have work to do."

Nick nodded, knowing a brush-off when he heard one, but he wasn't going to leave—nor was he going to let her leave—without saying something about what had happened between them.

He glanced at the receptionist, making sure she was still occupied with her phone call. When he was sure she wouldn't hear, he shifted closer to Annie and said quietly, "Annie, I think we should clear the air about yesterday. I just want to say—"

She immediately raised her hand just as she had on the street.

"We don't need to talk about this," she said, still not looking at him. "It was an accident, not a big deal and best forgotten."

Nick laughed then, although the sound didn't exactly hold any humor. "I'm not sure accident is the right word."

Annie seemed to almost flinch at his words, but since he couldn't see her eyes, he wasn't sure if she was upset, angry, or ashamed.

"Fine then," she said softly, "it was a mistake."

He knew he should just let it go. If she saw their kiss as a mistake, so be it. But he just couldn't do it. That kiss had only been a mistake because she was taken; otherwise it had been the most perfect kiss he'd ever shared with a woman, and he wasn't going to label it anything other than that.

"Oh, it definitely wasn't a mistake," Nick stated, his voice just firm enough that she raised her head to look at him, clearly startled by his conviction. "It was amazing, wonderful. Something I would love to share with you again, but—"

His words were interrupted by the sound of the double doors to the main offices opening. Into the lobby walked Finola and Tristan.

"Nick," Finola called out as soon as she saw him.

Chapter Nine

Annie immediately stepped back from Nick as soon as Finola joined them. She hadn't wanted to continue the discussion she'd been having with Nick, but she couldn't exactly say she was pleased to have Finola be the one who interrupted it.

Finola strode up to him, looking amazing in a white pantsuit, the fit tailored to every curve of her body.

She took his hands in hers and leaned in to kiss his cheek.

Annie noticed that Nick didn't react with the same enthusiasm, his posture stiff, but Annie still hated to see the other woman touching him in any way.

Because you know what hides under that human mask she wears, Annie told herself. Which was partially true. But not totally. Another part of her just didn't like seeing another woman touch him.

But she was going to have to let that feeling go. Nick wasn't hers. He never would be. Period.

"Are you here to talk with some of my employees?"

Nick nodded. "Yes. Is that still okay with you?"

Finola grinned at him as if he was just the silliest thing. "Of course. I can't be here, because Tristan and I have to go to Lincoln Center to meet with some of the directors who will handle our participation in the Fashion Week shows."

The receptionist, who was no longer on the phone, chose that moment to pipe in. "I could take him to whoever he wants to talk with."

Finola frowned at the woman, and Annie could see her pale gaze taking in the woman's long, wavy blond hair, perfectly made-up face, and formfitting, low-cut dress with matching five-inch-heeled sandals.

"Why, that won't be necessary," Finola said, her tone taking on the deceptively sweet quality that Annie had learned to recognize as a cover for her irritation.

Jenna clearly wasn't familiar with that particular trait, because she continued. "It's not a problem." She smiled widely at Nick. "I would enjoy showing the detective around."

Annie nearly groaned for the younger woman. She really had no clue what trouble she could potentially be in.

"Anna will help him, if he needs it. Won't you, Anna?"

Annie nodded, wishing she didn't have to be a part of any of this, but unlike the young blond receptionist, she knew it was always best to just agree.

"Well, we must run along now, but I will see you tonight," she said to Nick.

He nodded. "At seven o'clock, although Annie— Anna—is being very secretive about what we are doing." He glanced at Annie, but thankfully he didn't smile or wink. He did nothing flirty in the least, for which Annie was very grateful.

"Well, both Anna and Tristan are being very hush-hush. But I'm sure their choice will be delightful."

Nick glanced back at Annie, then over to Tristan, who'd remained slightly apart. "Anna and Tristan, huh? I didn't realize they were both going with us."

Finola laughed as if his comment was the most amusing thing she'd ever heard. "Of course they are coming. This is a double date."

Nick nodded, but didn't say anything more. Finola offered him another cheek kiss, then she and Tristan disappeared into the elevator.

As soon as the door slid closed, Nick said, "You are dating Tristan? He's your boyfriend?"

"No," Annie answered without hesitation. "Finola just wanted us both to go. I'm not sure why."

That wasn't completely true, but Nick didn't need to know anything more.

She noticed that he actually looked relieved at her answer. Then he validated her opinion by saying, "I don't like that guy."

Annie was about to tell him he definitely had good instincts, but decided that was just going to open up a can of worms she'd rather stayed closed.

Instead she offered to take him to whomever he wanted to question.

He nodded. "I would like to talk to Carrie Hall."

She nodded, heading back to the offices.

"So tell me," he said as he followed her through the bustling maze of magazine employees, "why does Finola call you Anna?"

She didn't slow down or look back at him. "Because she doesn't think the name Annie is classy enough."

"But Anna isn't your name."

She stopped in front of a closed door, now looking at him. "Well, that doesn't much matter to Finola White. She does exactly what she wants."

He studied her closely for a moment. "And doing exactly what she wants could entail making employees disappear, couldn't it?"

Annie didn't look away, knowing he'd read that as assent or as purposely avoiding the subject, which she was. But she chose to appear unshaken by his question.

"This is Carrie's office," she said instead. "Good luck with your interviews. If you need anything, you know where to find me."

She started to walk away, but Nick's voice stopped her.

"She shouldn't be allowed to call you by the wrong name."

Annie paused for just a second, but decided to keep going without acknowledging his comment. Nick was right: there were plenty of things that Finola shouldn't be allowed to do, but no one was going to stop her.

Nick didn't seek out Annie, realizing she wanted a break from him. Her walls were firmly up at the moment, and he knew pestering her wasn't going to help them come down.

Instead he focused on his work. He spent a majority of the day asking the higher-ups in the magazine what they could recall about the missing people. And although he wasn't surprised, he was disappointed that none of them had much to share. Some remembered them vaguely, others didn't remember them at all. And none had any details on what might have happened to them.

It was as if everyone at the magazine was hiding something. And maybe they were. Or protecting someone.

Frustrated, he decided he'd spent enough time at *Hot!* for today. He glanced in the direction of Annie's desk in the reception area, but then decided just to head out. He would see her tonight, which was going to be an exercise in torture to say the least. He found it virtually impossible to be around her and not want her.

But he did turn the other way, heading back to the lobby.

Just as he reached the lobby's double doors, they opened

and the old mailroom clerk stepped through. He didn't have his mail cart with him today.

"Hello," Nick greeted, but the old man only nodded, picking up his pace as he moved past him. Nick paused to watch him go, wondering what had him in such a hurry.

Late mail delivery, an urgent package pickup. Nick supposed there were any number of postal issues he could be dealing with.

Nick pushed the door open and stepped into the lobby. Almost instantly, a weird feeling overtook him, making his skin tingly. He saw the blond receptionist at her desk, but otherwise the waiting area was empty. And instead of acknowledging him as he expected, she just stared straight ahead.

At her computer, he thought, but as he stepped farther into the room, her gaze seemed to go straight through it, as if she was lost in thought.

Carefully, he approached the desk, that strange, uncomfortable prickling tingling up his spine. Especially when he got closer, she didn't respond.

"Hey there," he said softly, almost afraid of how she might react if he startled her.

Still she didn't acknowledge him.

He moved around more directly into her line of view.

"Jenna," he said, a bit louder this time, and this time she did lift her gaze to meet his.

His breath caught. Her eyes fixed on his, but her gaze was flat, empty. There was no sign of the smiling, flirting young woman he'd met before.

Just like Jessica Moran. Just like her, this woman was gone. Disappeared.

"Jenna? Are you okay?" he asked, even though he knew she wasn't.

Her head bobbed up and down in response, but it was as if she was on autopilot.

Nick actually jumped, startled by the sudden peal of the phone next to her.

She turned to it, her movements oddly robotic, jerky and abrupt. She lifted the phone, "*HOT!*, Jenna speaking, how may I help you?"

She waited, silent, utterly still.

"I will transfer you." She pressed the correct button, waited for the connection, then hung up the phone. And again, she just fell silent, staring straight ahead.

Nick started to ask her what was wrong, what had happened, but stopped. She couldn't answer him.

Instead he hurried back to the double doors, rushing through the inner office, not caring about bumping into people, not caring that he probably looked like a crazy person racing through the place. He had to get to Annie and show her this. He needed someone else to validate what he was seeing. And maybe if she saw it firsthand she'd realize she needed to talk. She needed to tell anything she knew about Finola.

When he barged into her reception area, she was talking to an older man. Nick recognized the man instantly as the mailroom clerk he'd seen the first morning in the lobby. The clerk who had noticeably been curious about him.

They both stared at him, confusion on their faces, as he rushed up to the desk.

"Annie, you have to come with me," he said, knowing he sounded breathless and pretty much crazy.

"What's going on?" she asked, clearly unnerved by his behavior. "What's happened?"

"You have to come see the receptionist out front. Something is wrong with her."

Annie glanced at the older man, but to Nick's surprise she stood up, not asking for any more explanation than that. She came around her desk, and did pause then. "Should I call for help?"

He shook his head, reaching for her hand. "No, just come with me."

He tugged her back through the hallway, this time trying to be a little calmer. He didn't want to draw any more attention than necessary. Not when he had Annie with him.

This place was dangerous. He was certain of that. And he did not want Annie put at risk.

He quickened his pace when the double doors were finally in view, shoving them open with more force than necessary.

The blonde at the receptionist's desk made a small squeak as they rushed in. Then in a perky, if somewhat startled, voice she asked, "May I help you?"

Nick came to a halt in the center of the room.

"Who are you?" he asked, immediately looking around for Jenna.

"I'm Chelsea."

Nick stopped scanning the room, realizing only the three of them were there. Jenna was gone. Now physically gone as well as mentally.

"Can I help you?" Chelsea asked again.

"Where did Jenna go?" Nick demanded.

Chelsea shook her head, confused. Then her eyes lit with sudden dawning.

"Oh Jenna, the usual receptionist."

Annie nodded. "Yes, she was here just a few minutes ago."

"She went home sick. She wasn't feeling well. I'm new here, I usually only work weekends, but I was called in today."

"Oh, okay. That's good. We were actually worried about Jenna," Annie said, her voice calm and composed, not at all what Nick was feeling inside. "Thanks for letting us know."

Annie then squeezed the hand she still held, urging him to follow her. He did, allowing her to lead him back to the main offices, but instead of returning to her desk, she led him down a side hall, away from the bustle of the other employees.

"Nick," she finally said once they were alone in a hallway that looked like it housed the janitorial department and a freight elevator. "What was that all about?"

"Jenna was not just sick," Nick said, that strange prickling sensation still lingering, making the skin on the back of his neck and down his spine tingle. "She was acting just like Jessica Moran."

Annie stared at him for a few moments. "Nick, the new receptionist said she went home sick."

Nick shook his head. "She didn't. And mark my words, that woman will never be back here. She's gone."

Annie stared at Nick, fear and guilt roiling in her stomach, threatening to make her ill. Was he right? Had another employee just gone missing, as easily as that?

Yes. She knew it was true. That receptionist had angered Finola by flirting with Nick, and just like that she'd been disposed of. But Annie couldn't tell Nick that. What good would it do? It would just get him hurt too—worse than hurt. Cast into Hell for all time.

"I'm sure she's fine," Annie said, trying to make her tone as calm and soothing as she could.

Nick frowned down at her for several moments, then nodded, although she knew he didn't believe her.

Behind them the doors opened, and the mail clerk appeared, now pushing his cart ahead of him. He frowned, seeming surprised to find the two of them back in this utility hallway.

"Hi Elton," Annie greeted him, trying to sound nonchalant, as if was perfectly normal for her to be back here with an agitated detective.

Elton wheeled his cart toward them. "Is everything okay?" The old man's eyes shifted back and forth between the two of them.

Annie nodded, offering him a bright smile. The fewer people who knew about Nick's concerns, the better for all involved.

Except Nick seemed to have different ideas.

"Did you see her?" he demanded.

Elton frowned, giving Nick a worried look. "See who?"

"The receptionist? You had to have seen there was something wrong with her."

"Who, Jenna?" Elton asked, looking at Annie.

Annie nodded, not wanting to say anything. It was best to keep this quiet, she knew it, and she didn't want to encourage any talk among the staff.

Elton nodded too. "Sure, I saw her. She was sitting at the front desk when I came through from the elevators. Why?"

Nick started to answer him, but Annie cut him off. "Just a misunderstanding. The usual craziness, you know this place."

The old man's eyes remained locked on Nick for a moment, and again Nick got that sixth-sense feeling of his. Something wasn't right with this guy.

This old guy knew and saw a lot more than he was admitting. Maybe he was involved with Finola, doing whatever it was that they were doing to these people.

"Well, I'm glad it was nothing serious," Elton said, maneuvering the steel cart past them toward the freight elevator.

Oh, he knew something. Nick was sure of it, but he didn't stop the old man. He considered following him and asking him some questions, but he decided right now wasn't the time. He needed to leave this place and shake off the strange sensations still clinging to him.

He needed to get some perspective, some control. Not to mention he didn't think Annie would let him confront the old guy. So he would wait.

"I'm going to get out of here," he said to Annie, not liking the feelings that seemed to be enveloping him.

Annie nodded, her gray eyes darkened with concern. She lifted a hand as if she planned to touch him, but then thought better of it.

"I'll see you tonight," he said, wanting to touch her as well, but not daring to, afraid that even the smallest touch would get out of hand. "Please stay safe."

She nodded, and he strode from the hallway, leaving her to exit after he was gone.

"You cannot keep doing this," Tristan said, not caring if Finola got mad at him or not. Frankly being cast back to Hell was starting to look like a good thing to him at the moment as he struggled to wrangle Finola's current soulless ex-employee into the backseat of his Bentley Supersport. Not an easy task given it was a two-door, with a backseat designed more for show than functionality. All floppy and useless like she was, it was a bit like trying to get a soggy hot dog into a nail hole.

Not to mention she was going to end up scuffing his black leather interior.

"She was annoying," Finola said, absently checking her makeup in her gold compact. She glanced over the mirror to watch Tristan's struggle as if he was a porter simply loading luggage into the car before a holiday trip.

Not as annoying as you, Tristan thought bitterly, and at this point he was talking about both of them: demon, and soulless body. Finally he shoved the woman into the back headfirst, quickly cramming her legs in behind. He slammed the seat back before she could stretch out.

Then he slammed the door just for good measure.

"She should have realized it was totally inappropriate to flirt with the man I want. And will have. And you cannot tell me she didn't notice our attraction to each other."

Really? Because he hadn't noticed it either, at least not on the good detective's part. Tristan managed to keep that thought to himself, but couldn't contain his next opinion.

"I don't think that Satan would consider her flirting with some mortal male you want to nail a breach of contract."

"Want to nail," Finola repeated, her tone indignant, although that emotion didn't appear on her face. Indignant must be one of the emotions she considered unflattering. "That's just crass."

Tristan fought the urge to snort. She was calling him crass when she was the reason some dumb but otherwise innocuous blonde was heaped into the backseat of his car like so much trash. While Finola idly inspected her already flawless makeup. That seemed crass to him, and what he'd said sounded remarkably like the truth.

She strolled over to his car and peered through the back window at the now-inert body sprawled awkwardly across the seats.

She wrinkled her nose, just briefly, then once she was satisfied the soulless was quieted down, she opened the passenger-side door and got inside.

Tristan went to the other side and slid behind the wheel.

He started the custom-made car, and the engine sparked to life with a low, throaty roar, like a wild beast, its power barely restrained.

Beside him, Finola arranged herself, then pulled out her sunglasses and settled back as if she was going on a leisurely afternoon joyride.

"And besides," she said after touching up her bloodred lipstick, "I didn't have a soul contract with her anyway."

She snapped her sunglasses case shut and tossed it back into her bag. Or tried. She missed as Tristan hit the brakes, jerking them to an abrupt stop inside the parking garage. He turned his head to gape at her.

"What?" he finally said, sure he must have misunderstood.

"I didn't have a soul contract with her," she repeated with a careless shrug.

"How can you say that like it's no problem?" he asked, totally stunned, although he was beginning to wonder why anything surprised him anymore. "Taking a soul with no contract is worse than breaching a contract. You know that, and you know Satan is not going to be pleased."

"Satan adores me. He won't care. A soul is a soul."

Tristan stared at her for a moment, amazed that she could be that arrogant. Did she honestly believe she was above the rules of Hell? The very rules Satan himself had established?

Maybe she was just insane. He wasn't sure at this moment.

"So where are we taking her?" she asked, genuinely unconcerned with her behavior and its potential outcome. "We have to make sure it's someplace where she can't wander back."

Tristan again bit his tongue. He'd been covering up Finola's messes for years now; he knew what he was doing. This one woman—what was her name? Jessica Moran. Jessica was a fluke. He took his foot off the brake, letting the car roll backward from the parking space. He wouldn't mess up this "disappearance."

"The Jersey Shore," he told her. "No one will even notice there's anything wrong with her there."

Finola nodded, apparently satisfied with his solution.

They were both silent as Tristan maneuvered through all the stop-and-go traffic trying to get out of the city, when Finola said, "I do hope we get back in time for me to have my nails done. I want to look perfect for my date with Nick."

Thinking of the date he and Annie had arranged, Tristan instantly felt so much better. He didn't respond except to smile, just slightly to himself. Suddenly he was very much looking forward to tonight's outing.

Chapter Ten

"What *is* this place?" Finola asked, peering out the window of her limo at the square, industrial building covered in retro-looking neon.

"It's a bowling alley," Annie said, suddenly wondering if she'd taken being a "normal human" too far. Finola White was a woman whose normal evening out was at the finest restaurants—in France. The most exclusive nightclubs—in Ibiza. Yachts and cocktail parties with New York's elite.

It was not beer and bowling with the blue-collar set.

"Bowling?" Finola frowned at Annie, completely validating her thoughts. She didn't even know what a bowling alley was. "Is this something Nick would like?"

"He said so," Annie replied, trying to sound more positive and confident than she felt.

"I see him now," Tristan said as soon as the chauffeur opened the door. Even Finola's usually brooding assistant editor looked upbeat about the prospect of a night of hitting the pins. In fact, this was the happiest Annie could recall Tristan ever looking, even though he still managed to make happy drip with cool ennui.

Annie followed them out of the limo, realizing their arrival had garnered quite a bit of attention. Several men with large beer guts and receding hairlines stopped to watch

Finola cross the parking area, her white visage as foreign to them as a ghost.

A ghost the men found both amusing and intriguing.

When they reached Nick, he was smiling, and he looked considerable less overwrought than he had the last time Annie saw him.

"I bet not many patrons of this establishment arrive in a stretch limo," Nick said with a chuckle.

Finola immediately looked over at Annie. "I believe you said the limo was acceptable for tonight."

Annie hadn't said that. She had simply agreed that a taxi might very likely smell like body odor and definitely would not serve Perrier, which Finola had decided meant they should take the limo.

"I think the limo is a nice touch," Nick said with an approving nod. His reaction instantly appeased Finola and Annie was off the hot seat. Finola stepped forward and looped her arm through Nick's.

"Well, shall we?" Finola frowned, looking up the building until she located the word "bowling."

Nick nodded, grinning, clearly finding Finola's confusion about bowling amusing. Adorable, even.

A tightness filled Annie's chest. An unpleasant feeling she didn't like, didn't want. A feeling that felt far too much like jealousy.

Tristan appeared at her side, drawing her attention away from the couple. Annie never thought she'd actually be relieved to have Tristan as a distraction.

"She won't make it more than a few minutes," he whispered, the almost smile lurking on his perfectly shaped lips.

Annie looked back at the other couple, who entered the bowling alley, their arms still linked and their heads close together as they talked. Nick laughed at something Finola said, and that tight feeling in Annie's chest squeezed again.

Tristan gestured for Annie to join them.

She followed the other couple, really hoping Tristan was right. She hoped Finola quickly realized Nick was not her type of man. And not just because he was in danger of being involved with a demon, but because Annie couldn't bear seeing them together.

She would admit that to herself, and herself only.

"I'm supposed to wear these?" Finola said, staring down at the pair of red, white and blue bowling shoes. The leather was worn and the once-white laces were a little frayed and dirtied to a light gray.

"Yes," Nick said, smiling at her dismayed expression. "They have leather soles so they won't scratch up the wood flooring on the lanes. Your boots are definitely out."

Finola looked from her white high-heeled boots back to the flat, shabby shoes that had likely seen dozens and dozens of feet.

Annie found Finola's disgust at having to put her pampered demon feet into them amusing and gratifying. It was hardly suitable punishment for all the awful things Finola had done, all the souls she'd banished to Hell. But beggars couldn't be choosers, and Annie was enjoying this moment.

Annie took a sip of her beer, then looked down to admire her own green and orange bowling shoes. She rather liked them.

Finola tilted her head, still staring at the shoes as if they might bite her. In fact, even though they were on the floor in front of her, she actually leaned back on the plastic bench as if to put more space between herself and them.

"But they are used," Finola said after a moment. "There must be some way to purchase new ones?"

Why, no you can't, Annie thought smugly to herself as she hid another smile behind her plastic tumbler.

Her smile vanished as Nick dropped to one knee and took Finola's foot in his hand.

"The shoes may not look terribly fashionable, but they are cleaned and perfectly safe," Nick assured Finola.

Annie watched in a combination of fascination and horror as he pushed up the leg of Finola's white, wide-legged trousers, then slowly pulled down the zipper on her white Gucci boot. His broad-palmed, long-fingered hands cradled her silk-stocking-covered foot and eased the bowling shoe on like the prince slipping on Cinderella's glass slipper.

The tightness in Annie's chest that had lessened at Finola's misery returned with breath-stealing gusto.

Could Nick genuinely be attracted to Finola White? Pampered, bratty, not to mention demonic, Finola White? Granted, he didn't know about that last issue, but still. Finola.

Annie looked away, taking a much larger swallow of her beer this time.

"I suppose they aren't so bad," Finola said, smiling widely at Nick. Wide and toothy like a hungry gator. Nick had no doubt this woman was a predator.

After what he'd seen today, he was sure Finola White was somehow behind whatever was happening at *HOT!* It was all just a little too coincidental that the receptionist should flirt with Nick, and then fall prey to the same malady as Jessica Moran. He was willing to bet the receptionist would not return to work.

He needed to figure out what was happening at that magazine, and soon. There were already too many casualties, and Nick now knew there would be more.

He rose from adjusting Finola's shoe, slipping a quick glance over to Annie. She sat on the bench, looking anywhere but toward him and Finola.

Nick knew she must be disgusted with him. First he'd come on to her and now he appeared to be flirting with her boss, but Nick knew he had to use Finola's attraction to him to get closer to her. To give her a false sense of security about him. Then maybe, just maybe, she'd let something slip.

Not to mention, he couldn't risk letting Finola know his real attraction was to her lovely, sweet personal assistant. That was far too risky, and Nick couldn't bear ever to look into Annie's stormy eyes and see only a blank stare aimed back at him.

Nick had to keep Annie safe. And the best way to do that was never to reveal to Finola how much he wanted Annie.

But that still didn't make it easy to see Annie looking so disappointed and disgusted.

"So what do we do now?" Finola asked, glancing around her to see what the other people were doing. To their left a large man walked up to the lane. He lined up the ball, then took his approach, swung back and released. In doing so, he flashed a substantial amount of hairy lower back and rear end in their direction. The group the man was with shouted and jeered, razzing each other loudly.

Finola didn't manage to hide her grimace, but she rallied and gave Nick a weak smile. "So we fling a ball down that strip of wood to knock over those white things at the end."

Nick grinned, not even having to force the gesture. It was easy to take amusement from this woman's complete disgust at the whole experience. Not to mention seeing this well-known diva so out of her own element.

"Exactly," he said.

Finola watched another man, this one much thinner and younger, but still not the type of person Finola was used to.

The guy did wear Levis and Nike sneakers, brand names.

But were they designer brands? Nick smiled to himself. This really was amusing.

Again his gaze flicked back to Annie. Although it would be more fun to actually be here on a date with her. Alone.

His gaze moved to Tristan, who surprisingly looked fairly at ease. He even wore jeans and a T-shirt—probably $1,000 jeans and a $500 tee—but he fit in. Somewhat.

"I think maybe I should let someone else start," Finola said, watching her surroundings with a barely restrained expression of horror.

Nick nodded. "I can start."

He took his turn, doing respectably, getting nine of the ten pins.

Tristan agreed to go next, and while his bowling skills were rusty at best, he did far better than Nick would have guessed.

Then Annie rose, choosing a purple ball. She stepped up to the lane, arranging the ball in her hand, lining it up, the whole time looking so damned appealing. Her hair, which was usually in a tidy bun, fell down around her shoulders, and Nick could see glints of deep red highlighting the brown. She wore a simple black long-sleeve T-shirt and dark blue jeans that clung to her in all the right places, showing what an amazing figure she had.

When she threw the ball, her perfect derriere was cupped by the dark denim . . .

Nick looked over at Finola, making sure the woman hadn't noticed he was practically drooling over Annie's amazing bowling form.

Finola wasn't watching either of them. She was peering warily into her plastic tumbler of beer. She dabbed at something floating in the golden liquid, then, with a wrinkle of her nose, set it aside.

The group of men in the lane next to them noticed Annie, however. Several sets of male eyes were on her.

Even Tristan seemed to have noticed her. The man's strikingly blue eyes wandered over Annie's body, taking in every detail as she bent down to pick up her ball.

Nick gritted his teeth. Annie had said Tristan wasn't her boyfriend and they weren't on a real date, but that didn't mean the vampire didn't want them to be on a real date.

"Spare!" Annie called from behind him.

He turned back to find her grinning, oblivious to the attention she was getting. Even when the other group of men cheered for her.

She grinned at them. Damn, she was adorable.

Nick congratulated her, managing to keep his desire for her out of his voice and expression. Her smile withered slightly, but she thanked him and returned to the bench.

"Is it my turn?" Finola said, eyeing the lane as the pins were swept away and new ones lined up. "Already?"

Reluctantly Finola stood, gingerly stepping up to the lane.

Nick followed her, pointing to the balls. "Just pick one that doesn't feel too heavy for you."

Finola picked one up, grimacing as she did. She set it down, then looked at her white palms as if she expected them to be covered with filth. She glanced at Nick, attempting a smile, then hesitantly picked up another one.

"Okay," she said, forcing another smile. "I guess this one will do."

Nick smiled, trying to make the gesture look encouraging rather than amused. She moved to the red line on the lane, her white designer trousers and stylish white silk and lace blouse making her stand out like—well, like a rich fashion diva—amid Average Joes.

"Now just roll it down the lane, aiming for those pins," he said.

Finola eyed the holes in the ball, wincing as she stuck

her perfectly manicured fingers into them. She balanced the ball between her hands, then she rolled, the ball heading very slowly down the lane only to eventually go in the gutter. The next two balls did the same.

"That was a good try for your first time," Nick said.

Finola shrugged, clearly not caring how she played, but obviously wishing she were anywhere else.

"Don't worry, baby," one of the guys from the group next to them yelled. "You still looked fine."

Another elbowed his friend and added, "She could be on me like white on rice."

They laughed raucously.

Finola looked over at them, her gaze surprisingly calm, and the group fell silent as if she'd somehow wordlessly put them in their place.

She strolled back to the table, taking her seat.

"Good try," Annie said softly.

Finola lifted an eyebrow and looked as if she was going to say something, but the waitress appeared.

The high school kid with a ponytail, multiple piercings in her ears and one in her eyebrow, and an abundance of black eyeliner, placed the greasy pizza they'd ordered in the center of the table.

"Can I get you anything else?" she asked around a large wad of gum.

"I would like a glass of wine. Preferably a decent pinot noir." Finola said.

The girl's brows drew together, the neon lights glinting off the silver hoop at the corner of one of them. "I think we might have wine coolers. And we have Mike's Hard Lemonade."

Finola stared at the girl for a moment as if she'd spoken in a foreign language, which Nick supposed she pretty much had.

"How about just another pitcher of beer," Nick said to

the girl, taking pity on her. After all, it wasn't her fault Finola had just fallen to earth from the planet *Pretentious Entitled Diva.*

The waitress hurried away, clearly glad for the excuse to leave.

"Why don't we take a break and eat?" Nick suggested, handing Finola a plastic plate that was so scratched from repeated use that it looked more like a floor tile than a dish.

Finola accepted it, studying it dubiously.

Nick slid onto the bench beside Finola. As he served himself a couple of slices of the pepperoni pizza, he debated what to talk to Finola about.

"So how are the preparations for Fashion Week going?" he asked, knowing topics that Finola felt comfortable with would make her more relaxed. And he wanted her relaxed around him.

Finola immediately grabbed onto the topic, a real smile curving her bloodred lips. "Fabulously. This year *HOT!* will be the star of the show."

"Are the magazines as important as the designers and models?"

Finola raised a pale eyebrow. "Oh, Nick, I own most of the designers and models. There is barely a successful person in the fashion world who doesn't have me to thank."

Nick gave her an impressed look, although he was mostly impressed with her huge delusions of grandeur.

"We've definitely worked hard to be a force in the fashion world," Tristan said, his gaze fixed on Finola as he spoke.

Finola nodded. "And our impact will move past the fashion industry into places the world can't begin to comprehend yet."

Nick nodded, although he found her grandiose statement weird. Was it this idea of tremendous self-importance that had triggered her to literally get rid of employees rather than just fire them? His gaze moved from Finola to Tristan and Annie, wondering if they found her words odd too.

Tristan watched Finola, but as usual his strange blue eyes were unreadable. Annie looked like she wanted to be anywhere else. She nibbled at her pizza, following each bite with a generous sip of beer. She shifted in her seat, and again Nick got the feeling Annie knew much more than she was sharing, but he couldn't really blame her for keeping silent. If his feelings about the receptionist were correct, and she was really gone, then Annie could be in real danger.

Nick thought about what he'd seen again, as he had all afternoon. That receptionist's behavior was so, so strange. Unnatural.

He took a sip of his beer, and realized that the prickling along the back of his neck had returned. He wasn't sure when, but he felt it like a cold draft stealing up his back.

And now that he thought about it, the bowling alley, too, suddenly felt different. Suddenly it seemed quieter. Yet Nick couldn't see that it was any less busy. He watched the group of men, who'd been boisterous from the moment they arrived. They still bowled, but even they were hushed.

The waitress returned with a plastic pitcher of beer.

"I require utensils to eat this," Finola said, gesturing to the pizza.

The girl rooted around in the pocket of her apron, pulling out a set of plasticware in a cellophane wrapper. She held it out to Finola, who reared back as if the girl intended to stab her with it.

"I prefer silverware," Finola stated.

"This is all we have," the girl said, placing the set on the table. This time she left without asking if anyone else needed anything. Nick didn't blame her.

"Well, that was rude," Finola said, but reached for the packet of utensils. "I would think with the amount of metal she has in her face, she might have some real silverware back there too." She glanced toward the waitress, who was headed back to the kitchen now.

"I guess this isn't the type of place you are used to," Nick said, telling himself he was imagining that the weird tingle along his spine was increasing. She immediately turned her attention back to him, offering him a wide smile.

"It's fine. Very proletarian."

Nick nodded, not quite sure how to respond.

"Anna actually picked out this place. She thought you would enjoy it."

Nick looked at Annie, who suddenly looked like a mouse cornered by cats. Her wide gray eyes shifted from him to Finola and back to him.

"I—I always like bowling as a first date," she said, smiling weakly.

"Sure, it's a great idea," Nick agreed. Of course anything would be a perfect first date if it included Annie.

"I think it was a great idea too," Tristan agreed. He took a sip of his beer, and almost looked like he went bowling all the time. Almost.

"You must have a great relationship with Anni—Anna," Nick commented, not really wanting to put Annie on the hot seat, but wanting to hear what Finola said. After all, she clearly hadn't been pleased with so many of her other assistants. After all, even if she hadn't actually gotten rid of them, she had had many.

Finola stared at Annie for a moment. "Yes, she is the best assistant I've had."

Nick nodded, watching Annie's expression. She didn't look proud or pleased; Nick could only describe her expression as relieved.

Again, he wasn't surprised.

"I'm sorry to interrupt," a voice said from beside Nick. He turned to find a large woman probably in her late thirties. She wore a bowling jersey sporting the name of her league and plain navy blue sweatpants.

She smiled timidly at the table as a whole, but then her gaze stopped on Finola. "I'm sorry, but I had to come over. You are Finola White, aren't you?"

Finola looked the woman up and down, dismay clear in her pale eyes, but then she managed a smile. "Indeed, I am."

The woman beamed. "I told my bowling team that was you, but they said there was no way you'd be here. But I knew it was. We read *HOT!* all the time and see you at all the awards ceremonies. You are a real celebrity."

Finola raised her eyebrows as if to say "obviously."

"Could we get a picture with you?" the woman asked, waving her phone at them.

Nick expected Finola to outright turn her down, and she did open her mouth as if to do just that, but Tristan spoke first.

"Here, let me take the picture."

Finola's eyes widened with dismay, but then she stood.

She posed beside the woman, looking like an elegant queen consenting to consort with a commoner.

"Closer," Tristan said, gesturing for them to move closer.

Finola stiffened as the woman looped a meaty arm around her, but she managed a strained smile.

"Wow." The woman beamed, checking Tristan's handiwork. "This is just amazing. Like I said, I get *HOT!* every month."

Finola returned to her seat and picked up her napkin.

Nick half-expected her to wipe herself down with it, but instead she placed it across her lap.

The woman thanked the whole table profusely, then, tickled with her celebrity sighting, returned to her lane where her girlfriends admired and giggled merrily over her photo.

"Those women might read *HOT!* every month, but they clearly skip over all the articles we do on healthy diet and exercise," Finola said, shaking her head.

Nick frowned, not only at her harsh words, but at the fact that the prickling feeling was intensifying again. He rubbed the back of his neck.

Finola looked around, seeming to realize no one else was speaking and she might have said something wrong.

"Well, enough magazine talk," she said with a wide smile. "What are your interests, Nick? Aside from tracking down the bad guys?"

Nick considered her question, still rubbing his neck. "I mostly just track down the bad guys."

"No grand romances? Surely a gorgeous man like you has had his fair share of past paramours."

Nick dropped his hand from his neck, although the feeling hadn't diminished. He focused instead on Tristan and Annie, sure they must feel the change in the atmosphere here. Maybe it was a real draft. Something tangible, not just something happening to him.

"Well," he said after a moment, "I certainly can't say I've had paramours. Or even grand romances. But I was engaged once."

"What happened?" Annie asked; then her eyes widened as if she was surprised she'd asked. A blush colored her cheeks.

"Failed romances always fascinate me," she added, hiding further embarrassment behind a sip of beer.

"I became very wrapped up in my work," he said,

feeling strange about the direction this conversation had taken.

And because my ex thought I was nuts.

"Well, I certainly understand work being all-consuming," Finola said with sympathy.

Just then a squeal sounded behind them. They all turned, their gazes returning to the group of women who'd been watching Finola. And in the middle of them was the one who had just had her picture taken with Finola. The woman pulled at her sweatpants, the garment clearly having nearly fallen down.

Nick blinked, telling himself he couldn't be seeing what he thought he was. It had to be another woman, because this person was easily three sizes smaller than the one who'd come over to ask for a picture.

How could that be? He blinked again. It had to be a different person.

"Oh no," Tristan said loudly, drawing everyone's attention back to him. He held his cell phone, peering worriedly at the screen.

"I'm sorry," he said, his eyes still scanning the screen, "but I just received a message from Donatella Versace. She is having a cocktail party and is highly upset that Finola and I are not there. I must have forgotten to add it to my calendar."

Finola placed her napkin on the table, already rising.

"Tristan, this is a huge oversight," she said, disappointment evident in her pale eyes. "I'm so sorry to cut this evening short, but I don't dare offend her completely by not making an appearance."

Nick nodded, glancing quickly over to the group of women again, but now Finola's fan was gone. The others talked animatedly about something, but Nick couldn't tell if it was enjoyment or concern that had them so lively.

"I hope you understand," Finola said to Nick. "I really

must go." She touched Nick's bicep, her long fingers curling around the muscle there.

The prickling intensified almost uncomfortably, but he didn't move away.

When he looked up from her hand, he noticed Annie's gaze also locked on the touch. Her mouth turned down and Nick got the impression she wasn't pleased.

Tristan rose to join Finola, both pulling on their coats. Only when Annie stood, too, did either of them seem to remember her.

"Annie, is it possible for you get a cab home?" Tristan asked. "I think Finola and I should take the limo directly to Donatella's."

Annie hesitated.

"Don't worry," Nick said, despite the strange feeling overwhelming him. He was not about to miss the chance to be with Annie alone. "I can make sure Annie gets home safely."

"I'm fine," Annie said. "I can get—" but Finola cut her off.

"That's sweet of you," she said to Nick with a wide smile. "So chivalrous."

Nick raised an eyebrow at that. More like opportunistic, but Finola would never know that.

"I'm happy to do it," Nick said.

Chapter Eleven

Tristan slammed the limousine door and turned to his boss, or rather the demon he was apparently expected to babysit.

"Finola, I don't know how many times I have to tell you, you cannot do this."

"Do what?" Finola said, looking up from her dog, who had been waiting in the climate-controlled cabin of the limo with a dish of designer dog food, a bowl of Evian and soft jazz playing.

Tristan was starting to wish he was the damned dog.

"You can't go all demon whenever someone upsets you. You are going to give away what you are."

Finola kissed her silly little mutt, then gave Tristan a look that said he was being utterly unreasonable. "No one even noticed."

"That woman was losing weight like a full season of *The Biggest Loser* on fast-forward," Tristan pointed out.

Finola frowned. "*The Biggest Loser*? Tristan, sometimes you make no sense."

Tristan didn't bother to explain; it wasn't as if the explanation would make her understand the risks she was taking with her erratic use of her demon powers.

"Finola, that woman noticed. The men you made silent noticed—or at least they will once they can talk again."

"Well, they shouldn't have been so rude," Finola said. "And I don't see why I have to ruin the aesthetics of my evening by being forced to look at unattractive people."

Tristan closed his eyes, telling himself not to raise his voice. Getting cast back to Hell through her was the worst thing he could imagine; not only would he lose the wonderful pleasures of the mortal world, but then this arrogant, self-centered, spoiled demon would win.

"Besides," Finola added after a moment, "I listened to what you said earlier today. I didn't break the the soul laws by just casting them to Hell. I actually made them better. Now that obese woman is thin. Those men will hopefully think twice before saying offensive things to a lady, and the young girl will no longer look like a transvestite pincushion. Why, she might even be able to find employment in a finer establishment now."

"You did something to our waitress too?" Tristan groaned. Of course she had.

Finola nodded, looking quite proud of herself. "I was practically a fairy godmother to those people. A fairy godmother from Hell."

Well, at least she got that right.

Still, she needed to understand the risks she was taking. If they messed up after working so hard, both of them were going to understand what Hell could really be like.

"I see your point," he said, keeping his tone calm. "But someone like Nick Rossi is going to notice things like what you just did. And eventually he's going to notice that those odd kinds of things only happen when you're around."

Finola stroked her dog, actually seeming to consider his words.

"Which is also exactly why you shouldn't pursue a relationship with the man. He's too perceptive. And we don't want anyone asking questions. Now especially."

Finola was silent a moment longer, then finally nodded. "I do see your point, Tristan."

He sagged against the car's leather seat, glad that finally Finola seemed to understand that she couldn't act any way she wanted and not expect repercussions.

Maybe he had finally gotten through to her.

"Now I have a bit of a bone to pick with you," she said.

Tristan raised an eyebrow in silent response.

"How did you forget that we had a cocktail party with Donatella Versace?"

Tristan almost smiled. Finola White might be a powerful demon, but no one would say she was the smartest.

"Well, I could certainly use another drink," Nick said as soon as Finola and Tristan exited the bowling alley. "How about you?"

Annie wasn't going to argue with that. She held out her glass for him to refill it.

After they both took long swigs, Nick shook his head, looking around the place. Annie did too, feeling more relaxed already now that her boss and—whatever Tristan was to her—were gone.

"Well, that was weird," Nick said, vocalizing her very thoughts.

Annie nodded. "Definitely one of the more awkward nights I've ever had."

"Why did you pick this place?" he asked, looking around him.

Annie debated making something up, but then decided the truth might very well offend Nick enough that he would never consider dating Finola again. Not that she thought that, after this, that Finola would want to date him. It seemed Tristan's plan had worked just as they had hoped it would.

"Finola asked me to show her how—working stiffs date."

Instead of looking offended, however, Nick laughed. The sound was wonderful. By far the best thing she'd experienced all evening.

Annie wasn't sure why, whether it was the relief at Finola being gone, or the beer, or just the enjoyment of hearing this man's laughter, but she giggled too.

Nick sobered, his gaze roaming her face. "You have a great laugh."

"You do, too. You have the best laugh," Annie said, wondering if he somehow read her mind. Then she blushed. Yeah, it probably was the beer making her react a little differently from the way she normally would. Heaven knows, she wouldn't normally tell him something like that. But it was true.

Nick's gaze dropped to her lips, just for a moment, and Annie shifted on her seat, wondering what he was thinking. Was he thinking about that kiss they'd shared? The kiss she hadn't been able to get out of her mind, no matter how hard she tried?

He smiled again. "Well, I bet you will never agree to a double date like this again, will you?"

She laughed again. "I didn't really agree this time. I was just told what was going to happen."

"Finola does that to you a lot, huh?"

She nodded, focusing on the plastic tumbler she held in both hands on the table in front of her.

"So why do you think Tristan agreed to come too?" he asked.

Annie frowned at the question. "I guess he just—just wanted to keep an eye on Finola."

"Why?"

"They are very close," Annie said, wishing he would get

off this topic of conversation. The beer had also slowed down her thoughts and she was having trouble coming up with excuses that sounded sensible.

Then one came to her, another thing that might solidify Nick's decision not to date Finola.

"I do think they have some sort of weird relationship going on."

Nick raised an eyebrow, although he didn't look particularly surprised. "Divas with benefits, huh?"

Annie laughed again. "Exactly."

"I was wondering if maybe he's actually interested in you," Nick said.

Annie laughed, then sobered enough to give him a disbelieving look, then laughed again. "Oh, I don't think so. I'm hardly his type."

Nick shook his head. "Don't believe that. He was checking you out tonight."

"No, he wasn't," Annie said, shooting him a look that said he was clearly crazy.

"He was," Nick said more emphatically. Then after a moment, he added, "And so was I."

Annie put down the glass that was halfway to her lips, her heart leaping in her chest, making it hard to take a drink. She hated to admit it, but she loved hearing him say that.

"I know I shouldn't say that," Nick said, again seeming to see into her head, know her thoughts. "But it's true."

"You seemed to be noticing Finola too," she pointed out.

"The only reason I agreed to this date was to see if I could find out anything about those missing people," he assured her. "Well that, and the fact that I knew you'd be here too."

She looked down at her plastic cup. She loved and hated hearing him say things like that.

"All night I wanted nothing more than to talk to you," he said, "to be close to you. But I also believe that Finola White is a woman who gets what she wants, and she'd get rid of anyone she saw as a threat."

Annie didn't answer, nor did she meet his eyes, afraid he'd see the truth there. That he was right.

Then he reached out, placing his hand on her arm.

"Annie, I know you don't want to get involved in all this. And I know you have your reasons, and I suspect they are very good ones. But you have to admit some strange things are going on at that magazine, and they seem to revolve around Finola."

Annie still didn't look up from her cup, but her fingers curled tighter around it. Finally she nodded, just a slight, almost infinitesimal bob of her head.

"Can I get you another pitcher?"

Annie started at the new voice, and looked up to see a different waitress at their table. Annie glanced around, hoping, praying, that the first one was all right.

Annie spotted her on the other side of the alley, but she looked different. After a moment Annie realized all her piercings were gone. Losing her jewelry was far better than her soul.

"I think we are fine," Nick said, drawing Annie's attention back to them.

The waitress nodded and left them.

"Annie, I just want people to be safe."

She met his eyes then. His beautiful deep amber eyes. She knew he wanted to make sure people were safe, that was his job, but in this case, he couldn't do that. But she could see that *he* was safe.

"Finola is a difficult, demanding and often unreasonable boss, and that is all I can say for certain about her."

Nick studied her for a moment, then nodded. "Okay."

They were silent for a moment. Then he asked, "So

why doesn't your boyfriend care that you're on a date with another man tonight?"

Annie didn't take offense at the question. It was better than talking about those poor missing people and having to lie to him about what she knew. The guilt of not being able to help them was too much. Too upsetting.

"I told you, Tristan and I weren't on a date. Not really."

He nodded, taking a sip of his beer. "Still, you were out with another man on what was being called a date."

Annie shrugged. "Truthfully, I didn't even tell Bobby. He was already at the theater—he's an actor, and since I work late all the time, he wouldn't even notice. And honestly, I doubt he would care."

Nick frowned. "He wouldn't care? I know if you were my girlfriend, I sure as hell wouldn't like the idea of you being out with someone else."

She supposed that kind of possessive comment should have offended her independent sensibilities, but the truth was, it didn't. His statement made her heart leap and heat curl, warm and wonderful, in the pit of her stomach.

She didn't want to be controlled. God knows she had enough of that in her career, but it would be nice to have someone care where she was, be interested in her enough to be worried, to be a little jealous. To want her.

Nice to have Nick want her.

As soon as the thought appeared in her head, she reprimanded herself and immediately said, "He has a lot on his mind. He's starring in a play. Well, he's acting in a play. But it's a pivotal role, so that's where his head is."

Nick made an impressed face. "So he's an actor."

"Yes, and he just got a part in a movie too. A horror movie, but it's destined to be a classic."

Again, Nick looked impressed, although she noticed his coloring seemed just a tad paler and he glanced around the bowling alley before saying, "I'm not much for horror movies; I guess reality has been horrific enough for me, but that all sounds very exciting."

She nodded, but her attention was focused on what he'd just said about his career.

"I bet your job can be awful. Which must be why—" She caught herself, realizing she was about to refer to something she'd discovered online while researching him for Finola. Something that would reveal that her stalking had gone beyond grilling him over lunch.

"Which must be why what?" he asked, his intelligent brown eyes searching hers.

Well, what could it hurt to tell him, since he already knew that Finola had asked her to find out all about him? "Well, I looked you up online, you know, for Finola—"

"Sure it was for Finola," he teased.

"It was," she insisted with a laugh, but she could feel her cheeks burning. "So when I was looking you up, *for Finola*, I read about quite a few of the cases you've worked on and the fact you took a hiatus after one particularly horrible case."

"The Midtown Murderer."

She nodded. "From what I read that sounded like a truly awful case." A serial killer who mutilated more than fifteen people before he was caught.

"It was," he agreed, but Annie could tell he didn't want to discuss it any more than that, and she didn't blame him.

But he did add, "He was soulless."

"There's a difference between conscienceless and soulless," she said before she thought better of it.

"Is there?"

She nodded. "Yes."

"And what is that difference?"

She shook her head, realizing she'd already said too much. "There just is, and you know it when you see it."

★ ★ ★

Nick studied Annie, analyzing what she'd said. She'd seen exactly what he had, hadn't she?

"You knew what I was talking about today, didn't you?" he said, his eyes roaming her face for her reaction. "You've seen them too, haven't you? The blank expression and empty eyes."

Her eyes remained locked with his for a moment; then she dropped her gaze to her drink. Her hands tightened on the cup, the plastic bowing in under her fingers, the remainder of her beer going up and down with each squeeze.

Like a pulse.

"Annie," he said, not sure what more he was going to say, knowing she didn't want to talk about any of this, knowing that she felt she couldn't. She thought her life was at risk too.

Instead he reached out a hand to touch her, to comfort her and himself. At the brush of his fingers against hers, he lifted his head, meeting her gaze. And he could see so many emotions swirling like storm clouds in her eyes, futility and sorrow and frustration; but right now, all he could seem to focus on was the longing.

His body responded, filling with the same need. Deep, desperate longing. Slowly he leaned toward her, and he wasn't sure, but he thought she leaned forward too. Their lips were so close he could feel her breath, feel her warmth.

Then just as their mouths would have touched, he pulled back.

He straightened, taking a deep breath, struggling to pull himself together. Annie did the same thing, pushing at tendrils of hair that clung to her flushed cheeks.

Nick gulped the rest of his beer, and they both managed to compose themselves.

"Maybe it's time to head home," he finally said, even

though he didn't want to leave her. Damn, that was the last thing he wanted, but he knew it was the right thing to do.

Annie nodded.

"We could share a cab," Nick suggested when they got out to the sidewalk, but Annie shook her head.

"That's not necessary. I just live a few blocks from here."

Nick knew this neighborhood; a couple of blocks in one direction wasn't too bad, but go a couple of blocks the other way, and the area got pretty sketchy.

But he nodded. "Okay."

She offered him a small, uncertain smile, waved good-bye and then began walking down the sidewalk. Nick began walking too.

It took her a few seconds to realize that he was the one strolling along beside her.

"What are you doing?" she asked, a surprised laugh escaping her as a cloud of condensation in the cold air.

"I'm not going to let you walk home alone," he told her, his tone leaving no room for debate.

Still she tried. "I'm fine. I walk around this area alone all the time."

"Well, not tonight. After all, I promised your date."

She rolled her eyes, but smiled, "Tristan was not my date."

Nick smiled. He liked teasing her.

"I really am fine," she insisted again, remaining rooted to her spot. Finally when the cold caused her to tremble, she relented. "Okay, but let's walk fast, it's darned cold out here."

Neither spoke as they hurried along the sidewalk, hands deep in their coat pockets, collars up around their faces. Just when Nick was actually finding their silence a bit stifling, they turned onto Waverly Place.

"This is my block," she said.

She walked past a few historic buildings to stop in front of one that was a large ten-story, pre-war construction built of weathered red brick with brown brick detailing.

"Wow, gorgeous building," Nick said, thinking of his own studio walkup in a rundown apartment building in Clinton.

"It comes at a steep price, believe me," she said, and he got the impression she wasn't just talking about the cost of rent.

He continued to admire the styling of the brickwork as well as the large windows and arched entryway. Absently he pulled his hands out of his pockets, breathing on his freezing fingers.

"Why don't you come up and get warm for a few minutes?" Annie said, her tone somewhere between welcoming and reluctant.

Nick knew he should say no, but he found himself wanting to see where Annie lived. He'd only seen her in public places; he wanted to see what her private life was like. What her taste was. What made her feel safe and comfortable.

He knew his curiosity was dangerous, and akin to torture since he couldn't be any more than her friend, but he found that if that was all he could be, he'd take it. And he still wanted to know about her.

Just being friendly in a purely platonic way. Oh yeah, he was torturing himself all right.

"Sure. I'd love to see inside this building." Somehow that sounded better than saying he wanted to see her place.

She smiled, the gesture still a little uncertain, but she walked up the front steps. She pulled out a keycard, waving the plastic square in front of a sensor.

She shoved open the tall, heavy glass and oak door and stepped into a large foyer. The floors of white and gray marble gleamed from the huge crystal chandelier overhead. To his left was a large desk of carved, dark-stained oak where the doorman sat. To the right was a sitting area with Queen Anne style chairs and a settee. Beyond the doorman's station was a wall of bronze tenants' mailboxes.

"This is amazing," he said. "It looks like something out of an old Hollywood film."

Annie smiled. "That's exactly what I said the first time I saw it. I just fell in love with it."

He didn't blame her. The place was fantastic.

"Hi there, Annie," the heavyset, balding doorman greeted as they walked farther into the room. "Cold out tonight, isn't it?"

"Freezing," Annie said, shivering for effect. Nick smiled, finding her adorable.

"Chester, this is a friend of mine, Nick Rossi."

Chester gave him an amicable nod.

"I'm up on the eleventh floor," she told Nick, leading him to the elevator that also looked original to the building with its wood panels and bronze trim.

Nick busied himself on the ride up admiring the small, stylized details of the elevator. The faded ivory floor buttons, the carved details in the wood, even the carpeting that looked almost art deco. Really, he was trying to focus on anything other than the fact that he was enclosed in a tiny space with a woman he still wanted to kiss.

Behave. Boyfriend. Just keep remembering that boyfriend. He did respect her relationship; if he didn't, he'd still be back at the bowling alley making out with her like horny teenagers. PDA be damned.

But instead he was here, focusing on every minute detail of an old elevator, determined to keep from giving in to temptation. Thankfully, after a moment, the elevator bobbed noisily to a stop and the door slid open.

"Here we are," she said with a sigh as if she too needed relief from the small space. She rooted around her purse for her keys, stopping in front of a door marked 11B.

"Actually Bobby should be home by now," she said over her shoulder, her tone hopeful.

Nick wondered if she sounded so hopeful because she truly wanted to see him, or because she wanted him there to act as chaperone.

Well, there was no better chaperone than a boyfriend, he thought dully.

"Bobby," she called as soon as they stepped through the door. There was no reply.

"Bobby," she called again, this time her voice taking on an almost desperate edge. She waited as if somehow Bobby would miraculously appear before them.

After several seconds, she turned back to Nick, giving him an awkward smile. "I guess he's not home yet."

"It wouldn't appear so," Nick agreed, trying to smile in a way that would put her at ease, but he knew it was more clumsy than comforting.

Still her gaze moved to his lips and stayed there. Her cheeks blushed a pretty pink, while her eyes darkened with misgivings and something else . . .

No, he wouldn't go there. He wouldn't acknowledge the longing he knew they both felt. Not again. That took them to very dangerous places.

"So show me around," he said. They needed to stay busy and focused on things other than each other.

"Oh. Yes." She nodded, or maybe she was trying to shake off the desire surrounding them, as palpable and overpowering as the hot steam in a sauna.

She led him out of the small foyer area down a short hallway.

"This is the kitchen."

To his right was a decent-sized kitchen, although what it lacked in size it made up for in style. Cherry maple cabinets and a granite countertop with flecks of rust and black and gray took up two walls. The room was saved from being too dark by opening through to the living area, separated by a granite-topped breakfast bar. The dining room contained an antique table with an ornately carved center pedestal. Around it were mismatched chairs that still managed to work perfectly with the table.

"And this is the living room," she said, waving a hand to present the room.

The living room was comfy and warm with oversized chocolate-brown furniture in a soft microsuede, the dark color broken up with lots of pillows in light rusts and creams and beiges. Between the honey-stained maple floors and the warm beige walls scattered with light-framed black-and-white photos, the place was cozy and richly colored, but not dark.

Nick's overall impression was one of homey warmth, but the place was also interesting and a little artsy. He could see Annie in every decoration and small detail, and he liked it very much.

Even as he told his mind not to go there, he could see himself curled up on the sofa with Annie, watching a movie, talking. He could see them sharing the morning paper and coffee at the antique dining table.

And he could see them making love in every room.

Just like she probably did with her boyfriend, he reminded himself. That image cooled his rising libido almost as effectively as a bucket of icewater over his head.

Or at least it did until he glanced back at Annie.

She walked over to a stereo in the entertainment center under the wall-mounted TV. He watched, admiring the way her tight little jeans hugged her cute ass and long legs.

She bent over to turn on some music, and he closed his eyes, trying desperately not to think about going over and grabbing her hips to pull her back against him. That perfect ass against his hard cock.

"Do you like classic rock?"

He blinked, realizing Annie had straightened and now looked at him quizzically.

"Umm—sure. Definitely."

She made a slight face at his obvious confusion, but then asked if he'd like a drink.

"I might have beer. I definitely have wine. Coffee. Juice?"

She walked past him to go to the kitchen and he realized her formfitting T-shirt was as distracting as her jeans, clinging to her nicely shaped breasts and slim torso.

Stop it, Nick. Stop it now.

He really wanted a stiff drink, but he managed to say, "Coffee, if it's easy to make."

"Super easy," she said, throwing him a smile across the breakfast bar. Nick remained on the opposite side, deciding a large slab of stone between them was probably a good thing.

"I bought one of those single-cup coffeemakers," she told him, seemingly oblivious to his libidinous thoughts. "Because most mornings I don't even have time to wait for a pot to brew before Finola is calling to demand that I do something."

She bustled around the kitchen, getting mugs and spoons.

"Finola must be hell to work for," he said.

Annie laughed, the sound humorless. "Hell is an apt word, that's for sure."

"I know *HOT!* magazine is hugely successful, but do you ever just think about looking for a new job?"

"All the time." She placed steaming mugs of coffee on

the counter along with milk and sugar. Then she came around to join him in the same room.

The partition and conversation had calmed his thoughts a little, but now as she gestured for him to join her on the sofa, his mind went right back to all the things he'd love to do to her among those pillows.

She sat down, her mug cradled in her hands, waiting for him to join her. He did, making sure he stayed to one end, with plenty of room separating them.

"I like your couch," he said, then realized how lame that sounded.

But fortunately Annie didn't seem to notice; instead she nodded, reaching out to run one of her hands over the soft material.

"I like it a lot too."

Nick wanted to groan as her small, delicate fingers continued to brush over the material. With any other woman, he might have thought she was doing it on purpose, but he just knew innately that Annie didn't think that way.

But that didn't stop him from reaching over to place a hand over hers, his only thought to stop that teasing, arousing motion.

Annie's hand stilled instantly, her eyes wide and questioning. He took his hand away as if he'd been burned, afraid where that simple touch could lead.

"I'm sorry," he said, shaking his head with frustration at himself and amazement that such a simple thing could push him over the edge. "I'm trying really, really hard to just sit here and have a nice, friendly conversation. But it seems like everything you do is a major distraction."

"I—I don't mean to—"

"It's not your fault. I just cannot remember a woman affecting me like you do."

★   ★   ★

Annie didn't know what to say, because she couldn't admit the truth. The truth was she felt the same way. God help her, she did. She'd hoped having him in her apartment, in the place she shared with Bobby, would make her realize her attraction to Nick was silly when compared to the relationship she had with Bobby.

But the truth, the horrible truth, was she had been aware of Nick constantly, even more intensely than before. She imagined him being here with her, a part of her life. Talking, laughing, making love.

She pulled in a shaky breath, trying desperately to get that final image out of her mind.

"I'm so attracted to you," he told her, his tone pained, apologetic.

And even though she knew it was wrong, she nodded with understanding.

"I—I am attracted to you too," she whispered, almost afraid to admit it too loudly. "But . . . I can't."

"I know."

They both fell silent, neither of them moving.

Finally Nick set his untouched coffee on the table in front of them. "I'd better go." He rose and headed toward the door.

Annie nodded, knowing that was the wisest choice, but still she wanted to beg him to stay. She hadn't felt this connected to anyone in so long, and she was terrified to let him walk out that door.

"Do you think we can be friends?" she asked.

Nick debated, then shook his head. "I don't know. I want to, but I think we both know that this temptation is hard to ignore."

She sighed, knowing he was right.

He smiled at her, and for the first time, she noticed the

twinkle was gone from his golden brown eyes. Sadness was in its place.

"Good night," he said and disappeared out the door.

"Good-bye," Annie said, suspecting even if they did see each other again, there would be a reserve between them that would bring its own sort of finality.

Chapter Twelve

"Oh for the love of Pete, don't tell me she's done something else." Satan didn't even look away from the football game he was watching.

"She has been using her demon abilities in a very public way."

That did capture the Prince of Darkness's attention. He spun in his oversized leather chair, his frown making him look very intimidating.

"What did she do? And where did this happen?"

"She silenced some men who were making rude comments to her. She rid a teenager of her piercings and she made a fat woman thin."

The devil stared for a moment, a very muddled look on his face, then he laughed, the sound booming through his cavernous lair.

"I actually find that quite amusing," Satan said, which seemed unnecessary after his laughter.

"Yes, Master . . . but she did these things in front of the detective."

Satan's amusement vanished. "I thought there was a plan to destroy any interest she might have in this detective."

"There was—is, but this all happened while the plan was being executed."

Satan rose from his chair and paced across his new brimstone flooring, stroking his beard as he thought.

"She is a loose cannon," he finally said, "I will give you that. But she is also very powerful, and perfect for her role. Do you know how hard it is to find demons who are willing to wear female humans' high fashion day in, day out? Six-inch heels. Stockings. Backless gowns. Spandex. Skinny jeans. And don't even get me started on the grooming rituals."

Satan strode back and forth across the floor a few more times. Then he collapsed back into his cushiony chair. For a moment, the game distracted him again as he watched one of the teams race down the field for a last-minute goal.

"Blast it!" he shouted, and his powerful voice reverberated so loudly through the cavern, it made even the ground shake. He gaped at the huge 82-inch flat screen, watching the instant replay.

"I'm sorry," he finally said, although still shaking his head at the outcome. "My favorite team, the Saints, irony I know, just lost the play-offs. Anyway, back to the task at hand. I will give Finola one last chance. If she is focused and doing her job, with only the occasional demonic attack, then I will let her continue as the head of this project. If you return to me and say she has risked the project again, then I will be forced to meet with her and sort out the problem myself."

"Which I hope doesn't happen," he said almost to himself. "I'm already dealing with this lust demon I placed in the government. He's gone rogue, utterly sex-crazed, sleeping with anyone. Fortunately no one is paying too much attention. He is a government official, after all."

He refocused again. "That's it. Just continue to keep me posted."

"Yes, Master."

★ ★ ★

"Good morning. It's Elton, right?"

The older mailroom clerk finished placing a bound pile of mail onto his metal cart before looking up at Nick. His coffee-colored skin was creased with wrinkles and his dark eyes hazed with age, but Nick instantly got the impression this man didn't miss a thing. And he was willing to bet Elton hadn't missed the strange state of the receptionist yesterday.

"Yep," Elton answered, returning his attention to his work, reaching for another pile of letters.

"I was hoping to talk to you."

"Well, I'm right here. Go ahead."

Nick smiled at the man's gruffness. "I'm Detective Rossi."

He started to reach into his jacket pocket for his badge, but stopped when Elton said, "I know who you are."

It was on the tip of Nick's tongue to ask how he knew, but he suspected his presence had been a big topic of discussion; maybe Elton had heard mention of him during his daily deliveries.

"So you probably know I'm here investigating the disappearance of a significant number of people who once worked for Finola White Enterprises."

Elton didn't react, still arranging his mail on the steel cart.

"One of the missing people is a woman who used to work in the mailroom. Sheila Bernard."

"I knew Sheila," Elton said, then glanced up at Nick. "But it don't mean I know what happened to her."

Nick nodded, not surprised by the man's response. It was about the most he got from anyone. "Since you knew her, maybe you recall something strange happening around the time she went missing."

Elton pursed his lips, shaking his head. "Not that I recall."

"No change in her behavior? Did she start missing work?"

"Can I help you?"

Nick turned to assess the man who'd suddenly appeared beside him. He appeared to be in his late thirties, perhaps early forties. His build and face were nondescript, just an average-looking guy. The only thing that truly stood about him was his eyes. They were a light and vivid blue. Almost like those of a husky. Eerie, almost hypnotic eyes, giving him an almost feral look. Nick had seen eyes like that, somewhere, but he couldn't put his finger on exactly where at the moment.

Instantly that feeling of prickly awareness returned. An awareness that made him on edge, wary. Last night, lying in bed, trying not to think about Annie and his desire for her, he'd wondered about his strange feelings yesterday. He'd convinced himself that it was adrenaline or just an awareness fostered from years as a cop.

But right now, as he experienced the sensation so intensely again, he knew he was kidding himself. He was really feeling something. Some vibe that came off certain people.

"Hello, Eugene," Nick said, reading the man's name from his work smock. He extended his hand. "I'm Detective—"

"Rossi," the man finished for him. "Yes, I've heard of you."

"Apparently news gets around this place," Nick said.

"Indeed it does," Eugene said. "Why don't you come to my office? We can talk there."

Nick considered pointing out he'd been in the middle of talking with Elton, but then decided to follow the younger man. Since Eugene had sought Nick out, maybe he had something he wanted to tell him. Or something he didn't want Elton to tell him.

Eugene led Nick through the bustling mailroom, noticing that the whole place seemed to vibrate with a driven intensity. Each person was engrossed in whatever task he was doing. Yet, despite the number of people working there, it was almost quiet, as if everyone was simply too absorbed in his work to chatter or laugh. Another thing that struck him was the number of employees working there. Finola White Enterprises was a large company, but Nick would estimate there were probably seventy-five or more hardworking mailroom employees. That struck him as overkill.

But no matter what, the place felt . . . strange. That was the best way to describe the vibe. Why this surprised him was a mystery. Everything about *HOT!* and Finola White Enterprises was strange.

"Have a seat," Eugene said, gesturing to a folding metal chair across the desk from his own computer chair.

Nick sat, looking around the small office of gray plywood walls. Some scheduling charts were tacked up behind him. A calendar. A poster about employee etiquette. Another poster of a mountain with an inspirational saying underneath. Other odds and ends, but nothing that struck Nick as out of the ordinary.

"So you are the mailroom manager?" he asked.

Eugene nodded, taking his own seat. "I am."

"Then you would handle all the hiring/firing?"

Eugene nodded again. "I do handle all the hiring and firing, although Ms. White has the ultimate say."

"And is she very involved in the mailroom?"

Eugene chuckled. "Presumably you've met Ms. White. I think you can probably tell the mailroom is not of much interest to her. For the most part, we go unnoticed down here."

No, that didn't surprise Nick. The mailroom was definitely too . . . what word had she used last night? Too proletarian for Finola.

But still, Nick found the word *unnoticed* an interesting choice. Ignored would seem a better word to him. After all, unnoticed—at least to the detective in him—seemed to imply there was something going on down here that perhaps should be noticed. If anyone was paying close attention.

"Well, I'm sure you've heard that I'm here investigating the disappearance of a number of Finola White Enterprise's employees."

"Yes, I had heard that."

"And one of those missing persons is Sheila Bernard. Did you know her?"

"Certainly," Eugene said, with a solemn nod. "She was one of our delivery staff."

"Meaning?"

"She went up to the different floors and distributed the mail to the actual offices and other employees."

"Like Elton does," Nick said.

"Yes."

"What did you think of her?"

"She was a hard worker, good at her job."

"Do you remember when she disappeared?"

Eugene pursed his lips as he considered Nick's question; finally he shook his head. "Sadly, not right off the top of my head. But I would have the information in my employee time sheets. She actually didn't show up for work for several days before anyone became aware that something could be wrong."

"Did she just not show up for work often?" Nick asked.

"Not that I recall."

"And no one was concerned until she'd been gone for a few days?"

Eugene smiled wryly. "Not many people would go straight to Missing Persons just because someone missed a few days of work. We aren't all suspicious detectives, I'm afraid."

Nick wasn't sure he bought that. It seemed to him that at least one person would find it strange that a good employee didn't call in when missing a day of work, much less several.

But Nick was going to give Eugene the benefit of the doubt.

"Maybe the fact you weren't too concerned when she didn't show up for work was because she'd been ill before that? Or acting strange?"

"Strange how?"

"Maybe spacey? Confused? Maybe even totally out of it."

Eugene shook his head. "I'm sure I would recall that."

"Well, if you could go through your records and get me her time cards, that would be a great help." He reached into his pocket and pulled out a business card. "You can fax them to me."

"Certainly."

Nick stood. "You wouldn't mind me talking to some of your other employees, would you?"

Eugene raised an eyebrow. "Of course not."

Nick regarded the man for a moment, getting the odd feeling Eugene was almost challenging him. A certain smugness brightened his eyes.

Nick suppressed a shiver as the prickling sensation became very intense.

"Excellent," Nick said, torn between wanting to get out of there and wanting to continue grilling this man. He had a feeling this case had just gotten more complicated than he'd thought. Maybe Finola wasn't the only one to blame for the missing employees.

But he stood and shook Eugene's hand, then left his

office. When Nick glanced over his shoulder, Eugene leaned in the doorway, watching him with those eerie eyes. Again Nick got the impression Eugene knew a lot more than he was saying—and he liked having knowledge that Nick didn't.

Nick spent the remainder of the morning talking to as many of the mailroom staff as he could, discovering nothing new, except for maybe the fact that they were a peculiar group of people. A majority were surprisingly nerdy, seeming more like brainiac computer geeks than people who would handle the mail. Then there were several who just struck him as eccentric. Only a handful seemed even remotely normal, but then again, he supposed there was a reason why they were all working underground away from the general populace.

Did that weirdness give one of them, or maybe more than one, the potential to hurt their fellow employees? It wasn't out of the realm of possibility, that was for sure. He was even willing to bet more than of a couple of them thought zombies were cool. Could they be trying to make their own zombies somehow?

He dismissed mentioning that particular idea to Captain Brooks. That was the kind of thinking that would get him pulled from the case and on yet another leave of absence.

But Nick did have to give his superior some sort of update. With the lack of physical evidence, and the fact that aside for one person who was technically found alive, there were no bodies, this was going to be a hard case to keep going.

The only reason Chief Brooks was taking an interest in it to begin with was because of the number of people who were missing.

Nick wasn't looking forward to telling him that he didn't

have any solid information yet, and he was afraid Brooks was going to pull him anyway when he shared what he did know.

Still, he gathered up the report he'd written and headed for his superior's office.

He rapped on the doorframe even though the captain's door was open and he was seated at his desk.

Captain Brooks looked up from another report he was reading and called for Nick to come in. Nick wandered into his office, reluctant to sit down. Reluctant to hand over the report.

"Well? Any leads?"

Nick hesitated again, then shrugged vaguely. "I'm getting closer, I think, to some real news. There's definitely a lot of strange things going on at that magazine."

Brooks nodded. "But do you have anything definite?"

Nick looked down at the report clutched in his hand, then finally shook his head. "Not yet, but—"

His boss raised his hand to stop him. "I'm right with you that there is something very wrong over there. But I can only give you so much time to check it out. We just don't have the money or manpower for a lengthy investigation. Especially when there is still no proof that these people didn't just walk away of their own volition."

"Twenty-one people?"

Brooks nodded in sympathy. "I hear you, but these are grown individuals, and aside for the one, who was actually found alive—"

"But mentally gone," Nick added.

"I understand that, but as of right now, we have no proof that these people didn't just walk away and start a new life elsewhere."

"Twenty-one people, all working for the same company, who just to decide to walk away and start a new life. Without contacting their families, or friends, or anyone."

"I know." Brooks nodded again. "But without evidence or bodies, we just can't prove any foul play."

"But I did witness foul play," Nick said.

Captain Brooks leaned forward, listening.

"Yesterday, I encountered one of the employees, a receptionist, who was suffering from that same almost catatonic state as the one woman who was found. When I returned later, she was gone. I checked several times today and she is still gone."

Brooks studied him for a moment. "Maybe she was simply sick. She could have called in today."

Nick had thought of all those things, but he also knew what he'd seen, what he'd felt. She was gone. He knew it.

And the thing that drove him really mad was that he'd been in the building when it happened. Another missing person, right under his very own nose.

"Just a little longer," Nick asked, but he tried not to sound too worked up. He knew Brooks would pull him if he thought the case was too much for him.

Too much for his fragile peace of mind. His sanity.

Of course, Nick was a little worried about his sanity too. He'd been feeling things, seeing thing since he'd taken this case that he hadn't since he'd had to leave the precinct. He didn't want to leave now. Or to have to drop the case.

Not when other people could, and likely would, get hurt. His thoughts went to Annie. He had to keep her safe.

Finally Brooks nodded. "A little longer."

"Thanks," Nick said, smiling for the first time this morning. "Thank you."

He placed his report on Brooks's desk and headed for the door, deciding it was better to exit before the captain could change his mind.

"Nick—" Brooks's cigarette-roughened voice stopped him before he could make a clean escape.

Nick came back to the doorway.

"I can see this case is important to you. I understand that, but don't let it overtake you."

Nick nodded, then walked away. Was Brooks seeing something in him? Something he'd seen last time?

Were all his strange feelings and the fact that he thought he'd seen weird things the beginning of ending up where he was a year ago?

Was he slipping again?

Chapter Thirteen

"So I've been thinking," Finola said from behind the dressing screen in the corner of her office.

Tristan made a noise indicating he was listening, although barely. He concentrated on the schedule of events for Fashion Week, deciding when and where to have *HOT!* make its presence known.

"I think the reason my date with Nick was such a failure was the fact that going to a—what was that place called again?"

"A bowling alley?" Tristan said, not quite sure what she was referring to. But he was sure the second day of Fashion Week was going to be a long, busy one. Several of their rival magazines would be in attendance those days and they were the people *HOT!* needed to target.

"Yes, that bowling alley. That was just too common for me."

"Well, darling, it was good to see what kind of life he leads," Tristan pointed out, as he made more notes. They needed to target the editor-in-chief of *Señorita*. As well as *Urban*. Soon *HOT!* would have a foothold in all the major fashion magazines in the States. Then the world.

"He is a working stiff," Tristan added. "That's always been an obvious flaw in his personality."

"That is true," Finola said with a loud sigh.

"Be careful with those pins," she muttered to the woman who stood behind the screen with her, fitting the dress she would wear to her Fashion Week launch party. "I'm fairly certain blood does not come out of cotton, by which I mean your clothing, not mine."

Tristan smiled slightly at that. He was glad to see the old Finola was back, focusing on things that were important. Clothing. Parties. Veiled threats. No more love with the common man nonsense for her.

And soon, after not finding one single lead, the good detective would be totally out of their lives. Things were back on track.

After a few moments, Finola appeared from behind the screen in a gorgeous white silk charmeuse with a plunging V-neck and a cascade of flounces down her back that spilled into a short train.

Tristan smiled approvingly. "Beautiful. Fiord has out-done himself this time."

"Hasn't he?" Finola walked across the office as if she were on the catwalk. The dress flowed and moved with her body, accenting all the right places.

Tristan actually felt his libido surge to life for the first time in a long time. Apparently, stress even affected a demon of lust's sex drive.

"Fortunately I have a few more days to get Nick groomed enough to be seen with me in this gown."

Tristan's libido shriveled along with his smile.

"Nick?"

Finola paused and glanced at him over her white, bare shoulder.

"It's true, I did not care for our date, but that was be-cause of the awful place we went. Eating with your fin-gers. Fat people ruining the view. Not to mention the abundance of body hair on so many of the men in atten-dance."

She shuddered.

"It's little wonder the date was a disaster."

Then she turned and smiled. Tristan did not like the determination glittering in her eyes.

"I'm certain there must be somewhere in between. Something not quite so common. Then from there, I can groom him into what I want. Just cultured enough to be presentable and just edgy enough to be delicious in private."

Tristan fought the desire to growl. Finola's dog had no such control. The little white beast growled from its place in its jeweled bed. For once Tristan felt that he was connecting with the animal.

Finola slipped back behind the screen.

"I'm going to discuss this with Anna. She should be able to think of something that is more middle of the road for us to do."

"Finola," he said, keeping his voice calm, or as calm as he could, "you really don't have time to pursue a man who is far too much work, and ultimately not right for you. Why not ask Will Campbell to escort you to your party? He would look wonderful on your arm."

Tristan searched his mind for other models and actors who had garnered her attention. There had to be someone she would consent to date. Someone who wasn't a detective more interested in the missing people from *HOT!* than the owner of it.

After a few moments, the lady who'd been helping her to dress, a small Latina who did some of the fitting and tailoring for the *HOT!* models during photoshoots, stepped out from the screen with the dress over her arm. She nodded at Tristan as she bustled out of the office.

Several seconds later, Finola stepped out, now dressed in a simple, yet expensive sheath dress. "I'm tired of those types of men. I want someone more manly, more down to earth. Someone more interested in my looks than his own."

Tristan blinked at her, wondering if she had lost her mind. Or she'd somehow gotten possessed herself.

"Besides, I always get what I want. And I want Nick Rossi."

Well, that at least sounded like Finola, but in this case her response was little comfort. He still had to think of a way to keep her from really dating this man.

But before he could formulate a single thought, much less a plan, Finola was heading toward the office door.

"Where are you going?"

Finola paused midstep. "To talk to Anna. She must know of something we would both enjoy doing."

Tristan stood to follow, as did her dog.

Finola's little lapdogs chasing after her, Tristan thought bitterly.

"Surely there must be some way to locate white lilacs at this time of year," Annie said, realizing that she sounded almost as demanding as her boss. But she was desperate. No one had or knew how to get lilacs in winter. And Finola likely wouldn't settle for anything else.

But when the man on the other end assured her that he didn't know of anyplace to find them, Annie forced herself to thank him politely and hang up the phone.

"More difficult demands, huh?"

Annie looked up to see Nick standing a few feet away.

Her heart sped up at the sight of him, her eyes moving over him, looking so handsome in a leather jacket and low-slung jeans.

She'd missed him.

Immediately she reprimanded herself. She couldn't possibly miss him. She'd seen him just the day before yesterday, and he wasn't a person she should be missing anyway.

"Hi," she managed. "What brings you here?"

"Just questioning a few more people," Nick said. "How are you?"

Glad to see you.

Stop it, she warned herself. She couldn't think like that. "I've been fine. Busy."

Nick smiled, his eyes twinkled and the curve of his lips looked so naughty. So kissable.

She suppressed a groan. She really had to get herself under control.

"Well, you are just the man I wanted to see," that familiar, gratingly melodic voice called, forcing her to pull herself together and act as if Nick wasn't sending all her senses into overdrive.

Nick turned that smile toward Finola, but Annie liked to think the glimmer in his brown eyes diminished a little.

"You're looking for me?" he said. "What for? And how was the cocktail party at . . . who was it again?"

Finola smiled sweetly, her tone apologetic, "Donatella Versace. And it was very much a letdown."

Tristan appeared in the doorway of her office, and Annie got the feeling he wanted to say something, but he just paused there, quietly regarding the group in front of him. Finola's dog, Dippy, peeked out from between Tristan's legs.

"Well," Nick said, "the gang's all here."

Finola laughed, then moved forward to touch his arm. "I was actually coming out here for two reasons. To discuss with Anna another venue for a second date, and then to get your number so I could ask you out myself this time."

Nick looked impressed. "Wow, you want another date? I got the impression our first didn't go so well."

Finola touched his arm again, this time her long, pale fingers curling around his forearm.

Annie was instantly reminded of a skeleton hand reaching out from the grave, clawing and rasping.

"Well, I thought our part of the date went perfectly," she assured him, her pale eyes glittering with desire.

Nick smiled back, and Annie had to look away, the image of the two of them too much for her to handle.

Because he's at risk, she told herself, then silently scoffed at her usual rationalization. She was worried about that, but the truth was she really did hate seeing that creature flirt with and touch the man she wanted. It was as simple as that.

"Did you think Anni—Anna—could come up with a better place for us to go out a second time?" Nick asked, and Annie did look up at him, narrowing her eyes slightly, but otherwise not reacting.

Why was he dragging her back into this warped dating game? He and Finola could think of their own dating spot. She wanted no part of it. Unfortunately that wasn't what Nick had in mind.

"Anni—Anna—was just telling me about her boyfriend's play," Nick said. "That seems like something you would be more interested in."

Finola's eyes lit up and her fingers ran up and down his arm from wrist to elbow and back. "The theater. Now, that I adore."

Nick smiled at her, then looked almost slyly toward Annie.

"Well, let's go tonight," he said. "Annie, I mean Anna, already said she was going. We could join her. Meet her boyfriend."

Annie pursed her lips, not keeping her irritation out of her eyes—that is, until Finola turned to her.

"Why Anna, you little minx, I didn't know you had a boyfriend."

Because you don't know anything about me, Annie

thought. Because we are not friends who suddenly hang out and double-date. No thanks to Nick.

But instead of showing any of her irritation, she smiled and nodded. And because, as she'd mentally pointed out to no one but herself, they were not really friends, Finola asked her nothing further about the man and her relationship with him.

"Well count me in too," Tristan said, stepping away from the doorway, offering the group a smile that looked decidedly more like a grimace.

Someone else seemed as thrilled at the prospect of this outing as she did. But why was Tristan even going? It wasn't like Nick had wrangled him into his little plan.

But Nick didn't seem put off by the idea.

"Great," he grinned, then he turned to Annie, his eyes practically dancing with wicked merriment.

Annie decided that maybe his naughty twinkle might not be as cute as he thought.

"What time did you say you were going again?" Nick asked, pretending to be oblivious to her less-than-pleased look.

Annie didn't answer for a moment, but then looked at Finola and Tristan, who also waited for her answer.

"The play starts at eight."

"Then let's all meet at seven-thirty," Nick said, still grinning from ear to ear.

Nick's cell phone rang almost as soon as he left the Finola White Enterprises building, and he didn't have to guess who the caller was.

"Detective Nick Rossi," he said in his usual greeting.

"Why would you do that?" the voice he was expecting demanded—well, demanded in a hushed tone.

"Do what?" he said innocently, rather enjoying the way Annie's irritation made her voice breathy.

He wondered if she talked as breathily when she was aroused for other reasons. His cock perked up, clearly curious too.

"I don't want to go to Bobby's play with you and Finola."

"And Tristan," Nick added.

"This isn't funny," Annie said, her voice no longer just irritated but dismayed too. That Nick didn't find amusing.

"You know why I did it. I still need to figure out some way to get information from Finola."

There was silence on the other end of the line and for a moment he thought she'd hung up.

"But why include me? And why Bobby's play?"

"That does seem a little masochistic, doesn't it?"

Annie sighed. "Yes. I just don't see the point."

Nick considered his actions, not totally sure himself, but he did want her to know he hadn't done it to be mean or make her life any more difficult. God knew, she didn't need that.

"I just—" he shrugged, "I just wanted you there. And I guess I do want to see Bobby too. I want to see the man who's getting the woman I want."

"Nick—"

"I know, I know. I shouldn't say things like that. Hell, I shouldn't even think things like that. But that's how I feel. And who knows, maybe if I meet Bobby and he's finally real to me I can stop thinking about you nonstop. I can actually realize these feelings I have for you have no hope of going anywhere."

Annie's end of the line fell silent again.

"Annie?" he finally said, thinking maybe they were cut off, or that she'd hung up disgusted with his inability to let her go, even when he knew there wasn't any other option.

"So what's going to help me stop thinking about you?"

Nick paused on the sidewalk, torn between the joy and sorrow her words roused in him. Part of him was so

damned glad she felt the same way he did. So damned self-
ishly glad, and another part just felt like shit. Shit for making Annie feel guilty and sad. She didn't deserve that.

"Annie—"

"You know what," she said suddenly, her voice no longer
soft and filled with painful regret. Now she sounded resigned but determined, clearly the way she handled all the
difficulties of her life, "it is probably good that you meet
Bobby. I'm sure it will make both of us see this attraction
between us is just a silly little thing—not real at all."

Nick felt her words like a kick to the gut, stealing his
breath and making him want to double over in pain, but
he managed to sound as confident, as accepting as she did.

"Yeah, it's a good thing."

Annie was silent again, for just a moment, then she said,
"Good. See you tonight."

"See you."

Nick hung up his phone and slipped it back into his
jacket pocket. He pulled his collar up around his neck and
strode in the direction of his apartment.

For the first time since impulsively setting this plan into
motion, he started to feel like maybe he'd made a mistake.
It was going to be damned hard to woo the woman he
suspected of nefarious deeds for information while he was
watching the woman he really wanted with the man she
loved.

Chapter Fourteen

Satan frowned, clearly not pleased to be interrupted again so soon. But that couldn't be helped.

"Finola has not given up on her romance with the detective. They are going out again tonight."

Satan set down the fork; he'd just been about to stab into what appeared to be a huge helping of Belgian waffles. Dripping with butter and syrup. To his right stood a very buxom redhead with dramatic eye makeup and glossy ruby lips. She wore only an apron and chef's hat.

Satan sighed. "She would have to interrupt 'breakfast for dinner' night, wouldn't she? She really is becoming a nuisance."

Satan rose and turned to his sexy chef. He bowed his red horned head to the woman's chest, running his long, serpent-like tongue across the swell of her large breasts above the apron bib.

"I will be back in time for my dessert."

The woman nodded, her eyes glazed with desire. The scent of lust was thick in the air. Mingling nicely with the warm, toasty scent of the waffles.

"Okay, let's put a stop to this impudent demon's behavior. Now."

★ ★ ★

Tristan mixed himself a double dirty martini, extra dirty, and settled on Finola's white leather sofa. He gazed out her window at her much-coveted view of the Central Park. He preferred his loft in the West Village with all its quirky charm, but Finola's ultramodern apartment was undeniably stunning.

He just could not comprehend why she would want to risk this lifestyle, her free rein in the mortal world and all its amazing perks. Just for a piece of ass. Hell, they could get sex anywhere. Why was this one man so worth all this risk and, frankly, headache?

He took another sip, then let his head fall back against the supple leather. Damn, he was tired. Babysitting a diva demon was exhausting. He needed a vacation.

Beside him the sofa dipped just slightly, and he opened his eyes to see Finola's mutt on the cushion beside him. The white fluffball watched him with expectant, unblinking black eyes.

"What do *you* want?" he muttered. "Satan knows, I've already done a full day's work without waiting on you too."

He lifted a hand to shoo the little pest off the sofa when a deep voice stopped him.

"Do you not care for my gift to Finola?"

Tristan looked away from the dog to see Satan himself standing in the center of Finola's monochromatic living room, his bright red skin standing out violently against the white backdrop.

Tristan instantly rose, dropping his gaze in the appropriate response of submissiveness and respect.

"It is—cute," Tristan replied, so shocked to see the Prince of Darkness in someplace so unexpected as Finola's living room.

"Hmm, cute," Satan agreed, his voice rumbling through the room like low, distant thunder. "Please relax."

Tristan tried, but that wasn't something he could do easily. The appearance of the reigning prince of Hell himself
could not be a good sign.

Damn it, he knew Finola was pushing her luck.

Finally Tristan mustered the nerve to lift his head, carefully looking toward his master. It was especially unnerving to see Satan here in an uptown apartment in his full
demonic glory. Standing nearly seven feet tall, he seemed
to eat up the whole room. His bare torso was broad with
flaming red skin pulled taut over massive muscles. His
black horns, not unlike a bull's, threatened to hit the chandelier in the center of the ceiling. And his deep-set black
eyes burned with an inner light. He was terrifying and
oddly gorgeous all at once. Even to another demon.

"Where is Finola?" he asked, glancing around the stark,
modern space.

"Tristan," Finola called as if on cue, stepping out from
her bedroom suite, "what on earth is that noi . . ." Her
question trailed off as she stepped into the living room and
saw their unexpected visitor.

"Master," she said automatically, coming to a halt and
dropping her gaze to the floor.

Her meek demeanor amused Tristan, although he was
careful to keep his expression respectful. Even though all
demons, no matter how powerful, were subservient to the
one and only ruler of Hell, it was still nice to see her submissive for once.

"Aren't you looking lovely tonight," Satan said in his
rumbling, mighty voice.

"Thank you, Master," she said, her voice extra melodic.

Of course she was going to pull out all her most appealing tricks; she knew she was in deep shit.

Satan strolled toward her, moving with a grace that
seemed to defy his size and cloven hooves. He reached out
and tested the fabric of her skirt between his large fingers,

his talon-like black nails threatening to catch the filmy material.

"Chiffon," he confirmed. "Very nice."

"Thank you, Master," she repeated actually daring to lift her eyes just slightly and smile at him. A flirty curl of her bloodred lips.

Tristan's breath held, waiting for a burst of rage from their prince at her brazen behavior, but instead Satan only chuckled.

"Ah, Finola, always so sure of yourself," he said, shaking his horned head.

Finola didn't say anything to that, but her coquettish smirk remained.

"So, my lovely little demon, why are you dressed so beautifully tonight?"

"I dress beautifully every day, Master," she said, her voice light and crystalline.

Satan chuckled again, but this time his hand shot out with startling speed and captured her chin between his thumb and forefinger. Those clawed nails of his, pressing just lightly into her pale, perfect skin.

This time, when Finola looked at him, all hints of flirtation were gone, replaced by genuine fear.

"Oh Finola, you know you are one of my favorites. As greedy and heartless and arrogant as myself." He stroked the sharp nail of his thumb over her full bottom lip. "But even I know that too much of any of those traits will get a demon into some very serious trouble."

Finola nodded slightly, clearly afraid to move too much for fear of that sharp talon.

"So again," he asked, his voice so low and deep Tristan had to concentrate to make out his words, "where were you going tonight?"

Even as quietly as the question was asked, Tristan didn't miss that it was in the past tense. He cringed, afraid what the question meant. Was Finola going straight back to Hell tonight? Was Tristan?

"I have a date," Finola answered, her verb tense indicating that she either didn't catch the tense of his question, or that she, in her uncontrollable arrogance, still believed the outing was going to happen.

Satan slowly removed his hand from her, a slow brush of his fingers over her skin. Then he turned away, striding back to the center of the room.

"Oh yes, a date with the human detective."

Finola lifted her head to frown at him, although Satan's broad back was to her.

"Yes," she said, not keeping the surprise from her voice.

Satan swung back to her, a smile curving his lips into a wide, unnatural grin. His black eyes danced with an orange flame.

"You're surprised that I know about this mortal male, aren't you?"

"No," she said, but it was evident she was.

"Oh sweet, evil Finola. You should know that I know about everything. At least I do eventually."

She nodded, her eyes lowering again to focus on the white carpeting. But not before she shot Tristan an unpleased look.

"You will not see this man."

Finola didn't respond, although Tristan could see her pale eyebrows come together just slightly.

Obviously so did Satan because he asked, "You don't understand why, do you, lovely?"

This time she shook her head.

"Look at me," Satan ordered.

Finola lifted her head, her eyes meeting his and for a moment, Tristan was impressed with her boldness. It would likely get her permanently banished one day, but it was extraordinary. Satan was right about that.

"You will not date this man."

Finola again didn't respond.

"Do you understand?" Satan asked, sounding more like a stern father than the purveyor of all evil. "This man is off limits. We do not need a human detective worming his way into places he shouldn't be. He's already suspicious of you. Of the magazine. There is no reason to risk our hard work. One day, when we are better infiltrated into the human world, I will not worry about law enforcement and the like. But right now it could just draw unnecessary attention to you and the magazine."

"I understand," Finola said.

"Cancel the date," Satan said.

Finola nodded and walked over to Tristan, holding out her hand. Even in submission, Finola managed to make him feel like her lackey.

Tristan reached into the pocket of his Armani trousers and pulled out his cell phone. He unlocked the screen, then handed it to her. She scrolled through the numbers until she found the number she needed.

Chapter Fifteen

"*Three Men and a Cockroach?*"

Annie turned to find Nick standing behind her, peering up at the vintage-style marquee, which was Annie's own nice way of saying old.

"It—it's a satire about humans' false sense of supremacy over the world around them," Annie explained, repeating what Bobby had told her so many times. Not that she'd gotten that message from the play when she'd seen it previously. As far as she could tell, it was about three guys with a strange and at times unnatural obsession with a cockroach. A cockroach that could talk.

But Nick was kind enough to simply nod as if that explanation made perfect sense.

"So are we the only ones here?" he asked, glancing around at the crowd.

"So far."

Nick nodded again, and Annie could see that their earlier conversation was still weighing on both of them, making things between them awkward. Annie hated it.

"Does Bobby know you are here?"

Annie nodded, then shrugged. "I think he does. I left him a voicemail to let him know we were coming."

Nick nodded again. And again she wished they didn't

have to have this uneasiness filling the air like a canyon between them, making it impossible to act normal.

She opened her mouth to tell him so, when her phone rang.

She pulled it out of the side pocket of her purse, checking the name on the screen.

"It's Tristan. They must be running late."

She answered, frowning when she realized it was Finola. Her boss spoke quickly, not giving Annie any room or time to ask questions. All she managed was a couple of "okays" before the phone went dead.

"What was that about?"

Annie looked at Nick, somewhat surprised as well as a little—disappointed.

Was she mad? Finola's announcement should have pleased Annie no end.

"That was actually Finola. She said that something came up at work and she and Tristan won't be able to make it."

Nick frowned. "I wonder what came up."

Annie shrugged, realizing his detective cap was on just as quick as that. "She didn't say. But I guess that means our play night is off."

Annie started to pull her coat tighter around herself, preparing to walk home, when a hand on her arm stopped her.

"Why do we have to cancel?" he asked. "I know I was looking forward to seeing a play about humans' false sense of something or other."

Despite herself, she laughed. "False sense of supremacy."

"Yeah that," he said, his eyes twinkling in that way she so loved. "I want to learn all about that."

Annie regarded him for a moment. Those eyes, and that smile. His goatee and tousled hair. God, she loved just looking at him.

"You don't have to do that. In fact, I think it might be

easier if we just don't." Despite herself, she felt that dull sense of disappointment deep in her chest again.

Nick nodded, and for a moment she thought he was going to agree, but then he said, "Do you know what would definitely make it easier?"

Annie hesitated to ask, but couldn't seem to stop herself. "What's that?"

"Wine," he stated. "Wine."

Annie laughed again, and he must have realized she was going to protest again, because before she could, he pointed through the glass door to where a bar was set up in the lobby.

"No, really, wine."

Annie shook her head at his persistence, but relented. "Okay, let's get some wine."

Nick reached for the door handle just as she did. For a brief moment, her icy fingers brushed against his much warmer ones. She snatched her hand away.

"Let me," he said, his voice low and husky, and for a moment, Annie didn't know if he referred to getting the door or touching her.

But then he pulled the door wide, gesturing for her to enter. Neither spoke as they made a beeline for the bar.

"Two glasses of your best—" he raised a questioning eyebrow to Annie.

"Chardonnay," Annie said.

"Chardonnay," Nick repeated.

Soon they each had a plastic tumbler of cheap white wine and they moved over to a quiet corner.

Annie took a sip, letting the warmth seep into her.

"See, don't you feel better?" he said.

She smiled, then nodded. "I do."

She usually felt better around him, she thought, but had the sense to keep that to herself.

Nick glanced around the lobby. Annie followed his

gaze. Neither spoke, just sipped their wine and watched the people arrive.

"You really don't have to do this," she said when the dwindling crowd indicated it was time to go to their seats. "It's really not a very good play."

Nick smiled at that. "With a name like *Three Men and a Cockroach*, I never had high hopes it would be."

Annie laughed, then gestured with her empty cup toward the bar. "We better sneak in another glass of wine, because we're going to need it. The play's *really* not good."

Nick chuckled and followed her to back over to the bartender.

By the time the lights came up for the play's intermission, Nick realized Annie had understated the truth.

"I think we should have brought in a whole bottle," he said as they both headed out to the lobby. "This play is beyond bad, it's awful."

"I warned you," she whispered.

"How many times have you sat through this?" he asked.

"This is my third time."

Nick made a pained face. "Dear God."

Annie laughed.

"Although Bobby wasn't bad," he said, feeling like he should acknowledge him in some way. Truthfully, Bobby's very small part as a deliveryman delivering cases of roach killer, of course, was the only part of the performance that had held Nick's attention. He was morbidly curious about the man who called the most adorable and sweet woman Nick had ever met his girlfriend.

Nick hadn't been completely surprised by what he saw. A tall, fit blond with traditional good looks and a toothpaste-ad smile.

"It's okay," Annie said, drawing his thoughts away from

the other man. "He's not good either. But acting is his dream and he won't give up on it."

"What about your dreams?" Nick asked. "Surely, working at *HOT!* isn't your dream. Not with Finola as a boss."

Annie smiled faded, and he wished he hadn't brought up her employer.

"It was my dream at one time, but not anymore."

"Annie, you should just leave. No job is worth working with a demanding boss like that."

"Ah, if it were only so simple."

Nick frowned. She'd said that before. That leaving wasn't an option, but why not? Somehow he knew that was a question Annie wouldn't answer.

"Do you want to stay for the rest?" she asked.

Nick wasn't ready to leave Annie, but he honestly didn't think he could make it through the rest of that nightmare.

Still he had to ask.

"Tell me, does the involvement between Leo and the cockroach take a—" he grimaced as he asked, "physical twist?"

Annie made her own pained face as she nodded.

"Oh God, how?"

Annie shook her head. "You really don't want to know."

He paused, pretending to consider the possibilities, then stated, "No, I don't think I can make it through that."

Annie smiled. "I kind of thought you were done when you suggested we take our coats with us."

"That obvious, huh?"

"Understandable."

Nick smiled, then he couldn't help saying, "I did enjoy one part of it, though."

"Oh yeah," she said tugging at her coat, "which part?"

He moved behind her to help her, holding the coat out so she could slip her arms inside, but once she had it on, he still didn't move away from her, his hands resting lightly on her shoulders.

He leaned in, his mouth close to her ear. "I loved the part where I could smell your perfume. Feel the occasional brush of your arm against mine. Feel the warmth of your body."

At his murmured words, she swayed slightly back against him, only to catch herself and step away.

She didn't speak for a moment, her cheeks flushed pink, her breathing coming in short puffs. But finally she seemed to gather herself.

"I should go backstage and say hello to Bobby."

Nick nodded, realizing without saying the words that she was telling him this attraction couldn't go where he wanted it to go. And he understood that. He did, but something about being close to her stole all his rational thought.

"Okay," he agreed. "I'll go with you."

Annie immediately shook her head. "No, that isn't necessary."

"I want to. Like I told you before, I think I need to meet him."

She hesitated for a moment, clearly debating whether that was a good plan. Then she nodded.

As Annie led Nick toward the backstage door, she considered his theory about having him and Bobby meet. Earlier he'd said that meeting Bobby would make him real to Nick. Well, Bobby was already real to her, and still she couldn't seem to control her attraction to Nick.

Just his lightest touch. His hands on her shoulders. His breath against her ear. Even his voice. All of him drove her to distraction. And she just didn't know how to make the feelings stop.

Focus on Bobby, she told herself. You have to remember Bobby is the man in your life.

No one stopped them as they headed back into the maze of old sets and props, following the sound of excited voices and laughter.

"Clearly, they don't know they suck," Nick mumbled and Annie found herself suppressing a giggle even though she was distracted and nervous. Or maybe because she was nervous.

He smiled too, that naughty grin that instantly drove her heart into overdrive.

Stop it, she told herself. Her thoughts could not go there. This meeting would be the moment, the turning point, where she got control of her feelings and did the right thing.

They continued to weave through the theater paraphernalia, toward the voices, when a movement in her peripheral vision caught her attention.

She almost didn't even give the slight shuffling a second glance, assuming it was one of the theater hands changing the set, or a janitor cleaning up. But something about the flashing image seemed familiar.

Whatever the reason, she stopped, leaning down slightly to peer through the wooden framework of an old set piece.

There, amid the fake castle sets and a plywood cutout of a stagecoach, she could see what was obviously a man and a woman intertwined. Hands roaming over each other's bodies, clothing being peeled up to reveal flashes of skin. A man's still-covered rear end and hips pressing between a woman's bare, spread knees.

Shock and embarrassment heated Annie's cheeks, and she started to straighten, prepared to move on. But again, a flash of recognition stopped her.

"That feels so good, baby."

The female's comment was followed by a low moan. A moan Annie knew very well, even though she hadn't heard it herself in many months.

"Oh, Bobby."

Annie closed her eyes, as the enraptured woman confirmed what she already knew.

Before she realized what she was doing, Annie ducked and weaved her way through the scaffolding and props, making her way toward them.

"Hello, Bobby."

Chapter Sixteen

Annie was surprised at how even her voice sounded. How utterly indifferent.

Bobby froze, one hand under the woman's shirt, cupping her breast, the other digging into her bare thigh.

The blonde gaped at her, her hair tangled in her face, her legs still spread wide to accommodate Annie's boyfriend.

The boyfriend she didn't even want, but had somehow felt obligated to be loyal to. A giggle threatened to spill out of her throat, but she managed to control it.

"This is Ally, I assume," Annie said, her voice filled with an unsurprised acceptance.

"Annie," Bobby said, pulling away from his blond actress lover, rearranging his clothing with embarrassed, jerky movements. At first, Annie thought it was for her benefit, but then he realized Bobby kept glancing to her right, and she realized it was the appearance of Nick that seemed to have him more unnerved.

That realization should have irritated her. That he was more concerned about a stranger's reaction than hers, but for some reason she found that ironically amusing as well. Another inappropriate giggle threatened to spill out of her.

"Who is this guy?" Bobby demanded.

"Really?" Nick said, a disbelieving look on his face.

"You're worried about me? I think I'm the least of your concerns at the moment."

Bobby stared at them, his eyes moving from one to the other as he obviously struggled for what to say.

"Annie," he finally said, his voice a little pleading. "I can explain."

Annie stared at him for a moment, then couldn't suppress the giggle that had been bubbling up inside her any longer. "Of course you can."

Of course he would say the most clichéd response to this situation ever. That was Bobby for you.

"I don't think I need it explained. I can see pretty clearly what's going on. I just feel a little silly that I didn't see what was going on sooner."

"Annie, please." Bobby started to take a step toward her, but she held up a hand to ward him off.

"Don't Bobby. There really isn't anything you can say to change this. And frankly, I don't want you to."

"Annie," Bobby said again, and he did sound truly torn, upset. Behind him, Ally looked upset too, but Annie didn't think it was for her benefit. She was sure the blonde's feelings had to be hurt because Bobby looked moments away from groveling.

Annie shook her head. "No. I don't want to hear it."

She turned and walked back through the sets, feeling a little dazed, but surprisingly calm, given that she'd just seen her boyfriend of the last several years having sex with another woman.

"Annie," Nick said, once they were back in the theater proper, his hand caught her arm, pulling her to a stop. His eyes roamed her face. "Are you okay?"

Annie stared at him for a moment, her mind whirling, although she still didn't seem to feel anything. Finally she gathered her thoughts enough to say, "I think I need a drink."

★   ★   ★

Nick kept glancing at Annie, who sat on the barstool next to him, calmly sipping her glass of white wine. If he hadn't witnessed exactly the same thing she had, he'd swear she was truly just a woman out to have a relaxing drink.

There was no sign she'd just caught her boyfriend banging another woman in the back of a theater. And frankly, her odd serenity worried and unnerved him. It was almost as if she was in shock.

God knows, Nick didn't feel as calm about the entire event as Annie appeared to feel. He was furious and disgusted on her behalf. And very certain that Bobby may very well be one of the dumbest men alive. Did the idiot truly not realize what he had in Annie?

Beautiful. Sweet. Funny. A smile that always managed to scramble his brain and make him rock hard.

Nick realized he'd only known her briefly himself, but she had affected him to the core. And if he had her, he sure as hell wouldn't let her go. He sure as hell wouldn't hurt her like Bobby just had.

He studied her. Bobby must have hurt her, but still he couldn't see any emotion on her face. Nothing. Add to that the fact she hadn't said a word since they arrived, except to tell the bartender what she wanted to drink, and Nick was really concerned.

"Annie," he said softly, not sure how to handle the situation. Being a detective, he was always trying to get someone to talk. A witness. A victim. A suspect. But sometimes people just needed time to process, not share.

But sitting here silent didn't feel right to him either. He needed to know what she was thinking, to help her any way he could.

"Are you okay?" he asked.

She didn't answer right away, her eyes on her drink, her

fingers on the stem, slowly twirling the glass back and forth, first right, then left.

Finally she met his gaze, her gray eyes dark like stormy seas—and like a churning sea, he still couldn't see past the surface. He still couldn't tell how she was feeling.

"I'm fine," she said, then turned her attention back to her glass.

He didn't believe her. "Do—do you want to talk about it?"

She shook her head. "No. I mean what is there to say?"

"That he's a stupid ass," Nick suggested.

She still didn't look at him, but he saw the corner of her mouth lift in a slight smile, the gesture reluctant like she did it despite herself. "Well, there is that."

"And you never should have had to see that."

"Well, yeah, I could have done without that too." She took a long swallow of her wine, almost as if she hoped the pale gold liquid could blot out the image.

"And that he is a fool for not realizing what an amazing relationship he had with you."

She took another sip of wine, then began twisting the glass again.

After a few twists, she sighed. "We didn't have an amazing relationship. We might have at some point, but that was a long time ago."

Nick waited, expecting her to finally show some pain. Some sort of anguish, but she surprised him by meeting his eyes and giving him another smile, this one just slightly bigger than before.

"He'll be happier with someone like Ally. A fellow actor is exactly the type of girlfriend he wants and needs."

Nick didn't return her smile. In fact, the irritation continued to well up inside him. She shouldn't be so generous to the jerk. He didn't deserve her understanding.

"And what about you?" he said, his tone harsher than he intended. "What about what would make *you* happy?"

She considered him for a moment, then shrugged. She took another sip of wine, this time draining the glass.

Nick watched her, his irritation not lessening. He knew this wasn't the time to be annoyed. She was already overwhelmed, but he couldn't seem to control the emotion.

She'd nixed his attention toward her, because she knew it was the right thing to do. She'd been determined to be a loyal and true girlfriend. Bobby hadn't shared that same belief, that same respect. By Nick's way of thinking, Annie deserved to feel betrayed, hurt, angry.

But rather than tell her that, he simply opted for, "I don't know how you can be so understanding."

She glanced at him, then back to her glass. She twisted it again. Twist. Twist.

"It's easy," she said after a moment.

"Easier for you than me." He was furious for her.

"I understand, because I know how it feels to want someone else too."

Nick chest tightened, and he didn't pretend to not know that she was talking about him. "But you didn't go there. You respected your relationship."

She nodded, not looking at him. "I did."

He opened his mouth to tell her that she should be proud of herself, that she'd done what she thought was right.

But before he could speak, she shifted on her seat, her knees brushing his outer thigh as she faced him.

"I guess I am angry."

"You should be," he told her.

"I mean I didn't really feel anything when I saw the two of them together. Well, maybe a little silly, but no pain, no anger, no regret. But you know what does make me angry?"

He didn't respond, his eyes locked on her, waiting for her to continue.

"Bobby actually took a chance. He wanted something different and he went for it. I wanted something different, but I was too scared to make a change. To reach for what I wanted. To reach for you."

He stared at her, his heart pounding, then he touched her face. Her beautiful face.

"I want to kiss you," he told her, his voice low and husky with need. "I've thought about you nonstop."

"Me too." She cupped her hand around his, pressing his fingers closer to her skin. "So how can I be angry with Bobby when the truth is, I've been aching to be with you?"

Nick closed his eyes, his body reacting violently to her words. Every cell in his body became painfully alive, and only Annie could make that pain go away.

She turned her head and pressed her warm lips against his palm, the simple gesture almost driving him to the edge of sanity.

He'd been holding his desire tightly in check for what seemed like forever, even if it had only been a few days, but now she was telling him all the things he wanted to hear.

He pulled his hand away from her to reach into his pants pocket and retrieve his wallet. He plucked out a few bills and tossed them onto the bar.

Annie watched his almost manic movements as if entranced. Then he grabbed her hand, needing to get her out of there and to someplace where he could hold her. He might be desperate and half-mad to be close to her, but he wasn't going to be as tacky as Bobby.

He was taking her to his place to love her senseless in private.

★ ★ ★

By the time they caught a cab and reached his apartment, snow was falling, coming down in large, fluffy flakes.

The street where he lived on the edge of Hell's Kitchen
was startlingly quiet, only the occasional car passing them,
the wet sound of tires on pavement. Otherwise the night
and snow gave Annie an insulated feeling, sort of surreal
and otherworldly.

Of course, it had been a rather surreal night. Now she
walked with Nick, his finger curled warmly around hers,
through the beginnings of what appeared to be the beginnings of a full-fledged storm, heading toward his apartment
and his bed.

If any time in her life deserved to be perceived as surreal,
this was it. What a strange, strange night.

Yet in this moment, she felt more alive than she had in
years. She actually felt excited about something, rather
than just making it through another day.

The cold air stung her lungs, the snowflakes, icy and wet,
chilled her cheeks and somehow heightened her awareness
of the simmering, hungry burn in her body. A burn that
sizzled deep inside her because of Nick. She was reminded
of another time, with Nick, in the snow. Just days ago—
although it seemed like she'd known Nick forever. Wanted
him forever.

Tonight, a kiss between them could go so differently.
Would go very differently.

She glanced over at him, just as he looked at her. He
pulled her to a halt, his gaze still locked with hers. Those
usually twinkling eyes of his now serious, filled with concern. Maybe even doubt.

"Annie," he started and Annie knew what he was going
to say, and she didn't want to hear his words. Words of ap-
prehension and uncertainty. She didn't want to think
about whether what they were planning to do was right
or wrong. She just wanted to give in to the desire that had

been welling up inside her since the first moment she saw him.

She placed her fingertips against his lips, her skin cold against his hot, moist flesh. Almost as if he couldn't stop himself, he pressed a kiss to where she touched him.

"Don't say anything," she whispered, "I want to be with you. I've wanted that from the very moment we met. And I'm really hoping you aren't changing your mind about being with me."

He stared at her, that concern still in his eyes, but some of it was replaced by the hot glow of desire, a desire that she reflected back to him.

Slowly, he caught her hand, moving her fingers away from his lips and leaned in to capture her mouth. And finally they were kissing again, but tonight there were no barriers between them. No more guilt or reservations. Now she could give herself wholly to this gorgeous man. And she did, opening her mouth to deepen their kiss.

As soon as Annie's lips parted, Nick knew what she was offering. It was exactly what he'd wanted when he'd dragged her out of the bar and back here to his apartment. But the cold air had sobered him up, and had allowed him to think a little straighter. Had made him realize that maybe she did need some time to adjust to the changes in her life.

But now, with her lips clinging to his, his noble thoughts slipped away again, blotted out by his need to hold this woman, feel her beside him, feel himself deep inside her.

She made a noise low in her throat, the sound soft, yet so raw and desperate. Exactly like he felt.

He captured her head between his hands, angling her head, deepening their kiss. Damn, she tasted so perfect, warm and tangy like wine and desire.

Her fingers curled into the front of his coat, tugging his

body even closer as if she was freezing to death and only his heat would keep her alive.

His hands left her face to move to her hips, pulling her tightly against him, his arousal rubbing against her.

"Nick," she gasped against his mouth, his name on her lips filled with longing, rough, insistent longing.

But the sound of his name, said with such raw need, made him come to his senses, just a little. His blood still thrummed through his veins, threatening to again block out any rational thoughts, but he fought to stay in control, telling himself not to just reach for her again, dragging her back against him like some possessive, chest-thumping caveman.

Hell, he was so riled up he could throw her down on the snowy sidewalk and make love to her right here.

Maybe he wasn't any classier than Bobby after all.

No. Annie needed and deserved more than animalistic sex. She'd had a total shock tonight. He needed to keep his own desire in check and make sure she was okay.

"Annie," he said, his gaze roaming her face. Her cheeks flushed a pretty pink. Her gray eyes hazed with lust.

He fought to stay focused, to keep his hands motionless on her hips.

"Maybe . . ." He shook his head, and an incredulous laugh escaped him. "Maybe we should wait."

She frowned, clearly not following what he was saying. She swayed toward him, her gaze dropping to his lips. His dropped to hers too. Pretty lips, pink and damp and slightly swollen from his kiss.

He leaned in too, then caught himself.

"No," he said, mostly to himself, but he could tell from her slight flinch and wounded expression that she thought his unintentionally harsh tone was aimed solely at her.

He immediately moved one of his hands from her hips to stroke her cheek. "Annie, I want you so badly."

"And I want you."

He caressed her cheek, his body, and his heart, reacting to the desperation in her voice. Couldn't she tell how much he wanted her? Yet, he saw uncertainty in her eyes.

"I just don't think we should start something like this tonight. After what you've been through—you've got to have time to deal with it."

She stared at him, her dreamy look totally gone, replaced by confusion. "You've been telling me you want me, and I want you too. Yet now that I can be with you, you are having doubts. I don't understand."

"I know. I know," he said, conflicted, "but I don't want to be rebound boy. Or worse, someone that you have sex with as payback to Bobby."

She didn't speak for a moment, then shook her head, her eyes filled with outright hurt. "I would never do that."

Nick realized that as soon as the words were out of his mouth. Annie wasn't spiteful, or the type of woman to make rash decisions. She was the type who always tried to do the right thing, even when the right thing wasn't easy.

Wasn't that part of what appealed to him? God knows, he didn't see much of that behavior in his line of work.

"No. You wouldn't. But what if it's simply too soon?"

Annie might not realize it, but he did not intend for this to be a one-night fling. He wanted to be with her. He didn't have any doubts about that, and he didn't want her to either.

"It isn't too soon," she told him. "If anything, it's been too long. Too long since I've felt this way. Too long since I've felt anything. And I have wanted you from the very first time I met you."

Nick still didn't speak, indecision warring inside him, even as his heart—and cock—leapt at her words.

"Please," she said, "make love to me, Nick. I just want to be with you."

A low growl rumbled in his chest. How the hell was he supposed to deny her a request like that? He couldn't. Even if he did turn out to be rebound boy.

For the second time that night, he caught her hand and tugged her toward his apartment building, rushing her up to his second-floor apartment.

Once inside, he dropped her hand and simply watched her as she took in his place with its shabby furniture, clutter, and lack of pictures on the wall, or decorations of any kind. Books and newspapers littered most surfaces and a mug of coffee from this morning sat on the table that served as his kitchen table, coffee table and desk.

"It's not exactly as nice as your place," he said, suddenly conscious of that fact that he'd never made much effort to make his apartment a home.

"Well, my place came at a steep price," she said. She'd said that before and Nick wondered what that meant.

She walked to the bookcase on the far wall of his living room. There, amid more books, were the only pictures of any sort he had. Old photographs in cheap frames.

"Family?" she asked, leaning in to study them closer.

He nodded, wondering what she'd make of his big Italian family, knowing they would love her.

"Can I get you a drink?" Suddenly scared of how quickly and easily his thoughts had gone to Annie meeting his family. And they hadn't even had an official date yet. How could he be so certain about this woman? So sure she was the one?

She stopped perusing his books and smiled at him. That sweet, adorable smile, and again, he just knew.

"I'm fine," she said and it took him a moment to remember he'd offered her a drink.

She continued her stroll around his small apartment, pausing once she reached the door slightly ajar to the left of his kitchen. She tilted her head and smiled at him, her flirty expression making his blood sizzle.

"Is this your bedroom?" She leaned forward, peeking into the crack between the door and the jamb.

He found himself returning her naughty little smile with one of his own. "It might be. Maybe you should investigate."

Her smile broadened. "Investigate. How very detective-like of you."

"Isn't it?"

She hesitated for a fraction of a second, then pushed the door open. Her smile widened. "It *is* a bedroom."

"You are an excellent detective."

"Why, thank you." She stepped into the dim room, and he followed her.

Chapter Seventeen

Annie entered the room, then stopped in the middle, unsure what to do now. Even making the move to get to his bedroom had felt amazingly brazen to her. Not that she hadn't initiated sex in her relationship with Bobby. But they'd been young, and their physical relationship had evolved from a naïve exploration of each other to sex. It had been gradual, and in that slow pace, there had been a certain security. A sense of control.

This felt wild.

She looked at Nick silhouetted against the light from the living room, his shoulders broad, his body lean. She knew there were sinewy, strong muscles under his clothing. Powerful muscles.

Bobby had been muscular too, but Nick had a leaner build, a lithe power like a wild animal. A tiger. A panther. Something that was beautiful—and potentially dangerous.

He walked toward her, and her stomach tightened with both desire and trepidation. But he didn't touch her. Instead of touching her, he moved around her to switch on the lamp on his nightstand.

He turned back to her, and she could see his warm brown eyes, and all of her fear disappeared. Looking into those golden brown eyes that she found so fascinating, she realized Nick would never hurt her.

Any fear she felt stemmed from the unknown. Like she was finally going to make love with a man versus a boy.

He walked up to her, stopping just inches away from her.

"You're sure?"

All fears left her. She'd told him she wanted this. And she did. Desperately. She wanted to know how it finally felt to be with a man who could make her heart race with just a smile. Who could send delicious shivers down her spine with the timbre of his voice. Who looked at her like she was the most beautiful thing he'd ever seen.

But she didn't speak. Instead she closed the space between them, and rose up on her tiptoes to press a kiss to those lips that she wanted to feel on every part of her body.

His lips moved against hers, but he didn't take control as if he somehow knew she was overwhelmed by the idea of him. He remained still, letting her experiment with their kiss. For the briefest moment they just clung to each other. Lips to lips, but very quickly that wasn't enough for Annie. She'd tasted him and she wanted more.

With more brazenness than she would have imagined, she brushed her tongue along the seam of his lips, teasing him into opening for her. He did, obedient, almost submissive. The idea that she could control his power excited her. Urged her on.

She tilted her head and kissed him deeply with all the passion she'd been keeping in check. He groaned, deep in his throat, but otherwise he still let her control their embrace.

Excitement raged through her as she reached for the leather jacket he still wore, tugging at the zipper, then pushing the garment off his shoulders. Her fingers returned to his shirt, fumbling anxiously with the buttons. After much pulling, and a little help from him, the shirt joined the jacket on the floor, and her hands could finally touch his warm skin and knead the taut muscles beneath.

As her hands stroked over his hot, smooth skin she realized he had a tattoo on his shoulder. Her fingers paused there, but in the dim light she could not see it clearly.

But there was one thing she did know very clearly: he felt wonderful, even better than she'd imagined. And she'd imagined him more than she'd even been willing to acknowledge to herself. Her hands sculpted over his shoulders, his chest, his sides, his muscles flexing and quivering with each caress.

She moaned, her hands sliding down his taut stomach to the waistband of his pants. The button popped open, and the zipper rasped as she eased it down. Metal sliding against metal like a relieved hiss in the quiet room.

His low growl joined the other sound as she slipped her hand down over his pelvis, coarse hair tickling her fingers as she wandered lower, finally reaching what she so desperately wanted to touch—see—taste—feel deep inside her. Claiming her.

Her fingers paused, just for a moment, his size startling her. Then her body responded with a hot, wet eagerness. Her vagina throbbed, almost seeming to plead with her to get that thick hardness deep inside her. Now.

She moaned and curled her fingers around him, stroking the velvety skin of his shaft. Her touch seemed to be the undoing of his submissiveness.

He caught her wrist, stilling her hand, but keeping it pressed tightly to him. He took control of the kiss, his possession leaving her breathless and weak. Then he pulled away; the only parts of them touching were her hand still holding his rock-hard penis, and his hand holding her wrist.

"I want to go slow," he muttered roughly almost as if talking to himself.

She moved her fingers, doing little more than wiggling them against his hot, aroused flesh. He groaned, the sound deep and guttural. Again she was reminded of a wild animal.

She realized he was working to keep himself tightly restrained. She could feel it in the air around them, but she realized that now the idea of him letting loose didn't scare her. She wanted him to take out all that wild passion on her. She wanted her body sore and aching from his fierce lovemaking.

She twitched her fingers again, smiling at his reaction. The tightening of his jaw as he clenched his teeth, the slow breath in deep through his nose, the dilation of his eyes beneath his half-closed lids.

"I want you inside me," she whispered as she gently squeezed him. She smiled, pleased with his sharp intake of breath and her own audacity. She felt bold and wild herself, new feelings spurred on by his intense reaction to her.

"Are you going to put this deep inside me?"

He nodded. "God, yes."

"Show me."

He growled again, his hands going to her clothing, easily divesting her of her layers until she stood before him in just her lavender bra and panties.

For a moment, the uncertain Annie returned and she fought the urge to cover herself. But Nick's low, hungry words stopped her.

"Annie Lou Riddle, you are the most beautiful woman I have ever seen."

Annie watched in dazed awe as Nick, in his breathtaking half-naked glory, slowly dropped to his knees before her. He remained still for a few moments, his face nearly level with her pelvis.

"I love these panties," he said, running a finger along the lace edging that disappeared between her thighs, stopping just short of brushing over the place at that was wet and pulsing, eager for his touch.

"Purple is one of my favorite colors," he said, looking up her with his naughty little smile.

"Is it?" she managed to say, her voice breathy.

"Definitely."

Again he traced a finger along the lace, this time hooking the edge with his finger. Slowly he peeled the silky material aside, baring her. She gasped as he leaned forward, closer to her. She could feel his breath on her exposed, damp flesh, and she struggled not to jut her hips toward his lips, so, so close to her.

"But I like pink better than purple," he murmured. He leaned forward and ran his tongue up the length of her lips, starting low and moving up, brushing just fleetingly over her aching clitoris.

She gasped, her hand sinking into his hair.

His tongue lapped over her again, this time going deeper, a hot raspy stroke of heaven. Her knees quivered, her reaction making her weak.

Another lick, parting her, lingering at that tight little bud that ached and throbbed for him.

"You taste delicious," he said, his breath hot on her wet skin. "And you are so pretty down here."

He licked her again, his tongue stopping on her clitoris, swirling around it, teasing it, loving it.

"Do you like that, baby?"

She nodded mindlessly, a rapid bobbing of her head. God, yes, she loved it. She tried to form the words, but only a moan escaped her, her fingers knotting in his hair.

More licking, more swirls of his tongue directly against her engorged, aroused flesh.

"Tell me what you like," he said against her, his words low and fierce, vibrating through her.

"I—" she gasped. "I like this."

"This?" More delicious torture with his tongue.

She nodded, her fingers digging into his hair, her body swaying, her desire making her weak.

"How about this?" He angled his lips, sucking on her clitoris.

Desire that was so intense it bordered on pain, radiated through her. But instead of pulling away, she tilted her hips forward, pressing herself tighter against him, knowing only more of his wonderfully torturous touch would give her the release she so desperately needed.

He obeyed her silent request, moving a hand to her rear end, pushing her harder to his mouth, and suddenly she wasn't the one demanding—she was the one submitting to his will, his amazing mouth.

Quickly, the waves of need grew, becoming more and more concentrated until she was lost to anything but the feeling he was creating inside her. She trembled, her muscles tightening as she surged toward release. His hand kneaded into her rear end, his tongue filled and stroked her. He held her upright, forced her to succumb to him.

And she did, a broken cry ripping from her throat as her body seemed to splinter, fragmenting into hundreds of crystalline shards of ecstasy. An orgasm more powerful than anything she'd ever experienced in her life.

And even after her violent reaction, he continued to tease her oversensitized flesh, with just fleeting strokes. She shivered, her body reacting again, even though she was weak; her legs shook and threatened to buckle under her.

With one last long lick, he rose and scooped her up into his arms. Normally, she would have stiffened, uncomfortable with being carried. Up in the air, against his hard chest. That required trust, and she'd lost that ability over the past few years. She'd learned to be cautious, guarded. Yet she didn't strain or balk as he carried her to his bed.

"Such a tiny thing," he said, then kissed her tenderly. She could taste her arousal on his lips. She found herself nestled in the middle of his bed as he straightened and regarded her for a moment.

Then he said, his tone almost reverent, "Do you have any idea how lovely you are?"

She shook her head. In truth, she didn't have much sense about herself at all. Not for a long time, anyway. She certainly couldn't recall a time, at least for a very long time, that anyone sounded so amazed by her.

"Well, you are." His voice was low and husky.

She watched in anticipation and admiration as he pushed his pants down over his lean hips, baring himself to her. Her eyes ate up the sight of his broad shoulders, muscled arms and chest, flat stomach . . . narrow hips and the amazing organ that jutted up against his taut belly.

She levered herself up onto her elbows, entranced by the beauty of him. Even after her intense orgasm, her body sizzled again, this time wanting to feel him deep inside her. Her vagina pulsed and she could feel moisture pooling between her thighs again.

"You are the one who is lovely."

He chuckled at that, the mattress dipping under his weight as he crawled onto the mattress beside her. Without hesitation, her hand came out to touch him.

He paused for a moment, clearly enjoying the hand that stroked over his chest. Then he grinned, a naughty twinkle in his eyes.

"Lovely, huh? My buddies at the precinct wouldn't let me live that one down."

She smiled too. "Okay, how about handsome, gorgeous, breathtaking?"

His eyes still twinkled as he leaned closer. "Mmm, definitely better than lovely, but they'd still get me razzed."

Her gaze dropped to his mouth, her breath escaping her as he got closer and closer, finally stopping only inches from her own lips.

"How about manly, macho, utterly masculine?" she whispered, her eyes moving from his lips to meet his gaze.

He leaned closer still. She could feel his breath against her damp lips. His heat.

"They aren't bad," he said, shifting forward to press a small kiss to the corner of her.

"But you think I can do better, huh?" she managed to murmur, arching upward as he kissed her jawline, then her throat.

"Oh, baby, I'm very, very happy with your opinion of me."

She gasped slightly as he nipped her earlobe, the small bite sending shock waves throughout her whole body. For a moment, she had a hard time not just giving in to his ministrations. But she wanted her chance to touch and love him. Even if his nibbling kisses were marvelously delicious.

"Maybe I can do better," she said, levering herself up to her elbows again.

He pulled back at her change of position, raising a curious eyebrow, then leaned back in to nibble at her bare shoulder.

Focus, she told herself. Focus.

She sat up further and placed her hands on his chest, nudging him back. At first, Nick didn't follow her direction, then he allowed himself to be pushed back against the tangled bedding.

Annie positioned herself over his prone, truly amazing body. She placed a hand on his chest, running it over him. His collarbone, his chest, stopping to tease his tight little nipples, then down over his hard belly.

"How about rugged?" she suggested, stroking down to

the curls covering his pelvis. She stopped short of his massive erection that pulsed at her exploratory touch as if it was trying to make sure all attention was focused on that part of his anatomy.

"Rugged is good," Nick said, his voice raspy and breathless. His obvious desire ignited Annie's, the sound of his voice like lighter fluid and a match to her libido. She was going up in fiery, intense flames.

But she managed to keep herself focused on her wonderful game.

"How about sexy?"

Her fingers toyed with the coarse, springy hair that surrounded his cock. She even brushed her fingertips against his testicles, only to move on to stroke down both of his thighs.

"Sexy would—would," he hissed as her fingers brushed dangerously close to the head of his penis. "It would be fine."

Again she caressed closer this time, wanting to touch him as much as he wanted to be touched. But she also wanted to play. To tease him. To drive him wild with the need.

"Hmm," she pursed her lips, pretending to consider other ideas. "What is the best way to describe you?"

He shook his head, the gesture agitated, a little frantic. "There must be something." She played with his pubes more, "accidentally" brushing the back of her hand occasionally against his arousal.

Finally, she paused her exploring and shot him a naughty grin of her own. "I got it."

He lifted his head, waiting for her to say, his eyes hooded, his lips parted, his breath coming in short pants of desire.

"What?" he managed to ask.

"I'll just tell them you're hung."

With that she curled her fingers around his thick erection and moved to lap the tip.

★ ★ ★

Whatever Nick had expected her to say or do, these two things weren't it, but he sure as hell wasn't disappointed with either, as a noise somewhere between a chuckle and a moan rumbled in his chest.

She continued to stroke him, but grinned at him, very pleased that she'd managed to surprise him.

"Only you could make that sentence sound so darn sweet," he managed to tell her, even though it was very difficult for him to concentrate with her small fingers driving him mad.

"Darn, I was trying to be as naughty as you."

He smiled, loving this lighter, teasing side of her. Loving her little Southern twang as she flirted. Loving the way her touch made him feel.

"You are very naughty," he assured her, the roughness of his voice saying exactly what effect her naughtiness had on him.

"You are a very big boy," she informed him, tilting her head to watch as she touched him, her fingers running up and down the length. Playing with the sensitive tip, then slipping all the way down to his testicles, which were tightening up to his body with the need to find release.

"Am I?" he asked almost absently. It was damned hard to stay focused as she touched him. He felt like a green teenager, fooling around for the first time. Conversation, even sexy banter, was beyond him at the moment.

"Yes," she murmured, then seemed to instinctively understand he couldn't follow the conversation any longer. So instead she decided to use her mouth in another way.

He groaned loudly as her tongue licked up the length of him. He muttered something incoherent, his fingers tangling in her hair, messing up her pretty little twist.

She didn't seem to mind as she continued to lick him like he was some delicious treat that she was savoring fully.

Then she took him deep into her mouth, hot, wet heat surrounding his aching flesh. Almost instantly he felt his orgasm rise up, rippling down his spine and through his abdomen, centering deep in his groin.

"Oh God, Annie!"

Reflexively he tightened his grip on her hair, but managed to gather his wits enough to loosen his hold. This moment of aggressiveness didn't seem to faze Annie. She still bobbed her head, her mouth taking his length in and out, her tongue swirling and licking and driving him precariously close to the edge.

And while he'd love to keep going, to release into her eager little mouth, that wasn't where he wanted to orgasm for their first time. He wanted to be buried deep inside her, watching her expression as they both came together.

With Herculean control, he forced himself up so he could reach her. She made a small disappointed noise as he tugged her away. His cock leapt in response to the noise.

Trust me, buddy, he said silently to his greedy cock, you are going to like where you are going next even better.

"Didn't you like that?" she asked as he slid her up his body. A little moan escaped her as he settled her over the top of him.

"I liked it way too much, but I want to be inside you." He reached down between her thighs, open to him because of how she now straddled him.

He slipped a finger inside her panties to tease the tiny little center of her sex. She automatically ground her hips forward at the touch.

He rubbed her there for a few moments, loving the reflex movement of her hips against his touch. Then he slipped lower into her moist heat to slip a finger inside her.

He gasped along with her, his cock pulsing against her rear end.

"Mmm, this is where I want to be."

She nodded, her eyes half-closed, her lips parted, pink and glossy.

"Please," she pleaded brokenly, riding his finger.

He would have liked the teasing to continue longer, and when he wasn't so out of his mind to be inside her, he would take his time. But right now, only one thing drove him.

He rolled her onto the mattress, then made quick work of ridding her of her panties and bra. She lay among his rumpled blankets and sheets, her hair mostly free of its twist, tangled wantonly around her pretty face. Her rose-tipped breasts puckered and pouted, begging for his mouth on them.

He didn't deny them, ducking his head to taste first one, then the other. She arched her back, offering them to him without hesitation. He suckled her for a moment longer, again annoyed with his impatience.

But he did feel like he was making love for the first time, and he couldn't control his desire. He swirled the tip of his tongue around her taut little nipple, then lifted his head to study her.

Maybe there was a reason for the inexperienced impatience he was feeling. Maybe he really was making love for the first time.

He gazed down at her beautiful face. Her large gray eyes, eyes that made him feel protective and possessive and happy and worried and so damned turned on that he could burst. Her pretty bow-like lips that he sometimes thought didn't smile enough, but when they did he couldn't seem to recall a prettier smile before hers. And her body that was curved in all the right places. Perfect, full, pert breasts, a small waist flaring into womanly hips and soft smooth thighs. She was perfection and there was little wonder he felt like a schoolboy finally getting to home base.

Then she looked up at him and nibbled her lower lip.

"Is everything okay?" she asked, her voice a little thicker with her accent, because of her uncertainty.

Didn't she realize how absolutely besotted he was with her? Then again, how could she understand when he didn't quite understand himself?

But instead of saying that, or thinking about the intensity of his desire for her, he simply nodded.

"Couldn't be better."

He moved over her, their chests pressed together, their legs intertwined, his cock pressing to the soft curve of her mons. He leaned forward, his arms braced on either side of her head, and pressed kisses to her lip. Softly at first, then growing with the uncontrollable desire that had overcome them both from the very first moment they had touched.

"Please," Annie whispered against his lips, which was all the urging he needed.

He balanced himself on one arm as he positioned himself to fill her. To finally be where he desperately wanted to be.

He slid in, just an inch or so. Annie's head arched back, the hard tips of her breasts brushing against his chest.

"Oh Nick. God, yes."

Their eyes locked as he slid deeper inside her tight, wet fire. Then deeper. And deeper.

Soon he filled her. Her muscles clasping him, accepting him, keeping him. He stayed motionless for a moment, just reveling in the glory of this connection.

Then she wiggled and her hands stroked down his back and over his buttocks, digging into his skin.

And he couldn't remain still any longer. He began to move, easing in and out of her, trying to remain steady, smooth. But all too quickly, their desire whirled out of control like a wild eddy of wind in a storm.

He thrust into her deep and hard and with a mindless

need for them both to reach the place where desire turned to bliss.

Under him, Annie writhed and bucked, demanding the same thing. Their lovemaking was rough and wild and so intense that when he felt her vagina spasm around him, her cry filling this air, he could do nothing but follow her response.

He thrust into her one last time, as deep as he could, and held there, shouting out his own orgasm, the force of it ripping through him. His muscles seized and his breath left him.

And damn it, nothing had ever felt more wonderful.

Chapter Eighteen

Annie woke, frowning into the darkness, trying to gather herself.

Where was she?

She started to move, to struggle upright when she felt hard warmth at her side and the comforting weight of an arm across her waist.

Nick. Her heart leapt at the memory of exactly where she was. She was with Nick.

She eased onto her side, so she could see him. He slept on his side, facing her, his pillow bunched up under his head. She studied his features, his mussed hair, his dark lashes. His sensual mouth accented by the scruff of his five o'clock shadow. His arm, strong and sinewy, holding her. Making her feel safe.

She sighed, letting her eyes drift closed again.

Nick. Having him close, holding her. His heat, his strength. She felt safer than she had in years.

She stifled back a yawn, snuggling closer to him, floating in that strange world between sleep and wakefulness.

Safer, she repeated in her mind. Safer than she'd felt in years.

Since . . . Finola . . .

Suddenly a cold chill, starting deep in the pit of her

belly, snaked through her. Uncurling throughout her body, into her chest, her limbs. A shiver wracked her, despite the blankets and Nick's warmth.

Finola. Oh God. Finola.

She looked back to Nick, his face peaceful. Beautiful. And . . .

Fear joined the iciness in her veins and she had to get out of bed, away from him. What had she done?

Carefully, she inched her way toward the edge of the mattress, sliding out of his hold, not wanting to disturb him. Not wanting to talk with him. Not right at this moment. She was too frightened, too confused. And she had to figure out how to handle everything.

Once out of bed, she tiptoed around, searching for her clothes. As if it wasn't hard enough to think straight, she sure as heck couldn't do it standing naked in Nick's room. But her hushed search in the dim light seemed another fruitless task. No clear thinking, no clothes. She was doomed.

Finally she found Nick's dress shirt. Better than nothing, she decided. She slipped the soft cotton garment on, smelling Nick's soap, his masculine scent. She resisted the urge to press the cloth to her face and breathe deep. Instead she worked the buttons closed as she walked over to the bedroom window, feeling the need to put even more distance between Nick and herself. Even as his wonderful scent surrounded her as surely as his arm just had.

She closed her eyes for a moment, determined to gather her thoughts. When she felt a little calmer—a very little— she opened her eyes and stared out the window, her thoughts still whirling. After a few moments, her gaze actually focused on what was going on outside, nature mimicking her swirling, turbulent thoughts.

Snow whipped and eddied through the air. A full blizzard raged outside, and she hadn't even realized. Nick's apartment was quiet and warm, the dim light cocooning them, shut away from the reality outside.

But the walls were really just a thin barrier against Mother Nature, just like they were only a thin barrier against Finola.

Reality would find her again. It always did. And her reality was very dangerous. Maybe even more dangerous than a blizzard. Certainly more unpredictable.

More unpredictable than the elements. Dear God, what had she been thinking? Nothing, that's what. No, nothing wasn't accurate. She had been thinking about one thing. How much, how very, very much she wanted Nick. And that had blocked out any other concerns. But now, reality was seeping in.

She made a small noise of despair, then quickly glanced over her shoulder to make sure she hadn't woken Nick. He was now sprawled on his back, one muscular arm flung up over his head. His other hand rested on his stomach. From here she could see the tattoo on his left shoulder, although aside for the impression of a vague image and some scrolled detailing, she still couldn't tell what it depicted.

She turned back to the window, staring into the storm. Snow came in torrents, battering the windows, swirling in a wild blinding vortex. She peered out, trying to see how much had accumulated, but at times the snow was so heavy she couldn't even see the streetlights below. The outside world was just a mass of white.

The analogy wasn't lost on Annie. Surrounded by White. Finola White. So oppressive and overwhelming that she threatened to block out every bit of light in Annie's life.

Annie had worked so hard to avoid doing anything that would incite her evil boss's rage. Annie had been so cautious and systematic and always trying to predict and avoid every pitfall.

Yet, tonight she'd done something that would so obviously anger Finola. Anger wasn't even a strong enough word. Yet Annie had blithely ignored the fallout of her desire for Nick. She'd lost any sense of self-preservation.

Truth be told, she'd never even considered what would happen when Finola found out that she, mousy, meek, often terrified Annie Lou Riddle, had gotten involved with the very man that her demon boss wanted for herself.

Annie couldn't contain the distraught groan that welled up from inside her. She rested her forehead on the cold windowpane.

She was as good as dead. Or as good as soulless, which Annie had come to know was worse.

What had she done? God, what had she done?

She closed her eyes, trying to stay calm. She would have to do something to rectify this. After all, at this point not only was her immortal soul in danger, but probably Nick's too.

She groaned again, having that awful, helpless feeling that if she could just go back and redo this night, she would. Not because she wanted to, but because it was the smart thing to do.

"Are you okay?"

Annie jumped as arms came around her waist. Behind her she could feel Nick's hard chest as he pulled her back against him. He rested his chin on her shoulder, and she realized the real scent of him was far headier than the fading smell clinging to his shirt.

She breathed in deep, trying to stay focused on what she needed to say. How she was going to end this before they got too involved.

"Wow, it's really snowing," he said, his low, husky tone tickling her ear.

She nodded, still unable to find any words. He was just so damned distracting.

"Looks like we could be trapped here for a while."

God, she wished it was forever. Just the two of them. Here. Safe from the elements out there that could hurt them.

"Are you okay?" he asked again.

No. But how did she tell him? What did she tell him?

He squeezed her tighter, then kissed the side of her neck. The sensitive skin right below her earlobe. Even as she told herself not to react, she found her head falling back against his chest to afford him better access.

He kissed her for a few moments, teasing her skin with his nibbling lips, his hands that had been at her waist slid upward, cupping her breasts through the cotton of his skirt, the soft material rubbing against her pebbled nipples, along with his skilled fingers.

"I like seeing you in my clothes," he said, his voice rumbling with pleased possessiveness.

She couldn't speak. But she needed to—she had to say something to bring this madness to a halt.

Being involved with Finola's current romantic interest wasn't just a risky situation. Or an uncomfortable one. It was outright dangerous. And she had to handle this—somehow.

She opened her mouth to tell him the whole thing had been a mistake. She could say that she wasn't actually over Bobby. That he'd been a rebound, just like he'd feared. But instead of any words, only a gasp came out as he squeezed her nipples, gently plucking them.

"Come back to bed. You are freezing," he whispered in her ear. "And I know a great way to warm you up."

Again she tried to speak, to tell him no. That should be simple enough. But the one-syllable word might as well have been like trying to speak an entire foreign language. She couldn't even begin to turn him down.

But still she didn't move; she just leaned heavily against

him, letting his talented hands explore her body. She closed her eyes, blocking out the storm outside as one of his hands slid lower, down between her thighs.

"Hmm, you are warm somewhere, aren't you?"

She nodded, struggling to remain focused on what she had to do, but as soon as he parted her and began to stroke her clitoris, all thoughts disappeared.

Tonight she was safe. And they definitely weren't going anywhere in this wild weather. Couldn't she just love him a little longer?

She turned in his arms, placing her arms around his neck and kissing him with all the passion that roiled inside her. She could show him how she felt tonight. Tomorrow would be a different story. Tonight she wanted to revel in her mistake.

"How could he have known?"

Tristan remained totally still as Finola paced. She came to a stop right in front of him. "How?"

Tristan repeated the same answer he had since Satan left them. "I don't know."

Finola had played the contrite favorite while their ultimate Master was here. Satan had requested that they show him their plans for Fashion Week. Their strategies to recruit the top executives of rival magazines. Gather more souls and more power.

Satan had been pleased, and so had Finola until Satan returned back to Hell and then Finola had shown her real feelings.

"I don't see how he could know, unless someone told him." She glared suspiciously at him.

"It was not me," Tristan assured her, also repeatedly. "I serve you, Mistress."

He kept his gaze lowered, knowing the quickest way to

please her was to play the submissive. Of course, he'd been "apologizing" for hours.

Finola was not to be appeased tonight. She did not like being called out by their overlord and she also did not like having to give up something she wanted. And she had very much wanted Nick Rossi.

Tristan knew he should just let her continue ranting at him, grilling him. But he couldn't stop himself from asking, "Why does Nick Rossi matter? Why do you want him any more than any other handsome mortal male?"

Finola stopped pacing, frowning at him. She was so angry that some of her demon traits had slipped through her human façade. Her pupils now vertical, diamond-shaped slits. Hints of her snake form.

"That is none of your business," she informed him, the last of the sentence coming out as a hiss.

Tristan couldn't recall ever seeing Finola this angry. But he wasn't surprised; she did not like to be called to task.

"However, can you explain to me why I am with you tonight?" she demanded. "Rather than on my date with my handsome human. Fucking my handsome human."

She just wasn't going to believe he wasn't involved somehow, not matter how many times he told her he wasn't.

But in one last attempt, he met her eyes. "Finola, I do not know. You know I support you. I am your ally, your servant, your friend."

Finola stared at him for a moment longer. Then slowly she walked over to him.

"And tonight you are going to be my lover," she stated. "You are going to provide me with what I thought was going to get from that mortal male."

Tristan nodded, lowering his eyes again. She couldn't think this was a punishment for a lust demon like himself.

Sex was never a punishment. And certainly they'd had sex before. Many times before.

So if this would somehow calm her temper, he was more than willing. Who was he kidding? He was always more than willing.

Finola slid her hand down his pants, curling her long, cool fingers around Tristan's hard cock, squeezing and pulling on the engorged organ. Her aggressive touch aroused him even more.

He groaned loudly, the sound echoing through Finola's bedroom suite.

Finola smiled at his reaction.

She ordered him to strip and lie on her bed. When he'd done what he was told, she slowly undressed herself, then straddled him.

She ground herself against him. He groaned, enjoying her roughness.

"Are you sure you have no idea who could have contacted our Master?" she asked, rubbing herself against him, harder.

"I swear, my Mistress."

She smiled then. "I will trust you, Tristan." She then mounted him, riding him rough and hard. Pleasuring herself over and over again.

Finally after satisfying herself until she was limp and exhausted, she allowed him to come.

Tristan shouted out his release, glad that she finally seemed to accept that he hadn't informed Satan of her actions and also glad that she had slaked her needs on him rather than still pursuing Rossi.

Finola rolled off him.

"You may leave now," she said; and Tristan, used to her abrupt dismissals in every aspect of their relationship, thought nothing of it.

He dressed and headed for the door.

"Tristan," she said and he turned back to look at her. She lay on her side, the sheet draped over her willowy body. Her pale hair like white silk over her shoulders. She looked almost angelic.

"You asked why I wanted him." There was, of course not need to state who she referred to.

"Yes," Tristan said, some of his peacefulness slipping.

"I wanted him because I shouldn't."

Tristan nodded, hoping that she'd just told him that because he'd asked. Not because she still wanted Nick Rossi.

Not because he'd become some forbidden fruit that she simply had to taste.

Chapter Nineteen

Annie stretched amid her warm sea of bedding, breathing in deeply, some of the sleepiness leaving her limbs. "Is that coffee? Are you bringing me coffee?"

"Ha, I knew something would finally wake you." Nick grinned.

But all too quickly her lazy happiness disappeared. A wave of concern flooded her. What time was it? Had she overslept? Was there a meeting or an appointment she needed to make, or one that she need to make sure Finola made?

She glanced at the radio alarm clock on his nightstand. A few minutes after ten. Oh God, she never slept this late! Finola would be furious. Annie had to get home and then ready for work. Right now.

She started to shove back the warm covers, then recalled that it was Saturday morning. And she hadn't heard her phone, which she kept near her at all times. It wasn't unusual to be spared Finola's early morning calls on a Saturday. But she didn't think she'd make it through a whole Saturday without a phone call. A list of demands.

But as long as her phone was quiet, she was going to take a moment to relax. Or try. She stopped pushing at the covers, but still sat upright.

"Wow, if I knew coffee would perk you up so quickly,

I'd have brought it in earlier." Nick said joining her on the bed. "Because I've been desperately wanting to do this."

He leaned forward and kissed her. She moaned, bittersweet desire filling her, because she knew this lovely moment couldn't last.

Just enjoy it a little longer. That's all she wanted.

When they parted, he held out one of the mugs to her, which she gratefully accepted, holding it between both her hands, tight, her emotions making her a little shaky.

She took a sip, then made a small noise of enjoyment.

"Good?" he asked.

"Perfect."

He grinned again, that smile of his as delicious as her warm, creamy coffee. This memory, his mussed hair and five o'clock shadow, his naughty little smile. Their lazy morning kiss and this coffee. She'd keep all of this close to her, even as she was forced to let him go.

"I wasn't sure what you liked," he said, pulling her out of her thoughts.

Everything, she thought. She'd liked every moment with him. Loved every moment.

"So I guessed. Lots of cream, and just a little sugar."

Only then did Annie realized he was talking about the coffee, not their time together.

She felt her cheeks grow a little warm, but she smiled, eyeing him teasingly. "Now how did you know that?"

"You keep forgetting: I'm a detective."

"Somehow I don't believe you really investigate things like how a person takes their coffee." She took a sip, closing her eyes in appreciation. "Although you did make mine just right. Lots of cream and just a little sugar. Perfect."

"You'd be surprised what minute details have played a role in some of my investigations."

She didn't doubt that. She'd watched plenty of crime shows in her life, although she imagined most investigations were nothing like those. But she did know the smallest things could be the big break.

"But in this case, it was dumb luck and the fact that I ran out of sugar," he admitted and she laughed.

He regarded her so closely that her laughter died on her lips.

"What?"

"I love your laugh," he said. "And I'm glad you do it when you are with me. I get the feeling you haven't laughed a lot recently."

She didn't know what to say, so she took another sip of her coffee. But when he didn't seem inclined to say anything either, she decided the best course of action was to make light of the situation.

"Is that another of your detective deductions?" she asked.

He shook his head. "No deductions needed. I've witnessed it for myself."

She stared at him for a moment, again not sure what to say. He definitely hit on a truth, but she didn't want to talk about all the events and problems that had made her so serious. Not right now.

Not ever. Sharing that side of her life would never be an option.

But unfortunately Finola was on her mind again. Like she always was. Which brought Annie back to the fact that she did have to tell Nick they couldn't be serious. Not until things changed with Finola. Honestly, maybe not ever.

But just like last night, she couldn't seem to bring herself to say those words. Those final words that would end what was the best thing that had happened in her life in for as long as she could remember. Maybe ever.

So instead she decided to turn her attention to something else. She took another sip of her coffee, perusing the room that she hadn't been able to see clearly in the dim light of the night before. Now with the gray light from the window coming in, she could see the furniture and decorations.

Well, okay, furniture. Nick didn't seem too big on decorating; not even a picture or two broke up the whiteness of the walls. Although he did have nice mission-style furniture in a dark, polished finish. Relatively new, from the looks of it.

"Sorry I'm not much on decorating," he said, watching her examination of the room. "I'm usually at the station or on a case."

"Ah, a workaholic, huh?"

He shrugged. "I guess, although more because there isn't any reason not to be. I mean, do I really want to come home and sit in my undecorated apartment?"

"Well, you could decorate it," she suggested.

"Mmm, true, but I'm also kind of lazy, so I was hoping to get someone to help me with that." He leaned in to kiss her, leaving no doubt who that someone was.

Her heart somersaulted in her chest, both from the kiss and from his desire to have her be such a part of his life.

But once they parted, she tried to get her emotions under control and into a realistic place. She couldn't think about things like being a real couple and decorating and making a home. Not when she knew, for both their safety, it was imperative to put a stop to this.

Just a little longer, she told herself. Just a few more moments of fantasy.

She turned her attention back to him. This time, her attention stopped on the tattoo on his upper arm and shoulder. She could finally see that as well. She leaned sideways slightly to get a better view of that shoulder. It was . . .

"A gargoyle?" she said, not really sure what else to call it. The artwork and detailing was very well done, depicting a strange face with horns and squinting catlike eyes and a wide, almost sinister smile. "I don't think I've ever seen anything like that before."

"Which is good," he said, sounding serious, but when she frowned up at him he smiled.

"It's just some odd thing from my imagination."

Annie studied the creature a little longer, then lounged back against the pillows. "I'm not sure I'd want to be in your imagination."

He glanced down at the ink drawing that took up a majority of his shoulder and bicep. "Me neither."

He smiled again, but once more she got the impression he wasn't totally joking.

She decided maybe it would be better to just change the subject altogether.

"So tell me about your family."

He didn't speak for a moment, like he was lost in thought. Thinking about his tattoo? The truth was it must mean something to him, otherwise he wouldn't bother to have it put on his body forever.

After a moment he seemed to realize she'd spoken. "I, um, come from a big family. Six of us. Four boys, two girls. I'm the one of the middle children."

"Wow, that is a big family," Annie said.

"Yeah, your typical large Italian family. Always something going on." He smiled. "Loud. They are going to adore you. Overwhelm you too, but they will like you very much."

Her smile slipped a little as intense longing filled her chest. She wanted to meet his family. She wanted to see what his childhood must have been like. So different from hers.

But that wasn't going to happen. It was too dangerous.

Still she couldn't help admitting, "I always wanted a big family. I was raised on a farm with just my grandparents, and I always imagined what it would be like to have brothers and sisters."

"Your grandparents? What happened to your parents?"

"My mother got pregnant at sixteen," she said. "She wasn't ready to be a mom, so she gave me to her parents— my grandparents—and she ran away to California with her boyfriend, who was not my father. I'm not really sure who my father is." She shrugged, surprised how little her mother's lack of interest bothered her. "We've talked a few times over the years, but my grandparents are the ones I think of as my real mom and dad. They really were wonderful parents. They still are, although I haven't seen them in three years."

Guilt and sadness made her pause, but she rallied and quickly added, "But they understand that I've very busy at the magazine and I am able to send them financial help, which I feel good about. But tell me more about your family."

Instead he said, "Finola keeps you so busy you can't even go see your family?"

Annie shrugged, trying not to show how much it bothered her. "Well, it's hard in the fashion industry. It's all so fast-paced and I just find it difficult to get away for anything, really."

"I think Finola is totally unreasonable about the amount of time she expects her employees to work. And that seems to apply to everyone at the magazine."

She opened her mouth to tell him again that that was just life in the fashion world, but her words were cut off by the faint sound of music.

A song she knew all too well. Chosen for its appropriate message. "You Can't Always Get What You Want," by the Rolling Stones. She frowned, knowing who was calling her, and the lyrics had never seemed so prophetic.

"I have to get that," she said, already scooting herself toward the edge of the bed. "Where is my purse?"

"The living room," Nick said, standing so Annie could slide past him. "I moved it out there, because it was going off like crazy all morning. And I didn't want it to interrupt your sleep."

Panic rose up in her chest, acrid and making it hard to breathe.

"All morning?"

Oh God . . . oh God. Finola. She'd been calling all morning and Annie hadn't answered. Oh God. She was in trouble. Big, big trouble.

"Why didn't you *tell me*?" she cried, not keeping any of the fear and dread out of her voice.

Nick followed Annie as she raced to her purse, which he'd placed on his cluttered coffee table. She rifled through a side pocket until she finally located her phone. But by the time she did, it stopped ringing.

She stared at the silent phone, her gray eyes round. "Oh God . . . five missed calls."

She pressed a shaky hand to her forehead. Then she swayed slightly as if she might pass out.

Nick strode to her side, putting an arm around her waist.

"Maybe you should sit down."

"No, I . . ." Her skin looked chalky, and she weaved again. "I've got to go."

"I don't think so." He led her to the sofa. "You look like you've seen a ghost, or worse."

She allowed him to ease her down onto the worn cushions of his couch. "Let me get you some more coffee."

But she suddenly seemed to realize she was seated and started to stand. He sat down beside her, placing a hand on her bare thigh to stop her.

"Annie? Just wait. What's going on?"

"I," her breath was still reedy, "have to get home now."

He didn't move his hand. "Is it Bobby?"

She blinked at him as if she didn't even know who Bobby was.

Finally she shook her head. "No."

"Finola?" he asked.

She nodded, this time slipping away from his hold and coming to her feet. "I have to go."

She didn't wait for his response as she scurried to the bedroom as if the hounds of hell were on her heels. He rose from the sofa too, following her. Leaning in the doorway, he watched as she scampered around gathering her clothes.

"Where is my other shoe?" she asked, her voice an octave higher than usual, her movements agitated.

Again Nick crossed over to her, catching her wrist and forcing her to stop her manic search.

"Your shoe is right there," he said calmly, pointing to the edge of his bed. The toe peeked out from the disheveled bedding that had slipped off the bed from her wild escape.

She made a noise, a combination of relief and thanks, but as she started in that direction, he held fast to her wrist.

She jerked to a halt, then spun back to him.

"Nick, please, I have to go."

"Not until you tell me what you are suddenly so panicked. Not to mention, you aren't going to be able to go anywhere. There has to be a foot of snow outside."

She frowned, then still not answering his question, glanced toward the window. This time when she pulled against his hold, he released her. She walked over to the windows, squinting even in the gray light. He joined her, blinded by the whiteness that seemed to envelop the city.

"Easily a foot," he said, glancing at her. "And it doesn't look like the plows have been through in a while."

The street was deserted aside from a few brave souls attempting to dig out.

Annie stared at the street below, but she didn't look any more relaxed by the knowledge that whatever—or whoever—was sending her into this utter panic would have to wait. Nature was taking precedence today over everything.

She stared a moment longer, then turned, beelining right back to her shoe.

"Annie, you can't leave now. And especially not in that dress and those shoes."

"I have to," she told him, as if that was explanation enough.

"Why?"

She slipped her foot into her shoe, then sighed. "That was Finola. She will expect me in the office."

Nick frowned, finding it hard to believe even someone as demanding as Finola White would expect her employees to drag out in this weather. On a Saturday, no less.

"You can't be serious."

She looked at him, her expression stating that she hadn't been racing around like a lunatic for her own amusement.

"But you didn't even speak with her. Or listen to her voicemails, if she left any."

"I don't need to," Annie stated. "If she called five times, then she needs me."

"Yes, and you need to stay here. At least until the plow goes through. Right now, you can't get a taxi. You can't even walk to the subway, not in those shoes and with the snow so deep."

She looked at him, her mouth drooping, her eyes filled with panicked frustration.

Finally she let out another sigh and her shoulders slumped. "She is going to be furious."

Nick went to the bed, dropping down beside her, their legs and shoulders touching.

"Well, that's too damned bad. You can't control the weather."

She nodded, but then said, "Sadly, she won't accept that as an excuse."

He wanted to tell Annie how ridiculous that all was, but he stopped himself. He knew Annie worked for a ludicrously unreasonable woman, and clearly she was used to jumping at every one of Finola's impossible demands.

Annie pulled in a deep, calming breath.

Clearly Finola had instilled real fear in Annie.

But why would Annie put up with it? Surely, getting fired would almost be a relief. Annie had mentioned helping out her grandparents financially, but still, even that didn't merit dealing with this kind of total anxiety.

And what other awful things could Finola do, aside from fire her?

He thought of the receptionist. And of Jessica Moran. The way they had been, empty shells. Could Finola somehow do that? As crazy as it seemed, Nick believed she could. Or maybe she could do even worse, and just make Annie disappear.

Nick glanced at her, her hair tangled, her skin still the color of milk. She worried her lip with her teeth; from her distant look it was evident she was still trying to figure out a way to get to work.

Yeah, it was definitely more than the fear of being fired that motivated Annie. This was genuine fear that pushed her to risk life and limb to go to work on what should be a day off anyway.

Finola had some kind of control. Dangerous control. Whatever Finola had done to the others in her employment, she wasn't doing it to Annie.

But rather than saying that, he suggested calmly, "Maybe

you should listen to your messages. Maybe she's telling you not to come in because of the weather."

Even he knew that was a long shot.

Annie looked at the phone still clutched in her hand, nibbling her bottom lip as she decided what to do. But before she could make up her mind, the phone began playing the Rolling Stones again.

She blanched, her skin growing even paler than it already was. Her gray eyes huge. But she managed to gather herself and answer it by the time Mick sang, "You get what you need."

"Hello." Her voice sounded thin, meek, and Nick was irritated on her behalf. She shouldn't be this afraid of anyone, much less her employer.

"I—I'm at home," Annie stammered, then fell silent.

Nick didn't react to her lie, which, from the hesitation and the quaver in her voice, sounded like a lie. But he agreed she shouldn't admit to Finola that she was at his apartment. Finola would find out they were a couple at some point, but Annie could not handle that admission right now. And truthfully, he didn't know if it was safe for her to say anything yet.

"The battery on my phone died and—and I didn't realize."

Nick grimaced. Oh yeah, definitely not a good liar.

They both sat silent as Finola clearly went into a long-winded tirade of some sort until finally Annie started to answer her again, each response meek and contrite.

"I understand."

"I'm very sorry, Finola."

"No, it won't happen again."

"Yes, I'm at home."

"I'm not sure."

"No, he didn't even come into the theater."

Nick frowned at her last comment. He'd be willing to bet the "he" Annie referred to wasn't Tristan.

"No, he didn't say where he was going."

"I'm not sure."

"Okay. All right. Thank you."

Annie lowered the phone from her ear and pressed the touch screen to end the call. Then she just stared at it held limply in her hand.

"Is everything okay?" he finally asked when it became clear she wasn't going to say anything.

"Yes, she was angry that I'd missed her calls, but she seemed to let that go."

"What did she want to know?"

"Mostly about you. How long you stayed after I told you she had to cancel. Where you went. If I knew anything about what you did."

Nick nodded. "It was wise to avoid telling her anything right now."

"Ever."

He frowned. "What?"

She shifted to face him. "I'm not telling her about last night, ever."

"Well, we certainly don't have to tell her exactly *when* our relationship started, but we can't avoid telling her something."

Annie began shaking her head even before he finished speaking. "No."

Nick regarded her, not sure how to feel about what she was telling him. But she continued to shake her head, her eyes focused on the bed rather than him.

"Annie, what are you saying?"

"This," she paused, then stopped, clearly struggling to find the words. She breathed in deeply. "This can't continue."

Hurt and anger swallowed him, stealing away his own breath.

Annie met his gaze when he didn't speak. Her gray eyes glittered with tears. "I don't want to end it." She shook her head. "God, I don't. But there isn't any other choice."

He fought back the deluge of emotions and said as calmly as could, "Of course there is a choice. There's a choice to pursue it. To just—be together."

She shook her head again.

"Yes. Yes we can." He reached for her hand. Her fingers were stiff and cold in his, but she didn't pull away.

"Nick," she said her voice so soft and shaky that he had to lean closer to hear her. "I can't. I want to be with you. But I can't."

Nick didn't know what to say, fearing his hurt and frustration would make any responses curter than he wanted, than she deserved. In fact, he knew from watching her with Finola that she shut down when anyone threatened her. And God knows, he never wanted her to feel threatened by him or his reactions.

But was she really going to let Finola play this big a role in her personal life? Why? Why?

Hurt crushed him, but his detective side became alert. Again he was aware her reaction to her boss was far from normal. He'd be damned if he wasn't going to figure out what was going on at that magazine.

But he wasn't going to lose Annie in that process.

"I know you are afraid of Finola," he finally said, when he was sure he could speak without letting any of his aggravation show.

He gently squeezed her fingers.

"And I know our relationship has put you in an awkward position at work."

She opened her mouth to speak, but he raised a hand to stop her. "I'm not saying we have to do anything yet. But

Annie, Finola would figure out soon enough that I wasn't ever going to be genuinely interested in her."

"That wouldn't help us either," she whispered, and Nick couldn't understand what she meant.

"Annie, I'm not going to let you just walk away from this, just because your boss is a spoiled diva who is used to getting whatever she wants."

Annie wished being a spoiled diva was the only problem. She would have no problems fighting Finola for him, if that were all she was. But Finola wasn't just that. And spoiled and diva just made the demon all the more frightening.

Still as she looked at Nick, knowing he couldn't possibly understand, her already broken heart shattered. Annie didn't want to give this up; a happily ever after with a man that she'd come to care about so intensely in such a short time.

But she didn't have a choice.

"Annie," he rubbed his thumb over her cool fingers, his touch soothing and arousing all at the same time. "You've got to explain why Finola has so much control over you. It can't be just because you are worried about losing your job. Frankly, it seems to me losing your job would be a godsend."

A godsend. Ha, yes, the perfect term. But even God couldn't help her get out of this job. That clause was actually written in the fine print of the contract she'd signed. Her soul was her collateral for a high-paying, high-profile, much-coveted job. And there was no getting out of the deal until her terms of servitude were complete. And that was seven more years of service to Finola White.

She glanced at Nick, then dropped her gaze back to their joined hands. She believed Nick cared for her and that he was being sincere in his desire to make it work by whatever means. But would even he wait seven years for her?

Would he even make it seven years, if he denied Finola what she wanted? Finola was not a person—demon—to be crossed, and if she was crossed, someone was going to pay. Annie was, of course, the easy target. But would Finola go for Nick too?

Annie liked to believe that was a no. That there had to be a contract between Nick and Finola. That he had to sign over his soul before she could banish him. But Finola seemed to do what she wanted. And there was still the fact that she had the right to banish Annie to Hell. Annie suspected stealing Finola's love interest was definitely a deal breaker.

In fact, there was no suspecting involved. She knew.

So, no matter how good Nick's fingers felt caressing her skin. No matter how sweet his kisses were. How passionate his lovemaking was. How he made her smile, and laugh and believe that maybe true love did exist, she had to walk away. And make sure he understood that she was serious.

"Annie," he said, his voice deep and hushed, another thing she loved about him. "I know you are very worried about Finola's reaction, but she is just your boss. She can't control your life."

That was where he was wrong. But she didn't say so. What was the point? It would just lead to more questions.

But when she didn't answer, maybe he mistook her quiet for acquiescence, and he pulled her into his arms, his hold feeling so strong and safe. His warm skin spicy, the masculine scent lulling her again into the false sense of security.

Maybe she was acquiescing. Her arms came up to hold him back. Just for a little longer.

But this was just a magical little stitch in time. Soon to

be gone, melted away like the snow cocooning them out-side. When that magic melted away, she was going to have to make him believe she didn't want him.

God, how would she do that? It was so darned hard to think with her hands stroking him, his chest, his bare shoulders, his hair. Her body growing hungry for him. And his hands touching her in return.

Right now, she couldn't think about it. But she knew this really was just a stolen moment. Soon cold reality would set in. But today, in the gray aftermath of last night's storm she just wanted to love him a little longer.

Chapter Twenty

Nick held Annie close, her skin flushed and warm from their lovemaking. The intensity of it, even now in the sleepy afterglow, astounded him. Even when he'd been buried deep inside her body, neither of them moving, just connected as intimately as a man and woman could be, there had been a wild passion between them. Something so powerful and bonding.

He'd made love to her slowly. Not wanting to rush. Not wanting to stop touching her smooth, perfect skin. But the unhurried, gentle caresses and kisses had been totally soul-wrenching.

Looking at her as she lay curled on her side, her breathing even, her hair tousled, her skin back to its warm, creamy hue, he knew he was going do this every day of his life. This was the woman he would wake up with every morning and go to bed with every night.

He'd never even allowed himself to think about having children, or being a father. In fact, he had always shied away from that idea. At first because of his job, then later because he had wondered if the job had somehow affected his sanity and then because of not even pursuing a relationship anyway. He'd decided that maybe things like marriage and children just weren't in the cards for him.

His gaze roamed Annie's pretty, sweet face. But now he knew, without a doubt, that he wanted that with her. To have children. To marry. To do all those things that he was afraid to do before.

Damn, could he really feel all this about Annie so soon, with such certainty? Then he found himself smiling. Yes, he was certain. In that same way he was when he was sure he'd caught the right man in a case. In the same way he just knew when a perp was lying. Or when a witness was hiding something.

In the same way he knew that prickling feeling meant there was something more going on in a situation. Something beyond rational thought or reason.

He lay very still, telling himself no. That feeling was just something weird that happened to him every now and then. It wasn't real, just a silly sensation of a tired, overworked mind.

His gaze drifted away from Annie's lovely sleeping face to the creature tattooed on his shoulder. He'd gotten that "thing" on his shoulder during his roughest time, telling himself he'd never forget what he'd seen, even if others wouldn't believe him. But now he wished he hadn't. He didn't want to remember it any longer. He wanted to believe in a normal, happy life without any of the shadows of the past.

His gaze returned to Annie. And he had found what would make him happy, happier than he'd thought possible. He wasn't going to lose her. Ever. He'd do anything to be with this woman.

He was glad to see her so peaceful after being so upset earlier. She had dozed off almost as soon as they'd finished making love. A damned near tantric session, if he did say so himself. But unlike Annie, he didn't feel sleepy in the least. In fact his body hummed, brimming with excitement, energized to the point of almost antsy.

He held her sleeping form a moment longer, breathing in the citrusy scent of her hair, and absorbing the sated warmth of her skin. But still he couldn't seem to settle down, and he was afraid his fidgeting would disturb her much-needed tranquility.

Carefully he inched away from her to get out of bed. Maybe a shower would soothe him. Really, a workout was probably a better solution, but the clanking of his weights would echo though his apartment and make too much noise. And the snow made going for a run almost impossible.

So shower it was. Hot water would relax him, and he always found the shower to be a good place to think. He needed to think about Annie and how to handle her fear and hesitation to deal with Finola. He also hadn't lost hope of discovering what was going on at *HOT!*

Hell, bringing down Finola White, who was still the most logical suspect, would also solve his issues with Annie.

Easing the top drawer of his dresser open, he pulled out some clean boxer briefs and headed to the bathroom. Whatever was going on at the magazine was not only affecting Annie's personal life, it was now affecting his too. And he planned to uncover all of Finola White's dirty little secrets.

It had been on the tip of Annie's tongue to ask Nick where he was going, but completely satisfied lethargy kept the words from ever reaching her lips. Instead she remained still, watching Nick move around the room through lazy, barely opened eyes, thoroughly enjoying the view, even though she had no energy to react to it.

Half-dead, she would still love the sight of him. His muscles rolling under his golden skin, his tight rear end darn near perfection, and his arms and legs long and powerful.

He was breathtaking. She sighed, letting her eyes drift closed after he'd disappeared into the other room.

She smiled slightly, even that motion somehow lazy and slow, but she didn't care about her languor. She simply felt too good, and it didn't take too long before she had fallen back into a light doze. That kind of in-and-out sort of sleep where reality and dreams seemed to meet, and Annie found herself floating as if she were lounging on a soft, billowy cloud.

She smiled. Her grin widened, enjoying the strange weightless feeling. She hovered and drifted as if there was no gravity to keep her anchored to the ground.

She looked around her, amazed at the vast emptiness that surrounded her, which was more awe-inspiring than overwhelming.

But then, she was no longer alone. Nick was sharing that vastness with her. And again she realized she wasn't worried or nervous or afraid. She was totally happy, at peace. The feeling was so wonderful.

Nick pulled her into his strong arms, his gentle hands caressing her as they both began to soar, upward. Light as a feather.

"Stiff as a board."

Annie's body reacted instantly to the melodic, yet somehow menacing voice suddenly echoing through the air all around them.

Startled, she released Nick, and as soon as she did, she began to plummet, her body not longer weightless but desperately heavy like thick chains and weights dragged her downward.

"Nick!" she cried, but he'd disappeared and there were no strong arms, no gentle hands to save her.

She fell and fell like Alice down the rabbit hole. But she wasn't Alice and she wasn't falling toward Wonderland.

She was going somewhere far more terrifying and evil and eternal. And very, very real.

The melodious voice surrounded her again, speaking with singsong glee, "You are going straight . . . to . . . Hell."

Annie jerked upright in bed, and a small cry escaped her. She looked around herself, panting. Her heart pounded so hard in her chest it actually hurt.

It was a nightmare. Just a nightmare. But it wouldn't be, if she wasn't careful. Hell was real, and she was teetering at the brink.

She had to leave. Now.

She pulled in a few more slow, deep breaths, willing her heart to stop racing and her breathing to slow down. Finally after another few moments of forcing herself to tamp down the fear strangling her, she pulled herself together enough to realize she could hear the water running from another room.

Nick must be in the shower.

She quickly slipped out of bed, rushing around the room for the second time today in a frantic search for her clothes. This time she found them move easily and hurried to tug them on.

She didn't bother going to the window to see if the plows had cleared the streets yet. It didn't matter. She had to leave even if it meant slogging through blocks and blocks of heavy, freezing snow.

Nick was her apple. Her temptation. And she had to put some space and clear thought between them.

She tiptoed quickly to the living room, locating her purse and coat. Wishing she'd worn pants and blouse to the play rather than a short sheath dress, she braced herself to step out into the wet, icy snow.

But as soon as she heard the squeak of a faucet being shut off, she forgot the elements, realizing she had to make her escape before Nick reappeared and convinced her to stay just a little longer.

She unlocked the dead bolt, then twisted the doorknob and she was in the stairwell that led down the several flights to the street.

As she circled down and down to each floor, she was again reminded of the descent to Hell. More fear chilled her to the bone even before she stepped outside.

She had to keep them both safe. And the only way to do that was to act like the last twenty-four hours had never happened.

When Nick wandered back to the bedroom, toweling off his wet hair, and saw the empty bed, he knew Annie had left.

"Damn it," he muttered, snatching up his dress pants from last night off the floor and pulling them on. He turned and headed to his apartment door. Taking the stairs two at a time down to the small foyer, he shoved open the door and peered up and down the wintery street.

He squinted against the blinding white, trying to see any hint of Annie, but there was none. The street was still eerily deserted.

And Annie, out there in heels and a short dress, was nowhere to be seen. Growling both at her disappearance and at the snow blowing in the open door, biting at the shower-warmed skin of his bare chest and feet, he finally shut the door with more force than necessary.

Damn it, didn't she know her just disappearing was his worst fear, his worst nightmare?

He climbed back up to his apartment, his ascent no slower than his descent. Once inside, he looked for his cell, which was on the nightstand, untouched since last night.

He flipped it open, ready to call her. But then he realized he didn't have her number. The only one he had was for her reception desk.

But as he stared, frustrated, at the small screen, he saw the icon that indicated missed calls. He scrolled to it and saw he had several calls from a number he vaguely recognized. Finola. She'd called him too.

He debated calling her back, starting the ball rolling toward discovering all the secrets of fashion's reigning queen, but he didn't think he could focus on being a detective when he was worried about Annie.

He returned his dresser to grab a thermal T-shirt and some jeans. If she could go trekking out into the arctic tundra, so could he. And he might not have her number, but he did know where she lived.

Annie didn't want to devalue the tremendous hardships of the people who'd survived the brutal conditions of Everest or other extreme physical endeavors, but she was willing to challenge any of them that hiking through snowdrifts and slush piles and scaling mounds of snow piled high by plows in nothing but a pair of four-inch heels was damned near on a par with their feats.

And even if it wasn't, it had been incredibly hard for her. But the time she reached her Greenwich Village apartment, her feet were numb to the point she was a little afraid to see what color her toes were.

Not to mention how her legs stung painfully from the cold and damp. Although they were at least a healthy pink. Okay, more a windburned red, but they were still getting blood.

She hobbled down the hall toward her place, her equally frozen and numb fingers barely cooperating as she dug around in her purse for her keys.

Finally she found them, and even though she was shivering uncontrollably, she managed after several frustrating attempts to unlock the door.

She just stepped inside and started to lean over to pry her shoes off, honestly dreading what she might discover inside the now waterlogged leather, when a familiar voice called what would have been an almost comically familiar greeting, if she wasn't so frozen, and so unready to deal with the speaker.

"Annie, is that you?"

Annie's paused, standing on one aching foot, her hand braced on the wall for balance, the other grasping the heel of her shoe.

Bobby. Really? She supposed she shouldn't be surprised to find him here, but somehow, probably because she'd moved on, she'd just imagined he'd be simply gone. Not very realistic, now that she thought about it, but then she hadn't exactly been the queen of realistic for the past several hours.

"Oh God, Annie," he said, coming into the hallway, finding her in the same awkward stance.

She looked up, realizing as she now blinked at water dripping on her face, that she was totally soaked. The cold had simply frozen the snow and ice to her hair and clothes. But now, in the blessed warmth of her apartment, she was melting.

Melting. Meltdown was a better word, and she was dreadfully close to that as well.

"Annie, where have you been?"

Annie frowned at Bobby for a moment, forgetting her miserable state.

"I was . . ." She shook her head, feeling strangely light-headed and confused.

Bobby stepped forward to place a steadying arm around her, being more perceptive than Annie could ever recall.

"Come on," he said in a soothing way, helping her

hobble into the living room. He settled her on the sofa, her aching muscles crying out with something between pain and pleasure at being allowed to relax.

Bobby reached for her left shoe, carefully and slowly wiggling it off her frozen foot. Her toes were painfully red, which was a relief when compared to what she thought she might find, and now they throbbed almost unbearably as heat seeped into them. But no frostbite. She'd take the agony.

"Where were you?" he asked again, after he'd disappeared into the bedroom and returned with a thick, soft blanket. She accepted it, not sure what to make of Bobby's attentiveness. God knows, he hadn't been that way for so long. Now, when things were over, it seemed strange to finally receive his attention.

"I was—" she hesitated to answer, not because she was afraid of hurting Bobby. He was with Ally now, after all. And she knew now he had been for a while.

But what was the point of talking about Nick? It was over before it began, and saying anything now just seemed senseless. And painful in a way that hurt far more than Bobby's betrayal.

"You were with that guy from the play, weren't you?"

Annie blinked, surprise making the answer for her. "Yes. How did you know?"

Bobby smiled. That perfect all-American smile. But this time, Annie thought there was a hint of sadness here, despite the wide display of pearly whites.

"It was impossible to miss."

Annie blinked again, utterly stunned that somewhere during the events of the past twenty-four hours, Bobby had suddenly become so observant, so aware.

She couldn't help herself, she laughed, all the emotions of the past day and a half—heck, from the moment she met Nick—bubbling to the surface.

Bobby regarded her, his brows drawn together in confused consternation.

"I'm sorry," she finally said, getting her giggling under control. "I just can't believe you noticed his reaction given the position *you* were in."

Bobby winced, then said sheepishly. "You never should have had to find out about Ally and me that way."

She shrugged, amazed that still she felt no pain over it. "It was a long time coming."

"Still, not my finest moment."

"No," she agreed, but again she couldn't be mad. At least he'd taken that moment. Bobby had gone for what he wanted and she wished she could do that same.

Instead, she had to settle for one night and now she had to walk away. Not that she had any other options now, anyway.

Sneaking away while Nick was in the shower was sure to have ended things anyway. She was sure Nick considered her a total coward now. Leaving without a good-bye, or even a note. She was sure Nick was pretty darned disgusted.

Yet despite knowing Nick was gone, she couldn't stop herself from asking, "So you could tell that Nick was interested in me?"

"Oh yeah. He had that possessive, ready-to-fight-for-your-honor look. You could just see he really cared about you."

She breathed in deeply at his bittersweet words.

"And you had a look of your own."

"I did?"

"Definitely. Who is he?"

Annie hesitated again, but then decided it couldn't hurt to tell Bobby who he was. "A detective. He's been at the magazine checking into some strange occurrences."

"Strange occurrences? You never mentioned that. Did you?"

Annie smiled. There was a glimpse of the Bobby she knew.

"No. I don't know much about any of it," she said, her smile fading. Liar. You total liar.

"You really like him, don't you, Annie?"

She blinked, forcing her guilt aside. Just like she always did. She opened her mouth to deny it, but couldn't say the words. She simply nodded.

"Then I'm glad we both decided to take some risks," he smiled a little self-deprecating. "Some risks are stupider than others. But I think we both needed to shake things up a little, didn't we?"

She squeezed his fingers back, giving him a shaky smile.

"When did you get so deep?"

He tilted his head, pondering. "Probably when I took that deep POV acting class with Professor Dunlevy. Remember that one where I had to stay in the point of view of an ostrich for three days?"

Annie stared at him for a moment, then just smiled. Now that was definitely the Bobby she knew.

But their shared moment of appreciation was interrupted by an abrupt rap on the apartment door.

Bobby rose. "I'll let him in?"

"How do you even know it's him?"

He gave her his best wise look. "You just said yourself, I'm deep."

Annie didn't have the heart to tell him deep didn't mean clairvoyant.

Chapter Twenty-one

Nick supposed he shouldn't have been surprised, but he was, when the door to Annie's apartment opened, and Bobby stood on the other side.

"Um, hello," he managed to say without sounding totally blindsided. "Is Annie here?"

Bobby nodded, an almost smug smile on his lips. "Yeah, come on in."

Nick didn't respond except to step inside the apartment. Did that self-satisfied little grin mean that Bobby and Annie had decided to reconcile? Was that the face of the man who knew he got the girl? Surely Annie wouldn't take this idiot back after what happened last night, both at the theater and afterward, with him at his apartment.

If she did take this turkey back, it was because she was afraid to take the chance and be with Nick. And he planned to tell her just that. Bobby did not deserve Annie. Plain and simple. And Annie didn't really want to be with this blond doofus anyway.

And he planned to tell her just that. He strode down the hallway toward the living room. He was not going to let Annie give in to this guy. She spent too much of her life giving in to those around her. He wasn't going to let her do that again, giving in to a man who definitely did not deserve her.

When he stepped into the living room and spotted Annie curled on the sofa, wrapped in a comforter, looking so young and bedraggled and miserable, all his intentions of telling her to stand up for herself disappeared.

Instead he stopped in the entryway, suddenly not sure what to say at all. Was he just barging in here to bully her like everyone else did?

"Hi," she finally said, when it became clear that he just planned to stand and stare at her.

"Hi." He took a step closer. "Are you okay?"

"Practically frozen, but yes, I'm okay."

He walked closer, wanting desperately to hold her. To . . . comfort her and soothe away that sad, bewildered expression from her face.

But he stopped a few feet from the sofa, pretty certain she wouldn't welcome his touch.

Instead he asked, "Why did you leave like that?"

She pulled the comforter tighter around her, whether in an unconscious gesture to protect herself or not, he wasn't sure.

"Because I knew if I didn't leave while you were in the shower, you would come back and convince me to stay."

Convince me to stay. Those words certainly seemed to validate his concerns. Was he just another person in Annie's life, coercing, pushing, bullying her into doing something she didn't want to do?

That wasn't what he wanted to do to her. He wanted her to be with him because that was truly what she wanted. Nick believed she cared about him in the same way he cared about her, but she had to make her own decisions on what she wanted.

"I—I just wanted to make sure you got back here all right."

She grimaced down to where her feet were hidden

under the covers. "My toes are hating me, but yes, I made it unscathed."

He nodded, not wanting to leave with that being all he had to say, but suddenly his plotted-out speech about how she was making a huge mistake letting this relationship go before she even gave it a chance, and how he planned to stand right there until she realized her mistake, just seemed like another way of making Annie submit. As hard as it was going to be, he had to let her make her own decision about him and about having a relationship with him.

"Good," he said, shoved his hands in the pockets of his leather jacket, uncertain what else to say.

"But there is no way you came all this way, in the snow, just for that," said a male voice from behind him.

Nick turned to see Bobby coming out of the bedroom. He hadn't even noticed the man had gone in there, he'd been so concerned with Annie.

Bobby looked calm, unconcerned as he walked into the kitchen. Of course, why wouldn't he? He was back in his apartment, with his girlfriend, while Nick stood here like a flustered fool.

Of course this was entertaining to him. He'd gotten Annie back, and as far as Nick was concerned, that made this particular play a tragedy.

"Okay," Nick said after a few moments of listening to Bobby moving around the kitchen. "I guess I should go."

Annie opened her mouth, whether to say "okay" or to say to "no, stay," Nick didn't know, because Bobby appeared back in the room.

"Sorry to interrupt," he said, "but I'm going to head out now. I just wanted to see if it's okay to come back over on Monday to get the rest of my stuff."

Annie nodded. "Of course."

Nick turned to look at the other man, for the first time

realizing there was a suitcase by the bedroom door, and a backpack slung over the man's shoulder.

Nick's tense muscles, muscles he didn't even know he held so taut, went weak. He almost felt the need to collapse against the wall.

Annie wasn't taking Bobby back. Bobby was leaving.

Bobby actually extended a hand to him then. "Good to meet you. Sorry it was in such an—awkward way."

Nick looked down at the other man's hand, then accepted it. Hell, he wouldn't have traded that awkward meeting for anything, although he didn't say that.

Bobby then did a silly little salute to Annie.

"Remember," he said with that toothy white smile on his lips, "we finally took some risks."

Nick didn't really follow what the man was saying, but Annie nodded.

"We took some risks," she agreed.

Bobby grabbed his suitcase and headed down the hallway to the apartment door. Nick heard it open, then click closed behind him.

He turned back to Annie, who still sat swaddled in her comforter looking just as dazed as Nick felt.

Nick started to ask if she was okay, but the apartment door opened again. Bobby came back into the room, giving them an awkward wave and sheepish grin.

"I just forgot my coat," he said, pointing to his jacket hanging on the back of the chair at the computer desk in the corner.

"Sorry," he said, snatching it up and waving it in the air like a trophy as he headed back to the door.

Both Nick and Annie watched him leave, before looking back to each other.

They both laughed.

"So you aren't getting back together with him," Nick said.

Annie shook her head. "No, absolutely not."

Nick nodded, wandering over to the sofa. Tentatively he sat down, leaving space between them.

"I thought when I saw he was here that maybe you decided to reconcile."

She shook her head, smiling like that was the most ludicrous thing she'd ever heard.

"Then why? Why did you run away?"

"I—I just felt like it was something I had to do. I am worried about Finola and her reaction. I'm worried about you wanting to force the issue by telling her."

Nick nodded. "I know. I don't understand why you are so afraid of her, but I do know you are."

Annie sighed. "I wish I could say something to make it make sense to you, but that's just the way it is."

Some of Nick's relief at discovering she wasn't with Bobby faded. "So you are saying there is no chance of us being together because of your boss."

That reason seemed so ridiculous to him, but he knew it was perfectly valid to Annie.

Annie surprised him by shaking her head. "No, that's not what I'm saying. But I do need you to accept some terms, that is if you are really serious about us being a couple."

Nick frowned. Terms? But he found himself saying, "Okay, tell me."

Annie was a little surprised, both at him and herself. But she guessed Bobby's talk about risks had made her realize she did have to take some. It wasn't as if these feelings for Nick were going to go away.

Heaven knew she'd done a pretty miserable job of staying away from him thus far. But she did need to ask a couple of things of him that would keep them safe. Or as safe as possible.

She sat up, turning toward him on the sofa.

"I'm crazy about you," she said.

Nick smiled at that. "Well, we're even there, because I'm pretty damned crazy about you too."

"And I know you don't understand my wariness toward Finola, but it's how I feel, so for this to work between us, we can't reveal anything about our relationship to her."

She could see from Nick's frown, he still wanted to know why. To know what she feared.

"Nick, she is a very jealous and demanding person, and it's hard enough to work for her without our relationship making her behave even worse."

That was the best answer she could give him, and to her surprise, he accepted it.

"Okay. We don't tell her about our relationship."

Annie smiled, relieved that one term was accepted, although the gesture didn't last, because she knew her next request was the one that Nick might not be able to accept. But for her, it was the only way they could possibly be together.

"And," she pulled in a deep breath, "I need you to stop investigating the missing persons cases at *HOT!*"

Nick didn't respond for a moment. In fact, he didn't even react. But then after a few moments, he stood up and Annie thought for sure he was going to walk out.

But instead, he paced across the room, then stopped and turned back to her.

"Why?"

Because it's too dangerous, she thought, but she knew she couldn't tell him that. That would reveal she knew so much more than she was sharing. Instead she told another truth, just not the whole truth.

"If you are still coming to the magazine, you will see Finola and she won't let go of her interest in you. She will still pursue you and that will put us in a position where the truth about us has to come out."

Nick fell silent again, but she could see in his intelligent brown eyes that he was weighing whether his own happiness was worth the lives of so many missing people and their suffering families. It wasn't, of course. Annie knew he'd probably have to put his work and this investigation first, but he managed to surprise her again.

"What if another detective takes the case?"

Annie didn't want another person to be at risk, but right now all she could think about was keeping Nick safe. Keeping him away from Finola and the awful truths that were hidden behind all the glamour and beauty and success of *HOT!* magazine.

"That is fine," she said, guilt pulling at her chest, but again, she knew she had to keep Nick safe.

She rose from the couch, shuffling to him, her blanket wrapped around her like a long cloak. She stopped in front of him, staring up at him, his dark eyes and beautiful mouth.

"I know I'm asking a lot, but it's what I have to do to feel like things will be okay for me."

Nick studied her for a moment, then dipped his head to capture her lips, his kiss hard and possessive and hungry.

"Okay, I'll do what you ask."

Relief and joy filled her.

She knew this was still such a risky thing, but it was the best solution she could come up with.

And in seven years . . . would he really agree to a weird, secret relationship for seven years?

She wasn't going to think about that right now. Right now, they were together in the best way she could devise. And she was going to allow herself to be happy about it.

She reached up and caressed Nick's scruff-roughened cheek, then pressed a kiss to his lips, so glad he had agreed.

But the kiss quickly changed from sweet and thankful to heated and full of passion.

More heat curled through her belly—and lower.

His hands slipped underneath the blankets, finding her body still covered in damp clothes.

He pulled back and frowned. "You're wet."

"Yes, I am," she agreed, her voice breathy from his wonderful kiss, then blushed at the unintentional double entendre of her words.

His smile was somewhere between naughty and affectionate, that particular combination absolutely breathtaking.

"Maybe we should get you out of those clothes then."

She allowed him to tug her in the direction of her bedroom.

Once inside, they kissed, again his talented fingers making short work of her damp clothes.

But before she was totally naked, he pulled back. "I sort of feel like we need to do something to seal our terms."

She laughed at that, her fingers moving to the buttons of his shirt. "Oh, I think we are doing that."

He smiled too and soon they were both nude, tumbling across the bed. When Nick slid between her thighs and thrust his rock-hard erection deep into her, filling her to the hilt, he paused, his brown eyes locking with hers.

"I would agree to anything to be with you. I would sell my soul to the very devil."

Annie stiffened under him, fear nearly blotting out her desire. Then he kissed her and began moving inside her and she managed to assure herself those were just words. A turn of phrase used hundreds of times.

He'd never know she'd done just that.

Chapter Twenty-two

Over the next couple of weeks, Annie was surprised how easily her plan worked out. In fact, it seemed to be working perfectly. Nick had pulled out of the investigation without much questioning from his captain, and in fact, no other detective was assigned.

Annie knew that didn't exactly sit well with Nick, but he told her the whole investigation was going to be short-lived anyway, because there just wasn't enough evidence.

Even Finola had seemed to have given up on Nick. Her whole focus now was Fashion Week. And though she wasn't aware of Annie's relationship with Nick, she wasn't making Annie's life any easier. Her demands were even more outrageous, the hours longer than ever, and every day was a struggle to make sure she didn't find a single reason to accuse Annie of breaching their contract.

Now that was more important than ever, because now she would not only lose her soul, she would lose Nick.

And today she was surprised that she came out unscathed.

Annie let out a sigh of relief as she finally reached her apartment. She wearily dug through her purse for her keys, finding the task of inserting the key into the lock almost too much.

But after a few attempts, she managed to unlock the

door and step inside. Immediately she was surrounded by the scent of something delicious cooking.

She closed her eyes, breathing in deep, suddenly her hideous day being so worth it.

"Hey," Nick said, poking his head out from the kitchen. "I was just checking on the lasagna."

"Lasagna." Annie moaned. She dropped her purse and shrugged off her coat, not caring that both ended up on the floor of her entryway closet. Then she went right to the kitchen and to Nick.

He was bent over the oven, and Annie came up behind him, curling over him to hug him, resting her cheek wearily against his strong back. Heat from the oven and more wonderful scents of home cooking encompassed her. Or maybe it was the heat of Nick and his wonderful scent that made her feel boneless and happy.

He finished checking the pasta, then straightened and turned in her arms. He kissed her, and she decided definitely he was the thing that made her feel at home.

"Another late night," he said, gazing down at her, his brows drawn together with concern. "You look dead on your feet."

"Not today," she said, then laughed at her private joke.

Nick's frown deepened and she gave him a smile. "I'm tired, but fine. Glad to be home."

"I'm glad you are, too."

They kissed again, something she was never too tired for.

"Go change," he said. "I'll get a plate ready for you."

Annie sighed as she wandered to the bedroom, amazed at how her life had changed. Nick was always there waiting for her when she was finally released for the night from work. He always had dinner waiting for her, whether he cooked or picked up takeout. And every night she slept in his arms.

She smiled as she changed into a pair of flannel pajama

bottoms and tugged on one of Nick's T-shirts. An NYPD baseball league shirt.

The past weeks had been heaven, and the time with Nick made up for the rest of her life that was still hell. But at least now she had something to keep her going.

"That smells so good," she said, shuffling out of the bedroom to the kitchen table, where Nick already sat, waiting for her.

"Well, this time I can't take credit," he admitted. "My mom sent it over."

"That was sweet." She sat down beside him, breathing in deeply.

"She's asking again when she's going to meet the woman who has me absolutely smitten."

"You're smitten?" she said, grinning coyly at him before popping a piece of garlic bread in her mouth.

"Just a little." His naughty smile out in full force.

She took a bite of the heavenly lasagna, moaning with appreciation.

"Once we get through Fashion Week, things should slow down," Annie said. "Then I should be able to go for a visit."

"They better slow down. You can't keep up this seven-day workweek for much longer. You look exhausted."

She knew she did. She was pale and there were purple circles under her eyes that expensive concealer was just barely covering.

"I know I look a wreck," she said.

"That is not what I said. I said you look exhausted. You always look beautiful. Especially in my T-shirt," he said, wiggling his eyebrows lecherously.

She laughed.

But Nick grew serious. "Finola cannot expect you to keep up this pace. It's ridiculous. It's superhuman."

He had no idea how accurate he was, but instead she

turned the topic to his work. She didn't feel like talking about Finola and her unrealistic, inhuman demands.

"How's your work going?"

Nick shrugged, taking a large bite of lasagna before he answered. "A murder investigation today. It shouldn't be too complicated. It looks like a straightforward case of a husband with a jealous mistress who decided to get rid of the wife once and for all."

Despite herself, Annie shivered at his words. That sounded a little too close to home for her. Annie wasn't the wife, and Finola wasn't the mistress, but she had no doubt the outcome would be the same if her relationship with Nick came to light.

Nick frowned, noticing her shudder. "Cold?"

She nodded, even though it wasn't true. "I think being so tired is making me feel chilled."

"Well, go in to bed. I'll clean up."

She smiled, feeling sad that she didn't have more energy. "It doesn't seem fair that you are always taking care of me."

"I like it."

Annie didn't doubt that. Nick was a natural-born care-giver. She pressed a kiss to his cheek, thanking him again for dinner, then she did head to bed, groaning with relief as she crawled under the warm covers. Her tired muscles relaxed and she drifted into a place somewhere between awake and asleep.

In the kitchen, she could hear Nick cleaning up. He really was the sweetest, most thoughtful guy she'd ever known.

He'd make an amazing father, and she smiled at the places her sleepy brain was going. She wondered what it would be like to be pregnant with his baby. She wondered what they would name him . . . or her.

She wondered if he'd wait seven years to do that with her.

Her eyes opened, all her warm, pleasant thoughts gone. In seven years she'd be thirty-five. Nick would be thirty-eight. Would he want to wait that long? Was it fair to ask him to?

She closed her eyes again and despite her restless, uncertain thoughts, exhaustion won out and she fell into dark, empty sleep.

Only later, although she had no perception of how long, dreams returned. Wonderful dreams. Arousing dreams.

Very deliciously real dreams. Dreams of Nick's wicked hands and mouth moving over her body.

Annie moaned, blinking her eyes open to discover she wasn't dreaming. Nick leaned over her, his T-shirt nudged her skin and his lips found her breast. He sucked lightly on one, then switched to the other.

Her hand came up to run through his tousled hair, pressing those naughty lips of his harder against her.

He obeyed, teasing her tight, sensitive nipple until she wiggled under him, her body begging for more.

He lifted his head then, his eyes dark and solemn. "I'm sorry to wake you. But I just needed to touch you."

Annie frowned, surprised by her seriousness. Not that they never made love seriously, but something felt different tonight.

But before she could question him, he ducked his head again, his tongue and lips teasing her nipples. Then when she was again writhing against him, he slid down her body pressing open-mouthed kisses across her stomach.

He eased down her pajama bottoms, baring her totally. Then he kissed the slight curve of her belly, her hips, the soft mound of her sex. Then he moved to situate himself between her thighs, her labia open to him. He touched her there, stroking one of his strong fingers lightly between them, her arousal slicking his fingertip.

Then he lowered his mouth to her, licking the dampness there, tasting her. He remained there, his tongue whirling and dipping, tasting every inch of her sex. His lips and teeth toyed with her, bringing her to the brink of release only to return to tender teasing.

Only when she was clutching him, digging her fingers into his broad shoulders, lifting her hips wantonly and demandingly against him, did he slide back up her body and penetrate her with his thick erection. But still he didn't let her have the release she desperately needed.

Instead he played with her, first taking her hard and fast and deep. But when the walls of her vagina began to clench him, quivering with her impending climax, he slowed down, sometimes barely moving at all.

Repeatedly being brought to the edge of the precipice, then pulled back was driving her mad, making her beg him for release, her words tumbling out, incoherent, desperate.

Finally he gave her what she pleaded for, driving into her over and over, his body filling hers completely until she screamed with the impact of her orgasm. He shouted too, joining her in the final almost brutal release.

Annie wasn't sure how long it was before she became aware of her surroundings again and able to form any sort of coherent thought.

"Holy cow," she finally murmured, rolling onto her side to curl against him.

Nick smiled over at her, looking as dazed as she felt. But again she got the feeling something still wasn't right. Something in his eyes looked different.

She lifted her head from the pillow, studying him for a moment. "What's wrong?"

He shook his head. "Nothing."

She wasn't convinced and he knew it. He rolled over onto his side to face her.

"Nothing is wrong," he said, his eyes roaming her face. "It's just that—I love you."

Annie stared at him, not sure that she'd heard his low, husky words correctly.

"You . . ." Her words stopped. She was almost afraid to say them in case she was wrong.

But he simply said them for her. "I love you, Annie."

Annie remained still for a moment longer and then she threw her arms around his neck, her body half on top of his.

"Oh, I love you too."

Nick watched Annie. A little smile curved her lips even in her sleep. He'd meant what he said and he was humbled and honored that she felt the same way, but this moment didn't have the blissful feeling it should. And that was because of him.

He carefully slipped out of bed and grabbed his boxers off the floor. He tugged them on, then walked to the living room. He sat down in the dark, the only light from the streetlights outside. But enough light to see his cell phone on the coffee table. He stared at it for a moment, then he reached for it.

The screen flashed to life, almost blinding in the dark. He hesitated again, then dialed his voicemail. He held the phone to his ear and listened to the message again, to the lilting, melodic voice on the other end.

Finola. She'd called after Annie had gone to bed. He'd recognized the number, but hadn't answered. He had listened to the voicemail, however. She wanted to see him. Wanted him to be her date for a party to kick off Fashion Week.

And he was going to betray his pact with Annie and do it. He didn't resent what Annie had asked him to do, give

up the case at *HOT!* He understood she was truly concerned about him, but he just couldn't stop thinking about
all those missing people. About Jenna and Jessica Moran.

And he couldn't stop worrying that the same thing
would happen to Annie if he didn't discover what was
going on there.

Chapter Twenty-three

The next evening, Annie got home even later than the night before, and Nick couldn't stand to see her as tired as she was.

He brought her a bowl of soup, which she accepted with her usual sweet smile.

"Thank you." She took one bite, then set it on the table, apparently too tired to even eat.

"Annie, you can't keep going this way."

She smiled again, telling him the same thing she had since they started seeing each other. "Things will get better after Fashion Week."

It was on the tip of her tongue to tell her they definitely would because he was going to start his investigation again. But he stopped.

He hadn't even called Finola back today. He'd pulled up her number several times, but couldn't bring himself to dial the number.

He didn't want to betray Annie. But looking at her now, he knew he had to do something. It was like that woman had some sort of power over Annie. Like she was a vampire, controlling her, then sucking away her life force.

"Annie, you have to quit this job," he said, but he'd already tried that many times. And his pleading had fallen on deaf ears, just as it did tonight.

"I'm fine," she assured him. "Nothing a good night's sleep won't fix."

"And I woke you last night when you so desperately needed to rest." He'd felt guilty all day about that too.

She roused then, moving closer to him. "Don't you dare apologize about that. That was the most amazing moment of my life."

He smiled at her. "I'm glad you feel that way."

She wouldn't when he finally told her what he intended to do. But he was doing it for her as well as the missing people. She wouldn't see it that way, but he was.

"You know, you've never told me about your tattoo," she said clearly nudging the conversation in a different direction.

She pulled up the sleeve of his short sleeve and inspected it closer. "It must signify something to you. Isn't that why people get tattoos?"

Nick glanced at it and decided he should tell her. After all, Annie loved him. If anyone could hear about his darkest moment and love him anyway, it was she.

"Remember you asked me about the Midtown Murderer?"

She nodded, her gaze on his face now rather than the tattoo.

"Well, that was a long, brutal case. His murders were violent, horrific. By far the worst killings I've ever seen. The women were just—" he shook his head at the memory. "They were mutilated."

He breathed in, remembering how awful and strange and just utterly frightening that time was.

"Nick, if this is too hard—" Annie began, but he stopped her.

"I want to tell you."

Her eyes moved over him, but she nodded for him to continue.

"The case was obviously very disturbing. And during it, I started to have—I don't know. The shrink says they were hallucinations brought on by stress. But whenever I got close to one of the bodies of his victims, I'd start having this intense feeling along the back of my neck and down my spine. I don't know how to describe it. I guess the best way is like hundreds of pins pricking me. Cold pins."

Annie listened, no doubt on her face, her gray eyes only solemn, maybe a little pained for him.

"I also started having dreams about a creature that looked like this." He tilted his head toward the tattoo.

"Finally we caught the murderer. The monster. He was cuffed in the interrogation room and I was supposed to go in and question him. Other detectives watched from another room, but I was the one who went in there alone with him."

Annie's hand, which had been resting on his arm, squeezed him. A gesture of comfort. Of support.

"I sat down across from him and began asking him questions," Nick shook his head at the memory. "He was evil. Pure evil. But as I looked at him, he started to change. He changed into this creature."

He touched his tattoo then.

"He sat right there, across from me, and let me see the monster deep inside him."

Nick fell silent, remembering that moment.

"What happenened?" Annie asked softly.

"I flipped out," he said with a humorless laugh. "I jumped up, screaming. The other cops had to come take me out of the room. While that monster just laughed. Laughed and laughed at my total breakdown."

"Did anyone else see it?"

He snorted. "Of course not."

"Was that why you had to take a leave of absence?"

He nodded, again chuckling although he felt no amusement. "A leave of absence, session after session with a shrink. You can't have a lead detective seeing monsters now, can you?"

Annie studied him for a moment, but rather than giving him indulgent sympathy like others had, she frowned and asked, "But why tattoo it on your body?"

He glanced down at it. "It's a reminder that I will never be frightened of a monster again."

Nick sat at his desk, reading over some eyewitness reports of someone seen at the site of a break-in. As usual, all the reports described something different. A hat, no hat. Facial hair, no facial hair. A yellow car, a white car.

No sooner had he read the word "white," than his phone rang. He glanced at the number and he paused.

Finola.

After the fourth ring, he pressed the answer button.

"Detective Nick Rossi."

"My, my, aren't you all official?"

"Finola," he said as if he was surprised it was her. "I was just getting ready to call you back."

"Well, you were taking too long," she said, her tone flirty and petulant all at once.

"I'm sorry about that."

She made a small noise like she doubted him, but then she said. "So, do I have a date for my party on Friday?"

"You do."

He could practically see her self-satisfied smile over the phone. "Excellent. I will have a car sent for you. Just text me your address."

"Sounds good."

Nick hung up the phone, his stomach sinking at the realization of what he'd done and what it would do to Annie. But after last night's conversation, he knew he couldn't let Annie's monsters frighten her any longer either.

★ ★ ★

"That's right," Annie told the caterer. "She wants the potato leek soup instead of the Manhattan clam. Great. Okay, good. Thank you."

Annie hung up the phone, then stretched. Well, she had Finola's dinner menu finally fixed. The woman even wanted all the food she served white. Really, that had to be the height of self-obsession, didn't it? But, whatever, it was done and hopefully Finola would be pleased.

Well, pleased until she came up with her next demand.

As if on cue, Finola's voice came over the intercom.

"Anna, I need you in my office. Right now."

"Right away," Annie answered, then stood, her muscles achy as she headed through the maze. Maybe she'd ask Nick to give her a massage tonight. He had amazing hands, large and strong.

She smiled to herself, realizing she was getting as spoiled as her boss. Okay, no one was that bad. But still she should do something nice for Nick for a change. She'd just been so busy and he'd been so good to her. But he deserved something nice.

He was an amazing man.

Anne rapped lightly on Finola's door and the woman looked up from her computer and waved Annie in.

Finola's dog stood up as Annie entered, and let out one little yip, but then circled a couple of times and curled back up in a ball as if it were too much work to do anything else.

"Anna," Finola said, "I need you to deliver something for me on your way home." She pointed to a garment bag hanging on the back of a rolling rack in the corner.

"The address is attached," Finola said absently, her attention never leaving what she was doing on her computer.

Probably solitaire, Anna thought wryly.

She crossed the room and unhooked the bag, draping it over her arm. Only then did she see the address.

She stared at it, the words and numbers written in Finola's loopy cursive. She read it again.

"Is there a problem?"

Annie looked up, trying to gather herself.

"No," she said. "I was just thinking that address seemed oddly familiar."

Finola raised a doubtful eyebrow. "It's Detective Rossi's address, but I don't know why you would know it."

"I—I must remember it from the research I did for you," Annie told her, surprised she could sound so calm.

Finola seemed to accept her explanation, with a dismissive wave. "Well, deliver that tonight. Nick is going to be my date for the party, and I'm sure he has nothing to wear. You may take it now. I'm finished with you for the day."

Annie nodded and left without further comment. She hurried back to her desk, gathering up her stuff. She was actually getting to leave early, and now she was going to go home and confront Nick.

Nick was surprised to hear the apartment door jiggling as a key was being inserted. Annie was home already? Before ten at night? That was unheard of.

He started down the hallway just as Annie barged through the door. Her gray eyes flashed and her pretty mouth was twisted in a furious grimace.

"Here you go," she said, shoving a white garment bag hard against his chest. His arms came up automatically to catch it. She then pushed past him into the living room.

She whirled on him, her expression still livid.

"How *could* you? How could you agree to go to Finola's party as her date?"

Nick wanted to groan. He should have guessed Finola

would say something to Annie. After all, Annie was little more than the woman's slave, expected to arrange every last detail of her life.

"I was going to tell you."

"Oh really?" she said, her voice more bitter and sarcastic than he'd ever heard it. It was unnerving, like discovering that Gandhi suffered from road rage.

"When were you going to tell? After this date? Or the next one? Or the next? Maybe I would just go into the office one day and happen upon you screwing her on my desk."

Nick blinked. Okay, her anger was even more shocking than his earlier reference, more like finding out that Mother Teresa was actually a nasty drunk.

"Annie, you know this isn't about an attraction to her. I love you," he stated. "And it's because I love you that I have to do this. I have to see what I can find out about those missing employees."

Some of Annie's anger seemed to diminish, and she looked somehow deflated, defeated. He actually could accept her anger better.

"But you promised you would let the investigation go."

"I can't, Annie." He dropped the garment bag onto one of the stools at the island and walked over to her.

He stopped just short of her, wanting to touch her, but not sure she would allow it.

"If she's involved, and I'm sure she is, she needs to be stopped. Not to mention you won't quit, and I can't risk you ending up like one of those past employees."

Annie raised a shaky hand to push the escaped tendril of hair from her bun out of her face. Her gray eyes shimmered with barely contained tears.

"Don't you understand?" she finally said. "If you keep prying, not only could I end up like one of them, but so could you."

Nick looked at her pleadingly. "No, I don't understand. Explain it to me. Tell me what you know. I promise I can help."

A bark of a laugh escaped her. "There is no way you could help."

"Of course I can. I have access to the best law enforcement in the city."

She shook her head. "Law enforcement can't stop them."

"Why not?" Nick just couldn't understand what she was telling him.

Annie stared at him for a moment, one tear rolling down her flushed cheek.

"They are demons."

Chapter Twenty-four

Nick didn't know what he expected Annie to say, but that wasn't it.

"Demons?" He couldn't keep the disbelief out of his voice.

"Yes," Annie nodded, "just like the one you encountered."

He frowned, not following her.

"The Midtown Murderer," she said, her expression beseeching.

Nick didn't react for a moment, but when he did it was to feel anger seeping into him. She was using his weakest moment against him. He'd told her about that dark moment, that moment when he was sure he was going mad and now she was using it to control him.

He couldn't believe it.

"That's low," he said to her, his voice raw and hurt.

Annie shook her head, her eyes looking genuinely confused.

"It's true," she said. "Demons are real."

He couldn't believe she was continuing with this. He'd spent hours in therapy sessions, hours coming to terms with the fact that he'd lost his mind, just for a moment. A way for his mind to deal with real-life horror. And now she was trying to convince him what he'd seen was true.

"Nick, please, you have to believe me. Finola, Tristan, they are demons. Just like the kind of demons in movies and books and folklore."

Nick shook his head and raised his hands. He wasn't going to listen to this. He headed toward the apartment door, but Annie followed.

"I needed a job," she said, the words tumbling for her mouth. "I needed a job badly and when I was offered the position at *HOT!* I was thrilled. Even when Finola explained the contract to me, I thought it would be okay. I signed the contract. And now I'm indentured to her for ten years. Well, only seven now."

Nick stopped and turned back to her.

"You expect me to believe this bullshit?" he snapped at her.

Annie winced like he'd slapped her.

"It's true," she said softly. Her eyes searched his pleadingly.

Nick closed his own to block hers out. He didn't know what to think. All he knew was he needed to get out of there.

Nick stepped out onto the sidewalk, the cold winter air feeling good. He breathed in deeply, hoping it would clear his head and help him understand what the hell just happened.

Demons. Sold souls. Annie selling her own soul.

It was crazy. Totally crazy.

He shoved his hands deep into his jacket pockets and started to walk. And as he walked he thought about what Annie had told him. He thought about the missing people. And Jenna and Jessica Moran.

He thought about his own feelings while at *HOT!* He thought about the things he thought he'd seen. He thought about the Midtown Murderer and what he'd seen with his own eyes then.

Then his thoughts returned to Annie. She wasn't a cruel person. In fact she was good to a fault. Accepting to a fault. She was genuinely terrified of Finola. She worked herself to the bone for that woman, not because she loved her job, but because she said she had to.

Annie wasn't a liar. And she wasn't the type to use his own fears and insecurities against him. To what end, anyway?

There was no denying that she was truly afraid. For herself. And especially for him.

When he finally stopped walking, he realized that he hadn't been wandering aimlessly. He'd had a destination, even if he wasn't conscious of it.

He looked up at the building in front of him. Finola White Enterprises.

Getting into the building was surprisingly easy, even despite the late hour. It was almost midnight now. He'd literally walked for hours. But the guard in the first-floor lobby had taken one look at his badge and let him in.

Nick immediately took the elevator to the fifteenth floor. When he stepped out he saw no one at the lobby's reception area.

He strode over to look at the desk. Everything was tidy, normal. He checked the large double doors, half-expecting them to be locked. They clicked open.

He walked into the back offices, the place even stranger at this time of night. Without the buzz of employees. The place looked cavernous, the red recessed lighting still glowing eerily.

Very Hell-like.

He wandered, looking here and there, not really sure what he was looking for. It wasn't as if he was going to find a big file box labeled "Contracts for Sold Souls" or anything.

Still he continued to look around until he finally made his way back to Finola's offices and Annie's desk.

Annie's desk wasn't as tidy as the front desk, but then she always had a zillion different tasks going on. To Do lists, appointment information. People to call.

He left her desk and tried Finola's office door.

It was locked. He considered trying to pick the lock, but decided he'd probably just end up getting himself in trouble.

He sighed, feeling a little silly even for trying to find any proof of what Annie said. After all, even if she was telling the truth, what did he expect to find? Satanic crosses? Pentagrams? The sign of the Beast?

Deciding he should probably just leave before he did actually get caught, he headed back toward the front lobby. But just as he reached the door, the skin at the back of his neck began to prickle and he had the strong sensation he was being watched.

He turned to scan the offices. He didn't see any signs of anyone. Any movement. He listened for another few seconds, then decided it was probably his own imagination getting the better of him. This place was creepy at night.

He twisted back toward the double doors, when he heard the distinct sound of a swinging door swishing closed.

A swinging door. He knew exactly where that type of door would be and he headed in that direction. The janitorial hallway, where he and Annie had tried to talk privately, but Elton had interrupted.

Carefully he pushed the door open, peering inside. The long, utilitarian gray hallway was empty. But probably any noise he heard was the nighttime cleaning crew working. Most office buildings had them and it would make sense he'd heard noise from back here.

But still he started down the hallway. The few doors that lined the hall were closed. He tested one, but it was locked. He walked a little farther down and decided there wasn't anything to be found in here, either.

Then he heard a noise. A sound like metal rubbing against metal. Faint, but distinctive. It seemed to be coming from the freight elevator. Nick got close, realizing the door was closed. Someone had just gotten onto the elevator.

Again it could easily be the cleanup crew, but his neck and back had begun to tingle again, so without any further thought, he pushed the UP button and waited.

After several seconds, the elevator returned to his floor and slid jerkily open. He got inside, realizing he didn't know which floor to go to.

Then he remembered that Elton had gotten into this elevator, presumably to go back to the mailroom. And the mailroom was on the lowest level. And the workers there *had* all made him very uncomfortable during his interviews. Lower level . . . Hell. Hell . . . demons. Ergo, the mailroom staff were all demons.

Nick knew it was a stretch, but what could it hurt?

He pressed LL.

When the doors opened, he found the mailroom lit up, but otherwise quiet. He stepped out and decided to look around. But as soon as he stepped off the elevator, the doors shut and it shuddered to life.

Nick checked to see if it would indicate which floor number the elevator was going to, but there were only UP and DOWN arrows above the doors.

He'd started to head into the mailroom when he paused and looked back at the elevator. The DOWN arrow was the indicator lit up.

Down?

He started back toward the elevators when he heard the

gears grind to a halt, then a slight pause, then the elevator began moving again.

Nick backed up, bracing himself, not sure what he would find on the other side of those metal doors. He thought about being in that interrogation room with that monster or demon or whatever it had been. He prepared himself for something just as horrifying. He glanced around for a weapon, wishing he'd remembered his gun.

Instead he grabbed . . . a stapler from one of the mail-room desks closest to him. At least it was industrial-sized.

The doors began to part and he positioned himself with the stapler, poised to throw.

But when the door opened, he found Eugene waiting on the other side, his hands clasped behind his back, a curious look in his eerie blue eyes.

"Have the NYPD stopped issuing firearms?"

Nick glanced at the stapler, then set it back on the workstation next to him. "I didn't bring mine."

"That doesn't seem wise when performing a covert investigation."

"No," Nick agreed, "it's really not."

"So would you like to tell me what you are hoping to find in the mailroom at midnight?" Eugene asked, stepping off the elevator.

As soon as the man got close to him, Nick felt that prickly feeling return, this time stronger than upstairs. Unable to stop himself, he rubbed a hand over the back of his neck.

"I was just looking around."

Eugene nodded.

Nick regarded the man. Could he be one of them? Could he actually be a demon?

The idea was still a stretch for him, especially when he stood in front of what appeared to be a normal, unassuming man in his mid-to-late thirties.

"I'm not," Eugene said so a matter-of-factly that Nick wasn't even sure the man had actually even said the words.

"You're not what?" Nick asked slowly.

"I'm not a demon."

Nick tried to remain composed himself. He shrugged. "Why *would* you be a demon?" He glanced over at the stapler, wishing he hadn't set it down.

Eugene sighed, then smiled almost in the way a person might when dealing with a slow child. "You are looking for proof of demons here. Which you probably won't find. But you might. This is kind of a sloppy lot."

Eugene walked toward his office, and Nick had no choice but to follow. He did pick up the stapler on the way by.

"That really wouldn't do you any good if I was a demon," Eugene said without looking back at him.

"But it could help if you're just a regular Joe," Nick said, again trying not to be totally unruffled by the fact that the man in front of him seemed to be reading his mind.

"True," Eugene said stepping behind his desk and sitting down. "I suppose it would sting a bit."

He gestured for Nick to take the same seat he had last time he was in this office. Nick hesitated, but finally sat down. After all, he had to find out what was going on here.

"What's going on is pretty huge, actually."

Nick stared at Eugene. "That is very unnerving, you know."

The man nodded regretfully. "I understand."

"So what are you? An alien or something?" Nick couldn't believe he was genuinely asking a question like that.

Eugene smiled, his demeanor still seemingly unflappable. "No. But I'm not human, either."

"Okay," Nick said, still wondering how he could be sitting here having a conversation like this.

"I'm a demon slayer."

Nick's eyes widened at that. Funny that this comment would be the one that surprised him enough to get a reaction.

"Well, not exactly a demon slayer," Eugene clarified. "More a demon controller. Demons can't actually be slain. They are eternal. But they can be monitored and controlled."

"Well, from what I've seen so far, you aren't doing a very good job," Nick stated wryly.

Eugene shrugged, giving him a look that said he couldn't argue. "But we are working on it. This is the largest assembly of demons we've ever had in one place. Usually demons work alone, but here they are working together. So all our moves have to be carefully planned and executed. But we are going to get the situation under control."

"We?"

Eugene nodded. "We're like a task force. Brought in by the government."

"Like the NSA or something?"

"Exactly."

"But how did you know I was here tonight? I mean I understand you can read my mind now, but can you read it all the time?"

Eugene shook his head. "No, I can only read it when I can see you. But we have been watching you."

"Why?"

"Because we did not want you drawing too much attention to the problems here. It's actually easier for us to clean up if not too many humans know there is a problem. We certainly don't want the NYPD involved. That would bring far too much attention."

Nick supposed he understood that. "So you know about all the missing people."

"Yes. Most of them are being kept in a safe place. Until we can figure out a way to get their souls back."

"So you can get your soul back from the Devil?"

"No," Eugene stated. "The Devil has soul bargaining down to an exact science. No loopholes. Totally binding. But the soul taking that has been done here did not follow the legal wording of the contract."

"So Finola is stealing souls."

Eugene nodded.

And Finola had a contract with Annie for her soul. A contract she could breach at any moment.

"Yes," Eugene said, confirming his unspoken concerns. "But we are getting closer and closer to figuring out how to get Finola under control. Annie will be safe. It just requires some stealth, because the goal is always to avoid making Satan aware that we exist."

"Well, he is the Prince of Darkness."

"Exactly," Eugene nodded.

"So are your headquarters below us?" Nick asked.

"Yes. It's a copper-encased workroom, because demons cannot cross barriers of copper. And the mailroom employees are members of the organization."

"Because no one pays attention to the mailroom."

"Exactly."

"Are they all inhuman?"

"No," Eugene said, his eerie eyes focusing on Nick more intently than before.

The prickling feeling, to which Nick had almost become oblivious, flared, and he suddenly felt a little uneasy. He gripped the stapler still in his right hand a little tighter.

"Don't worry. I have no intention of hurting you," Eugene said. "I cannot hurt anyone unless they are evil. You are not evil."

"Good to know."

Eugene actually smiled again.

"But why would you tell me all this?" Nick asked, still feeling not exactly wary, but a little unsettled.

"Because you are a human with special abilities. We have many humans with special abilities working with us."

"Who?"

"Elton. He's a seer, meaning he can see demons. We have several other working within *HOT!* And we can always use more."

"Are you recruiting me?"

Eugene nodded. "In a way. Because of being a detective, you are more likely to be in contact with evil than most people. And having you report any leads to our organization would be of the greatest help."

So I was never crazy, Nick thought. The Midtown Murderer was a demon.

"Yes. And because your detectives captured him, we were able to get him under control and back to Hell."

Nick frowned, a horrible idea hitting him. "So the man in jail isn't really a killer?"

Eugene sighed, and Nick felt a great wave of sorrow wash over him. "The man in prison is a killer now. When a demon possesses someone like that, some of the demon's evil stays inside him. Not true of all possession, but in this case, the man is a killer."

"If you gaze for too long into an abyss, the abyss gazes also into you."

Eugene nodded.

"Wait, was Nietzsche a demon slayer?"

"No," Eugene said. "Just a smart guy."

Annie leapt off the sofa as soon as she heard a key in the lock. She stood in the middle of the room, waiting for Nick to walk in.

He did, stopping as soon as he saw her.

"Nick," she said. Her eyes, already swollen from crying,

filled again as soon as she saw him. She'd been so afraid he'd left for good, thinking she was totally insane.

"I'm so sorry," she cried. "I never should have told you—"

Nick strode to her, pulling her tight into his arms, his cheek nuzzling against the top of her head.

"Annie, it's okay," he murmured, kissing her temple. "I know you were telling the truth. I know there are demons."

Chapter Twenty-five

Annie curled against Nick's chest, listening as he told the story about Eugene and the mailroom.

"I knew there was a reason I liked Elton," she said once he was finished. She rubbed her cheek again his broad chest, comforted by the steady beat of his heart.

"And," she added, "now you don't have to go to Finola's party."

Nick didn't answer and she lifted her head, eyeing him worriedly.

"You aren't going, right?"

Nick met her gaze, his eyes grave. "Annie, I'm not going to let her keep abusing you like she is."

"But this Eugene said they are close to helping us."

"Not close enough. You can't handle one more day of her crazy demands with the threat of losing your immortal soul hanging over your head."

Annie frowned at him, frustrated. "I've done it for three years. I can keep doing it. I have to."

"No," Nick said stroking her hair. "I will make a deal with her myself."

"No," Annie said pushing away from him. "Then we will *both* be indentured to her. What good will that do?"

"I will offer her *my* soul if she will destroy the contract with you."

"No," Annie said, unable to believe he would be so stupid. "Then I will lose you completely. She's obsessed with you. What do you think she'd have in mind for you as her indentured slave?"

Nick sighed, realizing Annie was right. "I suspect it would involve whips and chains."

Annie moved back against him, relieved he was seeing reason.

"I will be fine," she assured him again. "And soon it won't even matter, because she'll be gone, banished or whatever, by the slayers."

Satan sat on his balcony in a lounge chair. His head rested on the back, his eyes closed. A pleased little smile curved his wide lips. Heat wafted up from the fiery lake below his balcony and he waved his hand in the air in time to the sounds echoing from the countryside.

"Master?"

Satan raised his hand for silence. Then he continued to enjoy the cacophony of tortured screams from thousands of damned souls.

Finally, after a few more choruses, he opened his eyes.

"Don't tell me," he muttered.

"She is to see the mortal male tonight."

Satan roared, his angry bellow drowning out all other sounds. And when the echoing stopped, all of Hell was silent.

Annie checked her phone. She'd texted Nick nearly a half an hour before to tell him she was headed out the door. She'd hoped to be home long before the party started. Not that she didn't trust Nick. But she'd just feel better knowing he was at home. And she was with him.

She'd even bought a sexy little outfit to guarantee he

would be too busy with her to think about playing the hero.

But she was still stuck at Finola's apartment, making sure the florist was placing the dozens and dozens of white roses, which Finola had finally agreed to instead of the white lilacs, in the right places.

She'd also had to be sure the linens were correct, since the caterer had originally brought ivory tablecloths and napkins with golden accents instead of winter white with silver accents.

But finally it looked as if everything was close to complete. Tristan had arrived, and he would take over helping Finola, since her lowly personal assistant was not allowed at such an elite party.

Annie was happy to be Cinderella for the night.

She adjusted one last vase of roses, then went to find Finola. The diva demon was in her bedroom suite, a maid helping her into her gorgeous custom-made gown.

"Finola, the flowers and linens are all set."

"Good," she said, not looking away from her reflection in the mirror. "Just bring me a martini with three onions, and then go."

Annie nodded, repressing a sigh. She just wanted to get home and be alone with Nick for a whole, blessedly quiet evening.

She went to the bar, looking around for the bartender.

"He went outside for a smoke," Tristan said, appearing beside her. "Let's see how many times he does that tonight, before he finds himself cast into the universe's biggest ashtray."

Annie's eyes widened at his open reference to Hell and Finola's penchant for banishing souls there willy-nilly.

He sighed. "Don't mind me. I'm in a mood."

Annie didn't say anything, mainly because she didn't

know what to say. She slipped behind the bar and started to make Finola's martini.

The door chimed, announcing the party's first guest. Annie hurried to finish the martini, knowing Finola would be very upset if the guest saw her still there.

She scooped two onions into the liquor mixture, and was just ladling out another when she heard Tristan's greeting.

"Rossi, what are you doing here?"

Annie looked up to see Nick in the doorway of Finola's apartment. He wore the tuxedo Finola had provided for him. And Annie was sure her pulse would normally have sped up at the sight of him, if it wasn't skipping with dismay and fear.

"Finola invited me as her date," Nick said smoothly, not having spotted her yet.

"Really?" Tristan sounded almost as dismayed as Annie. "She did not tell me that."

"No, Tristan, I did not." Finola glided into the room in a cascade of white silk and diamonds. "I thought I heard your voice."

Nick smiled at her, but his smile slipped, just slightly, as he finally noticed Annie behind the bar. But the slip was enough to draw Finola's attention to Annie too.

"Anna, why are you still here?" she asked, her voice sharper than usual.

Annie didn't answer her, and Finola frowned, clearly furious at her insubordination.

"Anna, you may go now."

"No," Annie said.

"Annie, don't," Nick warned.

Annie stepped out from behind the bar, moving away from Finola toward Nick.

"I'm not going without you," Annie told him.

"Don't do this," Nick said, real fear filling his brown eyes.

Finola's pale gaze moved back and forth between the two of them, clearly confused. "Whatever is going on?"

But it wasn't either Annie or Nick who explained. It was Tristan. He moved to stand beside Finola.

"They are lovers," he said, then lifted his head as if he was sniffing the air. "Yes, definitely lovers."

Finola's eyes narrowed as she looked at Annie. "You dared touch what you knew was mine. Well, sweet little Southern Anna, you will pay dearly for that."

"No, she won't," Nick stated. "You aren't going to do anything to her, Finola."

"Aren't I?"

Annie stared at her boss, realizing that she looked different, her eyes becoming almost reptilian. Fear filled her. Both she and Nick were going to end up banished to Hell.

Why hadn't he just stayed home?

But Nick didn't seem to be afraid of Finola. He stepped forward, placing himself between her and Annie.

"I will make a deal with you," he said calmly.

"No," Annie whispered, reaching out to hold Nick's arms as if she could physically drag him back from Hell should Finola decide to cast him there.

"What kind of deal?" Finola asked, clearly intrigued.

"Release Annie from her contract, or I will go to my superiors at the NYPD with the fact that you are a demon."

Finola stared at him for a moment, then she laughed.

"Why would I ever agree to a deal like that? There's nothing in it for me."

"That's true," Nick agreed. "Nothing except for the fact that you will spare yourself from being called a demon."

"They wouldn't believe you anyway," she pointed out.

"That's true, but the news will run the story even if they think I'm crazy. And a rumor like that is sure to pick up steam when the fact comes out that over twenty people in your employment have gone missing."

Again, Annie was surprised when Tristan added, "That could very well be a problem. I can think of at least one of your superiors who would be very unhappy with a rumor like that."

"As can I," said a booming voice from behind them.

Annie turned to find a tall, slim man standing in the doorway of the apartment. He was balding, with a thin moustache and a beard that was groomed to a point. Behind a pair of wire-rimmed glasses, his small eyes appeared almost black. He stepped forward, a gold-handled walking cane in his right hand.

"I have to say—" his deep voice did not match his slight build—"I very much admire your ingenuity."

Both Nick and Annie remained silent.

"I'm sorry," he said offering his hand to Nick, who accepted it without pause. "I have not introduced myself."

He turned then to Annie. She hesitated before accepting his handshake, but when she did, his long, narrow fingers curled around hers, smooth and almost slithering, like several small snakes.

She fought the urge to brush her hands on her skirt once he released her.

"I am Satan," he said, offering her an amused smile almost as if he'd known what she'd been thinking. "Or Lucifer, if you prefer. Prince of Darkness always strikes me as so formal."

Annie inched closer to Nick and he pulled her against his side, his arm protectively around her waist.

Satan laughed, another booming sound that filled the room. "Oh, believe me, you two have nothing to fear from me. In fact, I have a real fondness for young love. And I want nothing more than to see you two lovebirds happy."

Nick's hold tightened around her waist, but they both listened, watching Satan pace back and forth in front of them, his cane thudding on the carpet.

"I actually have a deal for you that you both will like very much."

"We're listening," Nick said calmly as if he was talking to a used-car salesman rather than Satan himself.

"I will destroy the lovely Miss Annie Lou Riddle's contract with Finola White in return for your agreement that you will never discuss any of this with another living soul."

Nick frowned. "Discuss what, exactly?"

Satan chuckled, seeming pleased with Nick's need for clarification.

"You will not discuss the existence of demons within the fashion industry. You will not discuss the missing employees of *HOT!* and you will not discuss the fact that anyone working for Finola White Enterprises, including Finola White herself, is a demon."

Nick considered that for a moment. "And Annie will be free and clear to walk out of here today, no longer under contract, her soul completely her own?"

"Yes."

"And in return for our silence, no demons will bother us ever again."

Satan considered that, then smiled broadly. "Absolutely. Like I said, I enjoy a good love story. And all I want from you is silence on this matter."

Nick nodded, but before he could even finish the first bob of his head, Satan held out a contract and a pen.

Nick read the contract, then signed. Annie did the same.

"And the pink copy is yours," Satan said, handing them the bottom sheet of the contract.

"Now run along, you crazy kids," he said, gesturing to the door with his cane. "I have some things to sort out with my employees."

Annie and Nick immediately headed for the door. They did not have to be told twice.

Epilogue

Annie double-checked to make sure she had everything she needed, then she zipped her suitcase, glad everything actually fit.

"Ready," Nick called to her.

"Yes," Annie said, wheeling her suitcase out into the living room of their new apartment. It was smaller than her old one, but bigger than Nick's. And it was theirs, no strings attached.

"You ready to learn how to milk a cow, city boy?"

"Yes, ma'am," he said, attempting his best Southern drawl.

Annie grinned, feeling completely happy with her new life. She was finally going home again to see her grandparents after three long, long years, and she was bringing her wonderful detective fiancé with her. She'd started a new job as an assistant editor at *Comfy Home* magazine, and her head editor didn't show even the remotest signs of being a diva . . . or a demon. And she actually got to come home by six o'clock and had every weekend off.

Nick still worked as a detective, although he'd cut back on his caseload, only taking those strange cases where people claimed they saw things they couldn't possibly have seen. Things that other detectives thought were down-right crazy.

And Satan had stayed true to their contract: no demons from her past life had bothered either of them. She thought she saw Finola once through the window of an expensive, five-star restaurant, but since she and Nick had been heading to the next block to go bowling, she felt pretty confident she wouldn't run into her later. In return, she and Nick had kept quiet about what they knew. They might have felt guilty if Eugene hadn't said that was their best course of action anyway.

"I love you," Nick said, stealing a kiss as she passed him on the way out the door.

"I love you too," she said, feeling so very happy that she'd finally gotten the life she'd always imagined. And the man who'd been willing to fight demons to save her.

Tristan stood at the window in his office, looking out at the city skyline. He loved living in the human world and he didn't want to lose this.

For the past several weeks, Finola had behaved herself, and it seemed that Satan's wrath had finally whipped her into shape. She'd been fabulous over Fashion Week, and they had infiltrated several of the other larger fashion magazines, getting many legitimate soul contracts, even getting a few demons into some of the higher positions of other magazines.

But she was slipping back to her old ways. Just today, she'd cast her new personal assistant to Hell because the woman forgot to ask for extra foam on Finola's white chocolate mocha. So he'd spent yet another afternoon with a catatonic woman in the passenger seat of his Bentley as he drove to Jersey.

Tristan took a sip of his dirty martini, trying to decide

what to do to make sure he wasn't dragged down with her if she was indeed taken back to Hell.

He sighed. "Maybe I should just try to overthrow her myself."

"Maybe you should."

Tristan spun around, searching for who had just spoken. But his office was empty.

"Down here."

Tristan looked down, shocked.

Finola's dog sat in the center of the room, staring at him with beady black eyes.

Tristan blinked. "You can talk?"

"Yes, and I can listen too. How do you feel about staging a coup with man's best friend?"

Tristan walked over to the black leather sofa on the far side of his desk and sat down. For a minute, he doubted the sound logic of a takeover planned with a dog, but then a realization hit him.

"You were the one telling Satan about Finola's erratic behavior, weren't you?"

The dog nodded, his tongue lolling out the side of his mouth.

"Yes, and I'd do it again."

Tristan was impressed.

"So are you in?"

Tristan raised his glass. "Oh, I'm definitely in."

Love sexy paranormals?
Try Rebecca Zanetti's
CLAIMED,
out now!

"Do you think the Kurjans are near?"

He shook his head without opening his eyes. "No. I don't sense evil anywhere near us. We're probably safe for a couple of hours, then we should move again."

A couple of hours? Damn. She needed him in fighting shape. "Will drinking my blood help heal you?"

His lids flipped open, revealing those silver eyes that had haunted her dreams for fifteen years. Hunger, raw and pure, filled them. "Yes."

Emma gulped in air. The husky timbre of his voice caressed nerves she didn't want to own. "I won't become a vampire?"

His dimples winked at her. "No. Vampires are born, not made."

Fear and her damn curiosity blended until she could only whisper. "Okay." She held out her wrist and shut her eyes. And waited. The breeze picked up outside the cave, rustling pine needles and leaves inside the small entrance, and she shivered. Finally, she opened her eyes in exasperation. "What?"

Reaching out with his good arm, he lifted her chin with one knuckle, waiting until her gaze met his. "I want your neck."

Low and rough, his voice skittered need through her

midriff. Talk about direct. "Um, well, why?" Her mind reeled and she fought the urge to drop her gaze to his mouth. She lost the fight. He ran a tongue along those full lips and need rippled through her. How did he do that?

He waited again until she focused on him, her eyes widening on the pure confidence shining in his. "I've been waiting to taste you for centuries—I don't want you extending your wrist to me and looking the other way."

"What do you want?" She shouldn't have asked that. God.

For answer, he reached out with his healthy arm and lifted her until she straddled his lap. She should've protested, but the easy strength and warm hand on her hip caught the breath in her throat. Fascinating. Such true, raw power. She pressed both hands against the undamaged muscles of his chest, balancing herself. His erection lay thick and hard beneath her, and she fought the urge to clench her thighs against his legs.

He stared at her through half lidded eyes, his hands going to the buttons of her cotton shirt.

"What are you doing?" she breathed.

"I don't want to get blood on your shirt." His gaze dropped to the swell of her breasts over the plain white bra. Fire flared within those silver depths and she fought a moan.

"That's enough." She covered his hands with hers.

With a nod, he gently placed her hands on his thighs before clasping the shirt and drawing it down both arms. The lower buttons remained engaged, and the material trapped her arms at her sides.

He pinned her with a gaze so full of hunger she couldn't speak. "You'll give your blood?"

Emma nodded, her focus narrowing to the man before her.

Sharp fangs emerged from his canines and he growled,

reaching one arm around to cup her head and pull it to the side. Her neck stretched and vulnerability battled with arousal down her length. Every muscle in her body tensed to flee. His other hand gasped her hip, flexed, then slid up to her now bare shoulder, entrapping her.

There was no escaping him.

Tugging her closer, he buried his head in the hollow between her neck and shoulder. She tensed, waiting for the pain. Instead, he pressed one tender kiss to the rapidly beating pulse. She felt it to her core.

He inhaled, running his mouth along her collarbone and up to her ear, where he nipped. "You smell like spiced rum and peaches," he breathed against her skin, his hands holding her firmly in place. "Some dreams I could smell you, but not this strongly. Never this fully." He rose up, drawing in a deep breath. "Never so much I'd do anything to have you."

Quick as a whip, he struck.

His fangs pierced her skin, and Emma cried out, shutting her eyes.

Her blood boiled.

Raw need flared her flesh to life and a hum began deep in her core. What was happening? Without caring enough to stop and think, she pressed against him, so hard, so full. His mouth pulled harder, and her nipples pebbled into pinpoints of need. Something contracted in her womb, begging for him. He drank more, and she exploded into a thousand pieces. The room sheeted white and orgasm tore through her with the force of a furious tornado. She went limp, held upright only by his hands.

Sealing the wound, his tongue lashed across her skin and she shivered, nearly dazed. He held her in place and lifted his head away from her, his gaze piercing on her heated face.

She should be embarrassed, but a warm haze clouded her vision, her brain.

"Emma?"

She lifted heavy lids to focus.

His eyes burned hotter than molten steel. "I want you."

And don't miss ANGEL OF DARKNESS,
the first in a new series by Cynthia Eden,
coming next month!

He'd been created for one purpose—death. He was not there to comfort or to enlighten.

Keenan's only job was to bring death to those unlucky enough to know his touch.

And on the cold, windy New Orleans night, his latest victim was in sight. He watched her from his perch high atop the St. Louis Cathedral. Mortal eyes wouldn't find him. Only those preparing to leave the earthly realm could ever glimpse his face, so he didn't worry about shocking those few humans who straggled through the nearby square.

No, he worried about nothing. No one. He never had. He simply touched and he killed and he waited for his next victim.

The woman he watched tonight was small, with long black hair, and skin a pale cream. The wind whipped her hair back, jerking it away from her face as she hurried down the stone cathedral steps. The doors had been locked. She hadn't made it inside. No chance to pray.

Pity.

He slipped to the side of the cathedral, still watching her as she edged down the narrow alleyway. Pirate Alley. He'd taken others from this place before. The path seemed to scream with the memories of the past.

"No!"

That wasn't the past screaming. His body stiffened. His wings beat at the air around him. It was *her.*

Nicole St. James. Schoolteacher. Age twenty-nine. A woman who avoided the party streets. Who tutored children on the weekends. A woman who'd tried to live her life just right . . .

A woman who was dying tonight.

His eyes narrowed as he leapt from his perch. Time to go in closer.

Nicole's attacker had her against the wall. One of the man's hands was over her mouth, the better to make sure she didn't scream again. His other hand slammed against the front of her chest and held her pinned against the cold stone wall.

She was fighting harder than Keenan had really expected. Struggling. Kicking.

Her attacker just laughed.

And Keenan watched—as he'd always watched. So many years . . .

Tears streamed down Nicole's cheeks.

The man holding her leaned in and licked them away.

Keenan's gut clenched. Knowing that her time was at hand, he'd watched Nicole for a few weeks now. He'd slipped into her classroom and listened to the soft drawl of her voice. He'd watched as her lips curled into a smile and a dimple winked in her right cheek.

He'd seen laughter in her eyes. Seen longing. Seen . . . life.

Now, her green eyes were filled with the stark, wild terror that only the helpless can truly know.

He didn't like that look in her eyes. His hands clenched. *Don't look if you don't like it.* His gaze jerked away from her face. The job wasn't about what he liked. It never had been.

There'd never been a choice.

They have the choices. I only have orders to follow.

That was way it had always been. So why did it bother him, now? Because it was her? Because he'd watched too much? Slipped beside her too much?

Temptation.

"This is gonna hurt . . ."

The man's grating whisper scratched through Keenan's mind. Neither the attacker nor Nicole could see him. Not yet.

One touch, that was all it would take.

But the time hadn't come for her yet.

"The wind's so loud . . ." The man lifted his hand off Nicole's mouth. "No one's gonna hear you scream anyway."

But she still screamed—a loud, long, desperate scream—and she kept fighting.

Keenan truly hadn't realized she'd struggle so much against death. Some didn't fight at all when the time came. Others fought until he had to drag them away.

Fabric ripped. Tore. The guy had jerked her shirt, rending the material. Keenan glimpsed the soft ivory of her bra and the firm mounds of her breasts.

Help her. The urge came from deep within, but it was an urge he couldn't heed.

"Don't!" Nicole yelled. "Please—no! Just let me go!"

Her attacker lifted his head. Keenan stared at him, noting the gaunt features, the black hair, and the eyes that were too dark for a normal man. "No, baby. I'm not lettin' you go." The guy licked his lips. "I'm too damn hungry." Then he smiled and revealed sharpened teeth that no human could possess.

Vampire. Figured. Keenan had been cleaning up their messes for centuries. *A mistake.* That's what all those parasites were. An experiment gone wrong.

Nicole opened her mouth to scream again and the vamp

sank his teeth into her throat. Then he started drinking from her, gulping and growling. Nicole's fingernails raked against his face as she struggled against him.

But it was too late to fight. She'd never be strong enough to break away from the vampire. She was five feet six inches tall. Maybe 135 pounds.

The vamp was over six feet. He was lean, but muscle mass and weight didn't really matter—not when you were talking about a vamp's strength.

Keenan stared at the narrow opening of the alley. Soon, he'd be able to touch her and her nightmare would end. *Soon.*

"You're just going to stand there?" Her voice cracked.

His head whipped back toward her. Those green eyes—full of fury and fear—were locked on *him.*

Impossible.

She shouldn't see me yet. It wasn't time. The vamp hadn't taken enough blood from her.

Nicole slammed her hands into the vampire's chest, but he kept his teeth in her throat and didn't so much as stumble. Her neck was tilted back, her head angled, and her stare was on—

Me.

"Help me." She mouthed the words as tears slipped down her cheeks. "Please."

By the fire, she could *see* him. Every muscle in Keenan's body went tight. "I will." The words felt rusty and he couldn't remember the last time he'd talked to a human. No need for talk, not really. Not when you were just carting souls. "Soon . . ."

The vamp's head lifted. Her blood stained his mouth and chin. "Baby, you taste so good."

Her body slumped as her knees buckled. Kenton's wings stretched behind him even as his muscles tensed.

"Grade Fucking A," the vamp muttered and he eased

back. *Why?* The vamp planned to kill her. Keenan knew that. Nicole St. James was dying tonight.

Nicole's hand rose to her throat. Her fingers were shaking. Her whole body trembled. "Y-you're not real . . ." Her eyes never left Keenan.

"Oh, I'm damn real." The vamp swiped the back of his hand over his chin. "Guess what, sweet thing? All those stories you heard? About the vamps and this city? Every damn one of 'em tales is true."

Nicole didn't look at the vamp. She kept her eyes on Keenan as she inched her way down the alley. With every slow move, she kept her hands pressed against the wall.

"You gonna run?" The vamp asked. "Oh, damn, I love it when they run."

Yes, he did. Most vamps did. They liked the thrill of the hunt.

"*Why don't you help me?*" She yelled at Keenan and the wind took the words, making them into a whisper as they left the alley.

That was the way of Pirate Alley. Sometimes, no one could even hear the screams.

The vamp seemed to finally realize his prey wasn't focused on him. The vamp spun around, turning so that he nearly brushed against Keenan. "What the fuck?" The vamp demanded. "Bitch, no one's—"

Nicole's footsteps pounded down the alley. *Smart.* Keenan almost smiled. Had she ever even seen him? Or had her words all been a trick to escape?

The vampire laughed, then he lunged after her. Four steps and the parasite leapt at her, tackling Nicole to the ground and keeping her trapped in the alley. Glass shattered when she fell—a beer bottle that had been tossed aside to litter the ground. She crashed into it and the bottle smashed beneath her weight.

"You're gonna beg for death," the vamp promised her.

Perhaps. Keenan slowly stalked toward them. He lifted his hand, aware of the growing cold in the air. The stories about death's cold touch were true. Nicole's time was at hand.

"Please, God, no!" Nicole cried.

God had other plans. That was why an Angel of Death had been sent to collect her.

The vamp's hands were at her throat. His claws dug into her skin. The scent of decay and cigarettes swirled in the air around Keenan.

"Flowers," Nicole whispered. "I smell . . ."

Him. Angels often carried a floral scent. Humans caught a trace of that scent all the time, but never realized they weren't alone.

The vamp sank his teeth into Nicole's throat again. She didn't even have the voice to scream now. Tears leaked from her eyes.

Keenan knelt beside her. The first time he'd seen her, he'd thought . . .

Beautiful.

Now . . . covered in garbage and blood, still fighting a vampire, still struggling to live . . .

Beautiful.

It was time. His hand lifted toward her and hovered over her tangled hair. His fingers were so close to touching her. Just an inch, maybe two, separated them. But . . .

He hesitated.

Why couldn't someone else have come in the alley this night? A cop? A college kid? Someone *to help* her.

And not someone who was just supposed to watch her suffer.

A fire burned in his gut. She didn't deserve this brutal end to her human life. From what he'd seen, Nicole had been *good*. She'd tried to help others. His jaw ached and he realized he'd been clenching his teeth.

His gaze drifted to the vampire. It would be so easy to stop him and to take a monster from the world.

Forbidden. The order burned into his mind. He wasn't supposed to interfere. That wasn't the way. Wasn't allowed. He was to collect his charge and move on. Those were the rules.

He'd take Nicole St. James this night, and someone else would wait on him tomorrow. There were always more humans. More souls. More death.

Her hands fell limply to her sides as the vampire drank from her and her head turned toward Keenan.

There was gold buried in her eyes. He'd thought her eyes were solid emerald, but now, he could see the gold glinting in her eyes. Angels had strong vision—in darkness or light—but he'd never noticed that gold before.

Her eyes locked right on him. She was so close to passing. He had no doubt that she saw him then.

"Don't worry," he told her. The vampire wouldn't hear him. No one but Nicole would hear his voice. "The pain is already ending for you." His hand still reached for her. He'd wanted to touch her before. To see if her skin was as soft as it looked. But he knew just how dangerous such a touch would be—to both of them.

Keenan well understand what happened to those of his kind when they did not obey their orders.

Despite popular belief, angels were not the favored ones. They did not have choices like the humans. Angels had only duty.

"I don't . . ." Her words were barely a whisper. Had the vamp savaged her neck too much? "D-don't . . . want to . . . die . . ."

The vamp gulped down her blood, growling as he drank.

"Don't . . . let me . . ." Her lashes began to fall. The fingers of her right hand began to curl inward, and her wrist brushed against the jagged glass. "Die . . ."

There was so much desperation in her voice, but he'd heard desperation before. Heard fear. Heard lies. Promises.

But he'd never heard them from *her*.

Keenan didn't touch her. His hand eased back as he hesitated.

Hesitated.

He'd taken a thousand souls. No, far more. But her . . .

Why her? Why tonight? She's barely lived. The vamp should be the one to go, not—

Nicole let out a guttural groan. Keenan blinked and his wings rustled behind him. No, he had a job to do. He would do it—

Nicole grabbed a thick shard of broken glass and wrenched it up. She shoved it into the vampire's neck and caught him right in the jugular. His blood spilled over her as the vamp wrenched back, howling in pain and fury.

Her throat was a mess, ripped flesh, blood—so much blood. Hers. The vamp's. Nicole grabbed another chunk of glass and swung again with a slice to the vamp's neck.

Fighting.

She was fighting desperately for every second of life that she had left. And he was supposed to just stop her? Supposed to take her away when she struggled so hard to live?

You've done it before. Do it again.

So many humans. So little life. So much death.

"Bitch! I'll cut you open—"

The vamp would. In that instant, Keenan could see everything the vamp had planned for Nicole. Her death would be ten times more brutal now. The future had already altered for her. *Because I hesitated.*

"I'll rip your heart out—"

Yes, in the end, he'd do that, too.

She'd die with her eyes open, with fear and blood choking her.

"I'll shred that pretty face—"

Her coffin would be closed.

A fire began to burn inside Keenan. Burning hotter, brighter with every slow second that passed. *Why her?* She'd . . . soothed him before. When he'd heard her voice, it had seemed to flow through him. And when she'd laughed . . .

He'd liked the sound of her laughter. Sweet, free.

"Help . . . me . . ." Her broken voice.

Keenan squared his shoulders. What did she see when she looked at him? A monster just like the vamp? Or a savior?

"No one fuckin' cares about you . . ." The vamp yanked the glass out of his neck. More blood sprayed on Nicole. "You'll die alone and no one will even notice you're gone."

I will notice. Because she wouldn't be there for him to watch anymore. She'd be far beyond Keenan's reach. He didn't know paradise, only death.

She tried to push off the ground, but couldn't move. The blood loss had gotten to her and made her the perfect prey.

The vamp's claws were up. "I'm gonna start with that face."

Nicole shook her head and swiped out with the glass. The wounds didn't stop the vampire. Nothing was going to stop him. No one. Nicole would scream and suffer and then finally—*die.*

And Keenan would watch. Every moment.

No.

His hand lifted, rising in that last, final touch. His touch could steal life and rip the soul right of a body.

He reached out—and locked his fingers around the vampire's shoulder.

The vampire jerked and shuddered as if an electric charge

had blasted through him. Keenan didn't try to soften his power. He wanted the vampire to hurt. Wanted him to suffer.

And that was wrong. Angels weren't supposed to want vengeance. They weren't supposed to get angry. They weren't supposed to care.

Killing the vampire was wrong. Against orders. But . . .

She will suffer no more.